One More Time

A Nuclear Disaster Threatened By Criminals Must Be Prevented At All Costs

By

Nigel Seed

The Fifth Book In The Jim Wilson Series

www.nigelseedauthor.com

Copyright © 2018 Nigel Seed

The right of Nigel Seed to be identified as the author of this work has been asserted.

All rights reserved. No part of this publication may be reproduced, stored in a retrieval system, or transmitted, in any form, or by any means (electronic, mechanical, photocopying, recording, or otherwise), without the prior permission of the publisher. Any person who does any unauthorised act in relation to this publication may be liable to criminal prosecution and civil claims for damages.

This is a fictional work and all characters are drawn from the author's imagination. Any resemblance or similarities to persons either living or dead are entirely coincidental except where they are detailed in the factual chapter.

ISBN-13:978-1717120267
ISBN-10: 1717120261

This book is for Prakash and Chandra.

Acknowledgments

We are all travellers in the wilderness of this world and the best that we can find in our travels is an honest friend.
-Robert Louis Stevenson

I have been blessed with a number of honest friends who have helped me by reading my book at the embryonic stages and giving me useful criticism. They know who they are, but they deserve a mention for putting up with me. My grateful thanks to Pam and John Fine, Glenn Wood, Brian Luckham and Peter Durant.

The biggest debt though is to my wife who has lived this project with me and been supportive throughout, especially when I was struggling

16 July 1945

The people watching had been stunned into silence as the intense flash of light and the enormous fireball illuminated the desert. Some cried, a few laughed. The team leader of Project Trinity, Robert Oppenheimer, said, "It worked." The first atomic bomb had exploded.

They watched as the ball of fire rose and an ominous mushroom cloud formed and rose above the sands. Shortly afterwards it punched through the clouds. The effect was said to be indescribably beautiful as the peaks and ridges were lit with an unearthly light.

At the time nobody fully understood the effect the irradiated dust and debris would have as it fell back from the sky. Oppenheimer was heard to whisper a line from Hindu scripture, "Now I am become Death, the destroyer of worlds."

On the 6th of August 1945 a second bomb, of the same design, was dropped on the Japanese city of Hiroshima by a B-29 bomber piloted by Colonel Paul W Tibbets. It is estimated that 66,000 people died immediately and some 69,000 were injured. The fireball was estimated to be 370 meters across and to have reached a temperature of 6000º centigrade.

The horror of the Nuclear Age had begun.

Chapter 1

The cold clear waters of the Pacific lapped around his rubber boots as Jim reeled in the fourth fish of the morning. It was another good one and would make a fine addition to the dinner menu for the students back in the cabin. He was grateful for the thick woollen socks Megan had knitted for him over the winter. It would be months yet before the water warmed up and weeks before the last of the snow melted.

Dropping the fish into his keep net, he straightened his back and looked along the waterway that led out to the wide Pacific Ocean. The water was flat calm today and so he could hear the outboard motor gently chugging towards him. The boat came into sight around a small headland and he could see the silhouette of the single occupant.

He turned and waded back to the rocky beach with his rod in one hand and his catch in the other. He walked up the beach and through the few trees in front of the cabin. Laying his catch on the wide wooden veranda, he turned and walked back towards the water's edge to await the visitor. He stood and watched the boat turn into the small bay as the helmsman switched off and lifted the engine shaft out of the water. The boat drifted silently towards shore until the metal hull grounded on the stones and the boat came to a halt.

"Hello, boss. Nice to see you again. How's tricks?"

"Geordie! What the hell brings you out to the wilds of British Columbia?"

Jim gripped his friend's hand and smiled at him as he looked him up and down. Geordie's dark eyes were still clear and his grip was firm. He looked in good shape.

"Oh! I was just in the neighbourhood and thought I'd drop by to see if I could cadge a mug of tea."

"Come up to the cabin. Megan will be delighted to see you. The students are out gathering samples, so it's mercifully quiet for a little while."

They walked together towards the large cabin set back in the pine trees, the smoke from the log-burning stove wafting above as they mounted the wooden stairs. Jim paused to pick up his fish and then led the way through the door into the wide, open plan common room.

"So then, boss, what have you been doing with yourself since you left the army?"

"Keeping busy. The University of Vancouver took me on as an assistant lecturer and so I support Megan teaching the forestry and ecology students who come up here for their field assignments. Plus, I'm working towards a PhD so I'll be a doctor in a while, I hope, but not the kind who has access to pills. I'm working on biodegradable plastics and their effect on the marine environment with one of the university chemists."

"That's a shame; you could have had a look at my rash for me."

Jim smiled as he sat down opposite Geordie in the chairs next to the stove. "So when are you going to tell me what this is about?"

A flash of embarrassment passed across Geordie's dark skin. "Well, boss, we're putting the band back together and I've been sent to get you."

"I'm retired, Geordie, and loving it. Even the old trouble has eased off. I haven't had those nightmares for months. I get to sleep right the way through the night. So no, thank you, I've done enough running around getting shot at."

"I thought you might say that and that's what I told the Prime Minister when he called me in to see him."

"Unusual for a Sergeant to be called in to see the PM, isn't it?"

"It's Staff Sergeant now. I got promoted just after Ivan left the regiment and there was a bit of upward movement all round."

"Even so."

"Right, well, you know we had an election about six months ago?"

"I read something about it, but I'm not really very interested in politics, except those that affect the people round here."

"OK. Well David Orwell got kicked out and the other lot got in. The new PM is called Phillip Morton. It seems that, as part of the handover briefing, us three got mentioned and now a job has come up that Morton thinks is right up our alley."

"You've had a wasted journey. I'm really not interested, but you will stay for dinner, won't you? We'll find you a bed and you can go back to Mr

8

Morton tomorrow and tell him thanks, but no thanks."

Geordie stood up from his chair and walked towards the door where he had dropped his jacket as they came in. He fished in the inside pocket and withdrew a long cream envelope. He looked at it, paused, and then walked back across the room to Jim. As he held out the envelope he looked down at Jim. "Sorry, boss, but I have to give you this."

Jim took the envelope and slid his finger inside the flap to rip it open. He slid out the single sheet of heavyweight paper inside and opened it up. He read it carefully, and then looked up at Geordie.

"You know what this is, I take it?"

"Yes, I'm afraid so. It's your call-up papers. You have been called back into the army from the reserve."

"And I guess you have been told what happens if I chuck this on the fire?"

"I was hoping you wouldn't ask. I'm to call the Canadian authorities and have you arrested as a deserter. Morton really wants you back."

"And Ivan?"

"Same thing. I just hope I'm not the one who has to tell him. That temper of his is a sight to behold. Unless living in the Rectory down in Wiltshire with his Sarah has managed to calm him down."

The door swung open and Jim's partner, Megan, stepped in carrying an armful of logs with an over-excited Border Collie at her heels. She looked across at the two men by the fire and a sunny smile lit up her face.

"Geordie! How wonderful to see you!"

The dog dashed across the room to welcome Geordie and to receive his expected tickle behind the ears. Megan walked behind the dog, a little more sedately. Halfway towards the men she paused and looked at the two faces. She walked to the log shelf by the stove and put down the wood.

"What's wrong?"

Geordie stayed silent and avoided her eyes. Jim looked up and handed her the letter.

"I've been called back to the colours."

"English translation, please."

"I'm back in the army as of today."

"Why? How can they do that? You've retired. Do you have to go?"

Jim nodded. "I'm afraid they can. When you leave the British Army you go into the reserve until you reach the age of fifty-five and you can be called back if you are needed."

Megan turned away. "Oh bloody hell! When do you have to go?"

"Geordie?"

"We are booked on the flight to London from Vancouver tomorrow night. Sorry, lass."

Chapter 2

The government pool car, a dark green Jaguar with a tan leather interior that had met them outside the terminal at Heathrow, carried them quickly through the Buckinghamshire countryside until the entrance to the Chequers estate appeared before them, on their right hand side. The driver turned the car in through the ornate wrought- iron gates and drove along the approach road through the well-manicured grounds.

"Well, boss, looks like there are advantages to being Prime Minister if you get given a place like this as your country residence."

"True, but it must be a bit of a wrench when you get voted out of office and lose all this."

Geordie nodded as the car swung around and stopped on the gravel drive in front of the imposing house. They got out and walked towards the entrance while the driver retrieved their bags for them. As they approached the door it swung open and a chubby man in a dark suit stepped forward to greet them.

"Good morning, gentlemen. I hope you had a pleasant flight? If you would follow me you can wait in the library with your colleague. The Prime Minister is just finishing some other business and he will be with you shortly."

Geordie grinned and looked at Jim. "That's nice, mate, but don't call me shorty."

The butler looked over his shoulder at the well-built black man with a puzzled look on his face. Jim could have told him about Geordie's favourite joke, but the jet lag was kicking in and he really couldn't be bothered.

Their guide opened the beautifully polished door and ushered them in to a well-stocked library, with shelves lining every wall. As they walked through, a large figure rose from one of the leather chesterfield chairs.

"Do you two have any idea what the fuck this is about?"

Jim smiled. "Ivan! Nice to see you, too." He strode across the expensive Persian rug and gripped the hand of his old Sergeant Major.

"Sorry, boss. Nice to see you both too. I'm just a lot grumpy about being dragged out of retirement for whatever the hell this is."

"That's three of us. Megan is spitting teeth about me leaving just as the season starts to run up and with all the preparations for the students to do."

"How is Megan? Did you two get married yet?"

"If we'd got married you would have had an invitation to Canada. How about you? Have you married your lady vicar yet?"

"No, she's being difficult and this performance is not going to help. She's damned annoyed and of course thinks it's my fault."

Ivan turned to Geordie. "Hello, mate. You're looking well. How's Sam doing?"

Geordie sat down in another of the brown leather chairs and sighed. "Not too well. She moved out and went to live with her parents a few weeks ago. I think it's over."

Ivan sat back down in his chair and Jim took a third one. "That's a shame. I thought you two were well suited, even though she's way too good for you."

"Yeah, so did I, but there you go. With her going away on acting jobs and me being deployed so much, we were becoming strangers."

The door swung open and the butler reappeared bearing a silver tray with tea and biscuits, which he laid down carefully on the coffee table.

"The Prime Minister was very particular about making sure there were chocolate biscuits for Sergeant Major Thomas. Which of you is that?"

Ivan leaned forward and took one, then said, "That's me. How did he know about my secret vice?"

"I think Mr. Orwell, the previous PM, must have told him just now."

Jim looked up sharply. "David Orwell is here?"

"That's right, sir. They will be with you very soon."

As the butler left, the three soldiers looked at each other. Jim was the first to speak.

"Now I wonder what that means. Doesn't sound good for us."

Chapter 3

Geordie put down his empty tea cup and stood up to walk to the window. He looked across the driveway and the well maintained gardens with the pleasant pasture land beyond then sighed and turned back to the others.

"How the other half live, eh?"

"It's a bit different from a rectory in rural Wiltshire, that's for sure."

"And a lot different to a cabin in the forests of British Columbia," Jim agreed. "Mind you, I bet the PM never sees a black bear wander across his garden to get a drink."

Geordie sat back down. "You see that a lot?"

"We have an old bear that lives near us and comes down to the stream most mornings, now that he is out of hibernation. Every now and then he spots me sitting on the veranda and he stops and stares at me for a while, but we never bother each other. I give him a fish if he comes when I have any."

As Jim finished speaking the door swung quietly open and the butler returned. "Would you come with me, please, gentlemen? The PM will see you now."

Jim stood and automatically smoothed down his jacket, amused to see his companions doing the same before following the round faced man in the black suit. They walked across the wide hallway into a room opposite as the butler held the door open for them. Sitting at the table was David Orwell, a face Jim and the others knew well from their previous tasks for him. Across from him was another man that Jim did not recognise. This must be Phillip Morton, he guessed.

David Orwell rose with a wide smile and came to greet them. "Jim, Ivan, Geordie, so good to see you all. You're all looking well."

Jim nodded. "Yes, sir. Retirement agrees with me."

"Ah yes. Sorry about that, but let me introduce you to our present Prime Minister and all will become clear."

Jim looked across at the table and noticed that Morton had not moved and was waiting for them to come to him. His dark hair was perfectly combed and his lean face bore an inscrutable expression as he looked at the three men appraisingly.

Morton looked from one to the other. The broad shouldered, ever-smiling black man with the quick eyes he had met before, when he sent him to collect Jim Wilson. The large man with the scarred hands and the very short hair must be Sergeant Major Ivan Thomas. And that left the third man. Not as large as the other two, he nevertheless had an air of capability about him and he looked fit despite the touch of grey hair at his temples and the clear blue eyes that stood out against the tan that comes from outdoor living. He nodded as David Orwell made the introductions.

"Sit down, gentlemen, and let us get started." He paused while they all found seats and then continued. "We are faced with a problem and it is somewhat delicate. If it becomes known we will have a serious diplomatic incident on our hands and it will damage some crucial negotiations. I spoke to Mr. Orwell about it and he recommended that I bring you in to help us, since you have proven that you are both capable and able to keep your mouths shut. Unlike an awful lot of other people I have to deal with."

Jim looked along the polished oak table at the unsmiling PM. "I can't believe that with all the people at your disposal you really need to drag two of us back from retirement."

"Maybe not, but I have not been in this job long enough to find out who in the military I can trust with a task of this delicacy and importance. Which is why I have accepted Mr. Orwell's advice."

Jim looked at his two men and then back to the PM. "All right then, sir, tell us what you need."

"Very well. Not to put too fine a point on this, I need you to kill someone. This is a person who has the capability to damage this country in a very real way."

Jim stared at the PM for a second or two in disbelief. "Forget it, sir. We are soldiers and engineers. We're not assassins."

"Don't be silly. You have been soldiers for a long time. You must have been prepared to kill for your country."

"Yes, sir, in war or in self defense. Not murder."

"It isn't murder if you are obeying orders from your Prime Minister."

"In the army they call that the Nuremburg Defense. It didn't work for the Germans in 1945 and it doesn't work now. What you are suggesting is an unlawful command and we will not be obeying it."

Morton allowed a small smile to cross his thin lips. "I'm sorry, I'm not used to dealing with the military yet, so that was by way of being a small test to find out if you are honourable people. Mr. Orwell here trusts you implicitly, but I am still finding my way."

Jim tried not to show his annoyance at being played in this way. "Very well, sir, what do you really need?"

"As you said, you are engineers, so I have a task that should suit your talents. I want you to find King John's treasure. It would help the country to have a major input of gold and precious gems right about now."

Jim glanced at Ivan and then Geordie, who both shrugged their shoulders. He looked back down the table. He could feel the irritation rising within him.

"If my history is correct, that treasure was lost in about 1216 as King John tried to cross the Wash, in East Anglia. People have been searching for it for the last 800 years in an area that was covered by the tides twice a day and which has now changed completely. Frankly, sir, this is bloody ridiculous and a waste of our time."

Morton smiled slightly again. "You have my apologies once more. I now know that you are also realists and won't wander off on some kind of wild goose chase."

Jim drew a breath. "Fine, sir. If you have quite finished with our tests, can we please get to the point?"

"Certainly, Major. In February 1967 the Treaty of Tlateloico was agreed. This forbade the stationing of nuclear weapons in the South Atlantic. The UK signed up to this and kept its promise. However, in 1982, as you may recall, Argentina invaded the Falkland Islands and had to be ejected by force. It appears that the government of the time feared that the Argentineans might try again and so they secretly stationed nuclear weapons at the new military airfield we built down there. They apparently felt that was legal as Argentina had not signed up to the treaty. They did so in 1994. But by then the presence of these weapons had been forgotten by the politicians and they were left in place."

"I can see where that would be embarrassing, but what has that to do with us? Surely you could just send a team down there to pick them up and bring them home?"

"Oh yes, we thought of that, but once the team got there they noticed that two of the weapons, WE177 free fall bombs I am told, were too light. When they investigated they found that two of the weapons were just bomb casings. The active ingredients were missing."

Ivan leaned forward. "Bloody hell! Does that mean there are two nuclear weapons loose in the world and we're responsible?"

18

"I'm afraid it does. So you see the seriousness of our position."

Jim looked keenly at the past and present Prime Ministers. "You said that politicians had forgotten about these weapons, so how did this come to your attention?"

It was David Orwell's turn to smile. "I told you they were bright, didn't I? If anyone can find these damn things, it's these three."

Morton nodded. "We were discussing some negotiations that are about to start with Argentina when one of the Senior Civil Servants in the Cabinet Office said, 'It's a good job they don't know about the bombs we had down at Mount Pleasant.' It turns out that back in 1982 he was a junior clerk in the team that positioned the weapons there. Pure chance, or we would still have known nothing about it."

"Lucky, but I still don't see why you need us. None of us are trained in Special Weapons handling. I would have thought you'd need RAF specialists for this."

Morton paused with his teacup halfway to his lips. "If it was a straight job of picking the weapons up and getting them back here you would be right. As it is, these weapons are missing and you have proven you are adept at finding things. Plus, the big one, of course, is that, based on past experience, you won't speak about it afterwards."

Jim shook his head. "I'm sorry, sir, but I feel you have the wrong people for this job."

"Sorry you may be, but I have to insist. You are the people I want, you're back in the army and you are the people who are going to find these weapons and get them back. You can use any resources at the disposal of this government and, as Mr. Orwell has done before, I will give you a letter from me giving you that authority, but you must succeed. To be clear, I want all nuclear weapons back under proper control and no more super-secret programmes."

Chapter 4

Jim sat in the front seat of the government Jaguar taking the three of them back to London. Conversation was severely limited with the driver in the car with them, so he contented himself with watching the road and working out his next moves. The driver proved to be adept at negotiating the London traffic and soon stopped in Whitehall, just outside the Cabinet Office.

They got out and stood on the wide footpath to watch the car drive away. Then Jim turned to his two men.

"Coffee before we go and see our man?"

"Sounds good, boss," said Ivan. "And I guess we need to talk."

"We do. There's a small café across the road from the Foreign Office just over there." He pointed across the road. "We need to make sure we are all on the same page with this job."

They crossed the wide avenue that is Whitehall and walked the short distance to the café Jim had pointed out. Jim and Ivan found a table in a back corner while Geordie ordered at the counter. He joined them and sat down.

"I should have asked, have you two changed the way you take your coffee?"

Both said no and paused as the waitress arrived with the tray of steaming coffee and three energy bars. They waited until she had walked away before Jim spoke.

"Right then. We need to interview this Senior Civil Servant to find out exactly what was going on all those years ago. He has been told to expect us and to tell us anything he knows. The PM is worried that these may not be the only weapons stashed away in case of war."

"How do you know that, boss?" said Ivan, unwrapping his energy bar.

"He called me back as you two were heading out to the car. He feels that there was a lack of control in the euphoria at the end of the Falklands War and there could have been some unfortunate decisions made. He's already told his people to have this civil servant on standby to talk to us."

Geordie took a swallow of coffee. "So there could be more nukes around than we know about?"

"Possibly, and that's what we need to find out from our friend in the Cabinet Office. If he doesn't know, then we have to hope he knows someone who does."

Ivan put down his paper cup. "So this could end up being a longer job then?"

Jim nodded. "Again, possibly. At this stage we are just trying to find out what the hell went on back then."

"All I've got with me is an overnight kit. I thought I was done with needing a 'go bag' packed all the time."

"Me, too. How about you, Geordie?"

"I wasn't expecting this to turn out to be an urgent job, so I've got bugger all with me, except the hand luggage I took to Canada."

Jim stood up. "I'll go and pay while you finish up and then we are off to see the wizard."

Ivan and Geordie gulped the last of their coffee and joined Jim by the door to the street. They made their way back to the Cabinet Office and went in through the polished wooden door. The very attractive young lady at the security desk took their details and issued them with visitors' ID passes, while calling for someone to escort them to the required person. they needed to interview.

They were led along corridors to a door labelled Interview Room 3 and ushered inside. They had not been there for more than a minute or two when the door opened again and a bald man with a flushed face and a well-cut grey suit entered.

"Good morning. I'm Thomas Moffatt. I'm told you want to talk to me about my days in the Ministry of Defense."

"We do," said Jim. "Shall we all sit down?"

They took chairs around the nondescript table and Moffatt leaned forward with his hands clasped together in front of him. "How can I help?"

"The PM tells me you mentioned the special weapons that were positioned in the Falklands and you were on the project team that managed that. Tell me a little more, please."

"Very well. That was my first job after joining the Civil Service. I was a very junior clerk at the time. I got put on the team because they needed a clerk and they could get me a high-level security clearance readily because of my father's position. He was a senior army officer back then; dead now, of course."

"So where was this team and what did it do?"

"They based us down at Farnborough in the Royal Aircraft Establishment that was there then. It allowed us to have three separate small buildings, but we could be secure because we were inside the RAE compound. Our job was to manage the deployment of the special weapons to RAF Mount Pleasant in such a way that there was no trace of them in the usual security logs."

"Tell me about that, would you?"

"Special Weapons, as nuclear bombs are known, are very tightly controlled. Only specially authorised people can service them and the inventory checks are stringent with double key systems to the storage bunkers and things like that. They are checked again and again to ensure no tampering."

"So how did you manage to lose them from the system?"

"There was a weakness in the system which we exploited by putting two of our own people into the checking organisation. Effectively, two weapons from RAF Marham and two from RAF Leuchars were declared as BER, that's beyond economical repair. On paper they were shipped to the Atomic Warfare Establishment at Aldermaston in Berkshire to be taken apart and the usable parts were to be recycled. Of course, they never got there, but we ensured that the two bases got the required paperwork so they never asked any questions. We also sent paperwork, apparently from the AWE, to the Special Weapons control team to show that the bombs had been dismantled and so no longer existed."

"How did they get to the Falklands?"

"We had a cargo container specially adapted for them and they went as deck cargo on a freighter. The container looked like any one of a million others and was treated as such. Nobody raised an eyebrow."

The big Welshman leaned forward. "Can I ask a question, boss?"

"Of course, Ivan. Go ahead."

"Mr. Moffatt, you said there were three buildings. Why was that? Surely it would have been easier to have all the team together, wouldn't it?"

"Compartmentalisation. It was all part of the rigid security we were working under. None of the three teams knew what the other two were doing."

"So the work of your team could have been duplicated?"

"To be honest, I really don't know. We were forbidden to talk to anyone in the other teams. The only person who knew the whole plan was the team leader and he would certainly not confide in a junior person like me."

"Who was he?"

"That was Group Captain Arthur Hesketh-Brown. A very strict man, very correct and very, very security conscious."

"Do you know where he is now?"

"No idea. He must be quite old now, if he is even still alive."

Jim turned to look at his two men "Any other questions you can think of?" They shook their heads. "Well, thank you, Mr. Moffatt. If we think of anything else we'll get back to you."

Jim watched as Moffatt left and closed the door behind him, then turned to face Ivan and Geordie. "What did you get from that?"

"There's more than just the weapons positioned in the Falklands, by the sound of it, and if Hesketh-Brown is dead we are going to have problems."

"That was my take as well. We need to find him PDQ."

"How do we do that, boss?"

"Well, Geordie, if he is still alive then somebody is paying his RAF pension, so presumably they know where he is."

"So what would you like to do first, boss?"

"Ivan, can you take yourself down to the RAF personnel records office, wherever it is now. It used to be RAF Innsworth, but I think that's closed. Get me the details on Hesketh-Brown. Plus, we need a list of all the Special Weapons technicians and Special Weapons Officers who were posted to the Falkland Islands. Somebody must have been looking after these nukes and I guess we need to find out which one of them was there when someone did the deed. I think we need you to be there physically so you can explore their records and follow any leads."

"Right. What will you be doing?"

"After we pick up the government credit cards and authority letters that the PM promised us, Geordie and I are going to get educated about the handling of Special Weapons and I think the best place to do that is probably down at the AWE in Aldermaston."

Chapter 5

The three men stood on the jetty that jutted out into the Firth of Forth and enclosed the South Queensferry Sailing Club. Jim could see through the low-lying mist on the wide, cold river to the orange girders of the Forth Bridge stretching across the water to the north bank. As an engineer, he appreciated the beauty of such an iconic structure.

Geordie, next to him, looked around. "Quite a view, eh, boss? I can see why Hesketh-Brown would retire up here."

"Me, too, and, if the directions we were given are correct, his house is over there, looking across the beach and out to the bridge."

They all looked across the beach to the row of solidly built houses that fronted the sea wall. Queensferry was not a large town, so finding the address had been simple after they had driven down from nearby Edinburgh.

"Well, his wife told me on the phone that we should join them for morning tea about now, so let's make a move."

They turned and walked back to the road, then turned again and took the seafront towards the row of houses. Jim checked the address on the piece of paper in his hand.

"This is the one," he said, pointing.

They turned in through the small gate and went up to the front door. Ivan and Geordie stood back while Jim knocked. The door opened almost immediately to reveal a slender, silver haired woman with a wrinkled face wreathed in smiles.

"My, you are prompt. I do like that. I take it you are Major Wilson?"

"Yes, ma'am. And I guess you must be Mrs. Hesketh-Brown?"

"Dolly. Everybody calls me Dolly. Silly name, but I like it. Do come in. Arthur will be down very soon."

Dolly fussed them into a comfortable, but overdone sitting room. The chintz covered chairs were surrounded by framed photographs that seemed to cover every horizontal surface. The three men settled themselves in the chairs she indicated and Jim looked around.

"You have some remarkably good paintings in here, Dolly."

"Thank you, I did those quite some while ago, before Arthur became difficult. I haven't painted for years, though."

Jim looked at Ivan and then turned back to Dolly. "Difficult? I don't mean to be rude," he said, "but what does difficult mean?"

Dolly sat down on the arm of a chair and her shoulders drooped a little. She looked up at Jim and shrugged.

"When we left the RAF we moved back up here to look after my mother, who was getting a little frail. After she passed away, we decided to stay here as it is my home town. Then Arthur started to have problems remembering things and we took him to the doctor for tests. They showed that he has Alzheimer's. Some days he can be quite lucid. Other days he doesn't even know me. The good days are getting further apart. I hope you being here will make this a good day, but I wouldn't get your hopes up."

She stood up with a small groan and walked back out of the room. They could hear her clattering in the kitchen and then the doorway filled with a tall thin man. He stood and looked at them slowly before walking in and sitting down without a word. Jim took in the neatly fastened cardigan and the cravat that was properly knotted around the man's neck.

Dolly bustled back in to the room with a tray laden with cups, saucers and a teapot with a knitted cosy. She put the tray down on the coffee table and looked at her husband.

"Arthur, have you introduced yourself to these nice people? They've come all the way from London to see you."

Arthur looked at each of them in turn. He turned to Jim last and looked him up and down.

"I take it you are in charge? What do you need from me?"

Jim was mightily relieved. It seemed they had arrived on a good day.

"Well, sir," Jim said, "I need to ask you about a project you were involved with just before you retired from the Royal Air Force. Perhaps we should speak privately because of the security classification?" He looked at Mrs. Hesketh-Brown. "Sorry, Dolly, but we have to be careful."

"Never mind, dear, but if I leave he will get agitated and you won't get anything from him. I promise not to gossip."

Hesketh-Brown continued to stare at Jim. When he spoke there was a slight tremor in his voice and an uncertainty in his eye.

"How do I know you are who you say you are? I'm not supposed to talk about those days."

Jim handed over the letter from the Prime Minister that required all government servants to cooperate fully with the enquiries. Hesketh-Brown read the document and then handed it to Dolly who also read it, before handing it back to Jim.

"What do you want to know?"

"Thank you, sir. We know that you were tasked with prepositioning nuclear weapons in the Falkland Islands, in case of further Argentinean aggression, and we know you had to do it very secretly. We also know that you had three teams working for you and we need to know what the other two teams were doing for you."

"Ah yes. Good people on those teams. The best job I had in the air force after I stopped flying. Good people, really good people. Worked hard and kept the secret. Good people."

The old man smiled as he remembered. Then the smile faded and his eyes became unfocussed.

"Who are you? What are you doing in my house? Go away! Go away!"

Dolly jumped to her feet and took Jim by the arm. "You'll have to go. I'm sorry, but I thought it was going to be a good day. Please, quickly, before he gets more upset." She bundled them out through the front door and came out with them. "I'm really sorry about that, but once he gets confused he takes ages to settle down again. If you give me your phone number, I will ask him your questions when he is better."

"Thank you, Dolly. I'm sorry we've upset your husband, but please do call me if you can get any information from him. It really is very important."

They walked away from the house and sat on the sea wall, looking out at the bridge.

"Well, boss, that was a waste of time. What the hell do we do without him?"

"Never mind, Geordie, Dolly may be able to help us at some point downstream. In the meantime, we have to find those two weapons from the Falklands and the information Ivan picked up may help with that."

Chapter 6

Sitting in Edinburgh airport, waiting for the flight back to England, Jim ran through the list of Special Weapons trained people who had been posted to RAF Mount Pleasant. He tossed the list to Geordie with an irritated sigh.

"You have a go. I can't see anything that jumps off the page at me. It looks like we are going to have to go round and interview the bloody lot of them."

Geordie picked up the sheets of paper and quietly scanned through them. He looked up as Jim walked across to the window to stare out at the runway.

"The boss is a bit grumpy today," he said to Ivan.

"Yeah? Well, me too. I can see this stretching out for weeks or even months and I've got a church roof to fix, before the damn thing falls down."

Geordie grunted and went back to the two lists. There was nothing interesting until he compared dates. He looked further and checked between the lists again. He looked up as Jim came back and sat down again.

"Sorry, gents, just getting a bit frustrated, I'm afraid."

"Never fuss, boss. I think I may have something."

"Really? Well spit it out. If it looks promising, I'll buy us all a beer."

Geordie spread the papers out on the floor in front of them and, bending over, he pointed to two names on the lists.

"There was a Flight Sergeant posted down to the Falklands here, but there was no officer posted at the same time."

Ivan looked down. "OK, but so what?"

"While we were at Aldermaston they told us there always had to be two keys to open the weapons bunker and these could only be given to specially authorised people. Now if there was only one Special Weapons qualified person on the base he could not have opened the door to the store."

"And?"

"And so he would never have seen the weapons and could not have noticed they had been tampered with."

"OK, but again where does that take us? The RAF records person told me that the establishment list stated there had to be the two Special Weapons people in Mount Pleasant and that went on for a while, after the WE177 nukes went out of service, because nobody noticed the staffing anomaly until it became tricky to find qualified people."

Geordie grinned. "That's it. That's the opportunity for the bombs to be interfered with. With only two cleared people on the site they would have talked while they were working and the guy before the last Flight Sergeant would have known the next officer would not be security cleared for the task. Not sure how that helps, but I think that means this is the man we want to talk to." He pointed at a name on the list.

"Nice work, Geordie," said Jim, picking up the papers and looking them over. "Has to be worth a try as a start point. Do we know where he is, Ivan?"

The big Welshman turned and opened the bag at his side. "We do. I've got a second set of lists here with all their last known locations. The people are motivated to keep the records office informed so they keep receiving their military pensions."

He handed the papers to Jim who scanned down the list. He put his finger on the target name and looked up with a smile.

"What have you found, boss?"

"Well, not to be outdone by you, Geordie, I think I have a new clue as well."

Geordie took the list that Jim was holding out to him and looked at the relevant entry. He shook his head and looked up while passing the papers to Ivan.

"Don't see it. Are you going to give us a clue?"

"It's the address. It's a village down in the Cotswolds near Bath. I know that village and it's damned expensive to buy a house there. Lots of successful actors and even some minor royalty live round there. So, unless our boy won the lottery, I wonder how he afforded that on an RAF pension."

"Maybe he's got a rich wife?"

"Maybe, but we'll find out tomorrow when we drop in on him."

Chapter 7

Jim climbed out of the car and looked around at the neatly laid out gardens that surrounded the very pleasant cottage style house, set back from the road. He could not guess what a place like this would cost in this area, but it was certainly beyond what a Flight Sergeant's pension would stretch to. He and Ivan walked across the gravel drive to the front door while Geordie stayed in the car. The door swung open as Jim reached for the ornate brass knocker.

"Yes?"

Jim took in the chubby man who stood before him. Silver haired, with a small pot belly and still wearing his tartan house slippers.

"Good morning. I am looking for Mr. Brian Potts. Have I got the right house?"

"That's me. Who are you?"

"I'm Major Jim Wilson. I'd like to talk to you about your service in the Royal Air Force."

"Not interested. I've put those days behind me now. So you've had a wasted journey."

Potts stepped back and started to swing the door closed. The door stopped and swung back open as Ivan shot out his powerful arm and pushed. Without another word the big Welshman stepped forward and entered the house.

"What the ...?"

Ivan looked down at Potts. "We don't have time to mess around with you. You're going to answer some questions."

Potts looked into Ivan's determined face and swallowed. He looked at Jim and saw no relief there either.

"Who is it, dear?" A woman's voice came down the passage from what must have been the kitchen.

"Just some visitors who want to talk to me." Potts pointed a shaky finger at the doorway nearest to them. "In there."

Ivan stepped back to allow Jim to lead the way and watched as Potts closed the front door and followed on. The room was neatly furnished and had definitely been decorated with good taste. Jim and Ivan took the two armchairs while Potts perched nervously on the edge of the sofa.

Jim looked around and then back at Potts. "Nice house. Nice area, too. It must have set you back quite a bit. Pretty good for a retired Flight Sergeant."

Potts swallowed again and Jim noticed the tiny beads of sweat start to appear at his receding hairline. A short chubby woman, evidently the owner of the voice from the kitchen, bustled into the room, still wiping her hands on the tea towel. Jim and Ivan stood politely.

"Oh, sit down both of you. No need to be formal. Who's for a nice cup of tea?"

"Don't put yourself to any trouble, Mrs. Potts. We won't be here very long, will we, Brian?" said Jim turning back to the man on the sofa.

"No, that's right, dear. We won't be a moment and then we can go into Bristol like you wanted."

He'd done well to control his voice, Jim thought, though he marvelled that Mrs. Potts hadn't noticed her husband's pallor.

She shrugged and bustled out again. They could hear her quietly singing to herself in the kitchen.

"Right then, Mr. Potts, I'm guessing you didn't win the lottery and you didn't marry a rich wife, did you? So I think we both know where the money came from for this rather expensive house, don't we?" Jim asked.

"Do we? I've been careful with my money all my life. I had decent savings when I left the air force and with the retirement gratuity we had enough to move here."

"Really?" Jim raised a quizzical eyebrow. "And you will be able to prove all that to the Military Police when they turn up here, will you?"

"Military Police? Why would they come here? I've been a civilian for a while now."

"I think it's well past time for you to stop telling your cover story, Mr. Potts. We know it was you who stole the nuclear devices from RAF Mount Pleasant in the Falklands and I'm pretty sure you sold them to finance this very nice house. You will find that the Military Police are far less polite than us and it will be them rather than the local police, I can promise you that."

Potts' shoulders dropped and he leaned back into the sofa cushions and sighed. He looked at Jim and Ivan and they both could see the beaten expression in his eyes.

Ivan leaned forward and spoke almost gently. "Come on, Brian. Tell us the story."

Chapter 8

Brian Potts lay back in the soft cushions of the sofa and stared at the ceiling above him. He seemed shrunken and deflated. His voice when he spoke was calm and resigned.

"I was stationed at Marham at the time. My orders for a six-month tour in the Falklands had just come through, maybe four days before. Susan was in the supermarket when this guy came up and spoke to her by name. He said he wanted to meet me and would she give me the card he handed to her. She didn't think anything of it and gave me the card when I came in off the night shift. I rang the number and the guy who answered asked if we could meet; he said he had a proposition for me. Well, retirement was looming and I had put out some feelers for a job, so I thought it was one of them."

Potts looked across at Ivan, who was making notes in the pad on his knee.

"What's going to happen to me?"

"We'll worry about that later," Jim answered, "but being helpful now will make things easier for you. Carry on with what you were saying."

Potts eased himself up a little then continued. "So, we met up at a local pub that Saturday afternoon. I walked in and this swarthy man was sitting at a table in the bay window overlooking the river."

"Swarthy?"

"Probably the wrong word. He had that Mediterranean complexion and dark, almost black hair. It looked like he was overdue a shave. Turns out he was Greek. In any case, he bought me a beer and we sat at the table again where nobody could hear us. He told me had heard I was due to go off to the Falkland Islands and he wondered if I knew the special weapons officer who would be down there at the same time. I didn't and he told me the name. I knew the man; I had served with him before at Lossiemouth. I knew he was a complete waste of skin and I said so. The Greek just smiled at that and said that he knew that already, but it was nice to have it confirmed."

"Did he tell you how he knew all this?"

"I asked him and he just told me that money can buy information and left it at that."

Potts stopped and sat up as his wife pottered back in with a tray of teacups and a teapot. "I was having a drink anyway, so I thought I'd make you some as well dears. I brought you a plate of biscuits too so help yourselves. I'll take a cup out to your driver as well for you," she said over her shoulder, as she left the room.

They each took a cup and Ivan took two of the chocolate biscuits; giving in to his only weakness. Potts sipped his tea then carried on.

"Then he made me an offer. He knew that the officer, Johnson, was going to be the last special weapons qualified officer to be posted to Mount Pleasant, so he knew that nobody else would be able to go into the special weapons store afterwards."

"Why not?" said Jim.

"It's a security thing; there are always two keys so that nobody could ever be alone with the weapons. Once Johnson finished his tour down there the key would leave with him to be held by the special weapons project team."

Potts sipped his tea again and nibbled on a biscuit. Jim and Ivan waited and let the silence press their man.

"He knew about the WE177 bombs being in the Falklands and he offered me a serious amount of money to get a couple for him. He didn't want the whole bomb, he just wanted the active working parts from inside the casing, and he wanted me to modify them so they could be triggered by a timer."

"And you agreed?" said Jim incredulously.

Potts nodded sadly. "It was a lot of money. More than I had ever dreamed of having and he told me he was going to make sure that the bombs were only used to blackmail people in the Middle East. Well, after all the terror attacks that didn't seem so bad."

"I don't get it," said Ivan. "If you had to have Johnson there all the time, how could you interfere with the weapons?"

"That was the clever part. He knew Johnson was a lazy bastard and a drunk. He knew that he could be persuaded to hand over his key just so he could stay in bed and nurse his hangovers."

"But what about the rest of the station? Surely they would have noticed something?"

"No. You see, the WE177 Special Weapons had been taken out of service years before. The RAF no longer officially had any air-launched nuclear capability, so of course as far as the rest of the base was concerned there could not be Special Weapons there. The bunker was hidden away in case of an Argentinean sneak attack and not noticeable unless you knew where to look. People tend not to go wandering around in the weather they have in the Falklands."

"Go on then: so what happened?"

"I agreed to do it and it worked out just as he had predicted. Johnson didn't want to know. He was just as lazy as I remembered him and his fondness for the bottle had grown. He may even have been using drugs. He handed over the key and even thanked me for making his life easier. Then I had six months on my own to extract the active components and make the modifications."

"How did you get them out of the islands? You can't have flown them back."

"That's right. The security would have spotted them if I had tried to send them airfreight. I called the Greek when they were ready and we arranged that a fishing boat would come into one of the small coves near the base and I would take the bombs down there one at a time in the back of a Land Rover. It was a real pig of a job getting the devices onto the vehicle bed on my own; even stripped out, they're pretty heavy. It took two nights with the trawler standing offshore during the day. I nearly got caught bringing the Land Rover back the second night."

"And then?"

"And then at the end of the tour Johnson asked me to hand in his key to the project team when I got back to the UK."

"Did you?"

"No. That would have started questions. Remember, the WE177 was out of service by then and nobody outside a very small group of technical people knew they were still there. I've got both keys in my workshop in the garage."

"I take it you got paid?"

"Half up front and half when I delivered the second device."

Jim sat back in his chair and studied Potts. This had been unbelievably simple. All that was need was one inefficient officer and a corrupt technician. Amazing how the secrecy had worked against the safety of the weapons.

"So then when was this meeting exactly, and what was the name of this Greek and where was he from?"

"He told me his name was Niklas Christophides, but I have no idea where he came from. I'll have to look the dates up. They'll be in my diary from that year."

Chapter 9

They drove back through the winding country lanes towards the motorway. Jim, deep in thought, stayed silent. He looked round when Ivan tapped him on the shoulder.

"Come on then, boss, what did I miss? How did you know for sure that Potts was the one?"

"How do you mean?"

"When you told him you knew he had stolen the weapons and where the money had come from."

Jim smiled a little. "Oh, that. Just a bluff. I took a chance on catching him off guard. He's probably been waiting for that knock on the door since it happened. So I tried it on and it worked."

Ivan sat back, shaking his head. "Well, that was bloody brass necked! You had me convinced as well. Lucky. So what's the plan from here on?"

"We need to find Christophides and persuade him to tell us where the devices are now."

Geordie glanced across at Jim. "You do know that Christophides is a pretty common name in Greece? It's going to be worse than the famous needle in a haystack."

Jim smiled. "Maybe not quite that bad. The UK Borders Agency swipes the passport of everyone who comes into the country legally, so somewhere is a database of all the names for the time this guy came here from Greece. Potts gave us the date of his meeting so we get them to look a week either side and see what pops up."

"That could still be a hell of a lot of people."

"True, but I am counting on the fact that as an arms dealer he may have a flag against him on the database as a person to be watched for. If not, we just have to check everybody with the same name."

Geordie glanced across at Jim again, but said nothing. Ivan leaned forward in the back seat and tapped Jim's arm again.

"How do we know he's an arms dealer?"

"We don't for sure, but who else would have that kind of money to buy those two weapons? And who would know what modifications he wanted made to them?"

"Terrorists, maybe?"

"It could be, but I don't know of any active Greek terror groups at the moment and the rule seems to be to recruit people from the same background so you don't get betrayed. I reckon our Greek is a middle man, at least I hope he is or we may struggle to persuade him to talk."

♦ ♦ ♦ ♦

Geordie looked up from his computer. "Boss. The email from the Borders Agency has come in. We've been lucky. In the time period we gave them, only one Niklas Christophides came into the UK legally. It seems he's not Greek, he's a Greek Cypriot. There's no address information, though."

"So how the hell do we find him? It's a big island."

Ivan turned round in his chair. "I may have a contact who can help."

"Really? Who?"

"I served with a guy who settled out there when he retired. He was one of those people who could get you anything as long as you didn't enquire too closely how he got it. He went into fraud prevention when he left the army, but a couple of years ago he bought a place near Ayia Napa."

"How will he be able to help, do you think?"

"He may not know him, but he will know people who may know people, if you take my meaning. He's just that kind of guy."

"So give him a call."

"I'll call to make sure he is there, but probably best if I go and see him. A thing like this is better done face to face."

Geordie perked up. "And I know my way round Cyprus. I did a six-month tour there with the UN a few years ago."

Ivan nodded. "That might help. How about we all go, boss? We've got nothing here and it gives us a bit of flexibility on the ground."

Chapter 10

Geordie drove the hire car out of the airport and almost immediately they found themselves on the main A3 road to Ayia Napa. They skirted the British Sovereign Base Area at Dhekelia and were parking outside their hotel in less than an hour. While Jim and Geordie checked in, Ivan found a phone box in the lobby and called his friend. He came back to join the other two with a smile on his face.

"He's going to come down here right now to meet us. He sounded bored so we are a bit of excitement for him."

"A phone box is rather old school, isn't it? Did you tell him what we need?" Jim asked.

"No signal for my mobile here and, no, I thought I'd leave that to you."

Jim nodded and they picked up their bags and headed for the elevator. Thirty minutes later they were sitting outside on the terrace, overlooking the bright blue Mediterranean and nursing an ice-cold beer each when Ivan looked up at the glass door of the terrace.

"Here he is," he said, standing and walking towards a man in a pale blue shirt and khaki shorts. Ivan called a waiter over, ordered another beer, then steered his friend to the table. "Gents, this is Mike Donald. He's the guy who can find anything and get it for you. At least he used to be."

"Nice to meet you all," said Donald in a soft Scottish burr. "Ivan tells me you need my help. What can I do for you?"

Jim looked around quickly to ensure they couldn't be heard. "We need to find a man called Niklas Christophides. We think he might be an arms dealer and we need to find him quietly."

"An arms dealer? That may take a while; people in that kind of business tend to be very private."

Ivan smiled. "That's why we thought of you. If we go to the police and ask, then Christophides will know about us before we get an answer."

"That's probably true round here; everyone seems to be related. OK, I'll see what I can do. So why do you need to find him?"

Ivan glanced at Jim, who shook his head slightly. "Sorry, mate, I know it sounds rude, but we can't tell you. Just so you know, it's serious."

"Well, if I don't get to hear that, you can buy me dinner to compensate. There's a cracking place down on the beachfront. The owner is a friend of mine."

♦ ♦ ♦ ♦

With dinner finished they sat watching the sun go down, sipping a very acceptable local brandy. "So when can you start asking around, Mike?" Ivan asked.

"Already started. I had a word with the owner here and he has put the word out to his contacts. I've called a couple of other mates who have also started looking around. We should get an answer soon, if he is on the island."

"Not wanting to be pushy, but how soon is soon?"

"I'd be surprised if I can't give you something tomorrow."

Chapter 11

The large white villa was almost invisible from the road, nestled among the pine trees on the lower slopes of Mount Troodos. As they drove closer Jim could see the high wall that surrounded the estate with a solid-looking wooden gate set back from the road. Geordie swung the car up to the gate and stopped. Ivan pointed wordlessly to the two security cameras that swung inwards to look them over. There was a keypad and speaker unit mounted next to the gate and Jim got out and walked over to it. He thumbed the call button and waited.

"*Yasas?*"

Jim leaned closer to the microphone. "Do you speak English?"

"Yes. What do you want?"

"We want to speak to Mr. Christophides."

"Who are you and what do you want to speak about?"

"My name is Major Jim Wilson. I am in the British Army and I want to speak to Mr. Christophides on a matter of business."

"What business?"

"That's between Mr. Christophides and me."

"Wait."

The microphone stopped humming and Jim turned to look down the slope towards the Mediterranean. It seemed arms dealers made enough money to buy a very pleasant view across the plain to the sunlit sea that sparkled in the distance. Ivan and Geordie got out of the car that was starting to heat up in the sunshine and walked across to join Jim enjoying the view. It had been decided before they arrived that they would not give any hidden microphones anything to pick up, even when they seemed to be alone.

There was a loud click behind them and then the hum of electric motors as the large gate swung open. A uniformed guard stood inside with a pump action shotgun slung over his shoulder. Without a word he waved to indicate they should drive in. They got back in the car and as they passed the guard he pointed along the sweeping drive to the villa.

Geordie drove beneath the cool shadow of the fir trees and swung the car to a stop outside the portico covering the front door of the villa. Jim noticed they were being watched from the shade of the trees by yet another uniformed and armed security man. As he opened the door and climbed out, a small, smiling man with jet-black hair walked down the steps towards them with his hand stretched out in greeting.

"Welcome to my home. A surprise having the British Army visit me up here, but a welcome one. Come in out of the sun, I am having cold drinks brought to the pool for you. Come, come, follow me."

A little stunned by the effusive welcome, Jim followed Christophides up the four wide steps into the cool of the house, Geordie and Ivan behind him. Jim looked around as they walked in and followed the small man towards the pool glistening behind the wide glass doors in front of them. The house was very tastefully decorated. Jim had expected to see weapons or martial paintings on the walls, but there were none.

"You have a beautiful house, Mr. Christophides."

"Thank you, but I can take little credit for it. My role is to provide the money so that my wife and my daughter can have what they want. My wife had wonderful taste and she has taught my daughter to carry on now she is gone."

"Gone?"

"Yes. You must know the business I am in? A rival decided he would frighten me away from a big deal by killing my wife and threatening my daughter. A foolish thing to do."

Geordie glanced at Ivan then said, "Foolish, sir?"

"Oh yes. I sent a message to anyone else that would try and hurt my family. I had him and his two sons handcuffed to the railing of his motor cruiser and then we sank it. A shame really, it was a lovely boat, but in my business weakness is punished harshly and the message was received very clearly."

Jim looked at the small Greek. "Are you serious?"

Christophides looked at Jim with cold eyes. "I am always serious about business, Major, and Greeks take family very seriously, too. He should have known that. Now come and sit here in the shade and tell Alessandro here what you would like to drink."

Jim contemplated the young man in the white jacket who stood patiently waiting for them. His broad shoulders and narrow waist showed he was a man who kept himself fit. The slight bulge of his jacket at his waist showed he had a larger role in the household than just fetching drinks.

The drink orders taken, Alessandro left quietly. "He looks a useful young man."

"Oh, he is. He is one of my household staff; they are all trained as bodyguards as well as their normal duties. As I was telling you, it is not good to be unprepared in this business and there are many people who would be happy to take all this from me."

The drinks arrived and the three men sipped their cold beer appreciatively and waited for the waiter to withdraw.

"So, Major, what can Niklas Christophides do for you today?"

Jim leaned forward slightly in his chair. "Mr. Christophides, I need to be delicate here. We have discovered that two rather dangerous weapons have disappeared from a Royal Air Force armoury in the Falkland Islands. We are given to understand that you may know where they are and might be willing to help us recover them."

The Greek looked steadily at Jim and then his eyes drifted to take in the other two soldiers.

"And what is in this for me? I am a businessman, you must understand. If I am able to find this information for you, what do I get in return?"

"I suppose I could offer you money, but clearly you have plenty of that, judging by this beautiful house. So it has to be something else that you value."

Christophides raised a finger from the arm of his chair and Jim registered Alessandro moving forward and reaching under his jacket. "I do hope you are not about to threaten the welfare of my family, Major?"

"No, sir, that's not on the table at all. The British don't engage in that sort of blackmail. No, it's something much more to your advantage."

The Greek waved his hand slightly and Alessandro relaxed a little. "You intrigue me, Major. What have you got to offer me if not money?"

"Mr. Christophides, how would you like to stay in business?" Jim looked steadily at the Greek. "Let me explain. Your business relies heavily on keeping a low profile and not dealing with people who might cause difficulties to other more powerful people."

"Explain some more, if you please."

"If the US government was to gain information that you had been supplying weapons to terrorist groups who attack them, then I don't think you would stay in business very long."

"I do not deal weapons to these madmen. They are too unstable and dangerous."

"I'm sure that's true, but I doubt if the Americans would check too carefully before they shut you down, just in case, and if the information came to them from a friendly government, why would they doubt it?"

"You have my attention, Major. You have a way with words. But now it is time for my lunch. You will stay and join me, of course, so you can explain exactly what you need afterwards."

Chapter 12

Christophides refused to talk business across his table, but proved to be an affable and interesting host. His lovely dark-haired daughter joined them and spent almost the whole meal speaking quietly with Geordie. The conversation of the rest of the group roamed far and wide, although every time it came near to weapons, the Greek steered it back to lighter topics. After a large lunch and some very acceptable local wine, Christophides stood up and motioned for them to follow him out onto the wide terrace that looked down into his garden.

"Did your wife design the garden for you as well, sir?" said Geordie, admiring the view.

"No, my friend, that was all me. I wanted to save the native plants of my island and here between the mountain and the plain is the ideal spot. Perhaps you would like my daughter to show you around?"

The girl smiled sweetly and led Geordie away to the white stone stairs that led down to the garden. Christophides watched them go and sighed. He turned round towards Jim and rested against his stone balustrade. "Well now, Major, tell me all."

"As you may know the two weapons we have to try and find were air launched. More importantly, they were nuclear."

The small man spread his hands to show surprise. "Surely air launched weapons would be useless unless you also had an aircraft capable of dropping them?"

"Ordinarily that would be true, but these have been removed from their bomb casings and modified to be usable on a timer."

"Dangerous in the wrong hands, Major. I see your problem."

"Very dangerous. So you can see why we need to find them urgently. Any help you could give in locating them would be welcome and I'm sure my government would be appreciative."

"How appreciative?"

"So appreciative you would be allowed to carry on in business without interference."

"Ah, my daughter is bringing your handsome friend back from the garden. I will see what I can do for you, Major. Can I contact you tomorrow?"

Jim nodded as Geordie rejoined them. Christophides' daughter walked away into the house with a smile at the group. Christophides started to usher them towards the door when his daughter returned with a small red box in her hand.

"Calanthe, what have you there?"

"A small present for my new friend, Geordie. It will look better on his dark skin than it does on me."

She walked across and turned Geordie around, then opened the red box and withdrew a large gold medallion on a gold chain which she draped around his neck and fastened for him. She turned him back to face her and stepped back to admire the effect.

"It looks good on you. You must promise to wear it always until you find what you are looking for. Promise?"

Geordie looked down. "I promise, but what is it?"

"It is a medallion of St Anthony, the patron saint of lost things. He will help you in your search."

"Thank you, bonny lass. Maybe I'll bring it back to you when the search is over."

Calanthe smiled and watched as he turned and joined the others as they walked towards the door. Christophides took his daughter's hand and they walked behind the three men, then stopped at the head of the stairs to wave as they drove off.

Ivan looked at the medallion and grunted. "That girl seemed quite taken with you."

"Obviously someone who appreciates true masculine beauty," said Geordie, smiling and fingering the chunky gold medal.

Ivan turned to Jim in the back seat. "I played along, boss, but what were we playing at back there? That whole thing was way more civilized than I expected. We know damn fine that Christophides is the bugger who bribed Potts and got the weapons."

"Subtlety, I hope. If we knew that he had them we would be obliged to call in the heat. If we pretend he is helping us we don't have to and we all stay friends and he cooperates rather than being obstructive. It always pays to avoid cornering a rat."

Ivan sat back in his seat and looked out of the window. "I hope you're right and we haven't just been played for suckers:"

Chapter 13

Jim joined his two men on the hotel terrace for breakfast the next morning. Having filled his plate and picked up his coffee, he walked across to their table overlooking the azure Mediterranean.

"Morning, boss. Any news from Mr. Christophides?"

"Strangely enough, yes, Ivan. It seems it was quite easy for him to tap into his contacts and find out where the weapons went. Surprising, eh?"

Ivan grinned. "Looks like you were right about not cornering him then. So where do we have to go to collect them?"

Jim speared a small sausage from his plate. "Not as simple as that, unfortunately. It seems they have been sold and shipped separately to a couple of individuals. He had names and rough locations, but not exact ones. We are going to have to go and find these damn things and then work out how to recover them."

Geordie wiped the crumbs from around his mouth and off his new medallion. "So where next on the magical mystery tour?"

"Two choices. Zimbabwe or Belize."

"Really? Who the hell would want nukes in places like that?"

"We'll have to find them and ask them. Can you two go find a computer and get us booked to whichever one is easier to get to? Book us a trip by way of London, will you? I need to sort a couple of things out before we head off."

♦♦♦♦

Three days later Jim leaned across the aisle of the aircraft and tapped Ivan on the arm. As the big man woke up Jim pointed to the illuminated sign telling them to fasten seat belts as the aircraft lined up for a landing in Harare, Zimbabwe.

The aircraft landed hard. Maybe the pilot was unused to landing on airfields at around five thousand feet above sea level. Jim looked through the aircraft window at the scrubby grass alongside the runaway as they taxied to the terminal. The heat was already starting to build with the hard sunlight on the fuselage.

The terminal had seen better days, but at least they were able to get through passport control once the bribes, customary in this part of Africa, had been handed over. Further bribes were needed to get the hired Land Rover out of the airport and through the military security gate. They took the road into the city, passing locals, who could not afford the broken-backed buses, walking along the roadside.

They drove into the chaotic city until they found the start of the A5 highway that would take them to their destination in Kwekwe. An hour out of Harare they came to yet another military checkpoint and after the vehicle was searched the disappointment of the searchers on finding nothing to steal had to be assuaged by paying the soldiers yet another bribe.

As they drove clear of the checkpoint Ivan leaned forward in his seat. "Here's a thought, boss: when we do find this device, how the hell are we going to get it out of here with all these checkpoints?"

"That's why we spent the day in London on the way here. I was setting up our exit strategy."

Geordie glanced across at Jim. "So when do we hear what that is, boss?"

"I thought I'd keep that one as a surprise for you. A magician never reveals his tricks, but I promise it'll be fun."

Ivan grunted and sat back, returning to watching the scrubby bush land pass the window. He had hoped to see herds of antelope or zebra running across the plains, but so far, nothing.

They passed a slow-moving train on the surprisingly narrow gauge railway that every now and then came close to the road. Then they were driving into the town of Kwekwe. The highway took them into what looked like the town centre, with a traffic roundabout overlooked by the onion dome of a mosque and a small row of shops close alongside. Geordie turned the Land Rover off the road and into a parking slot in front of a butcher's shop.

"As good a place as any to start asking, eh?"

Jim agreed. "It'll do nicely. Take a shop each and see if anybody knows him. Paul Verstegen, remember, provided Christophides was telling us the truth. Keep it low key; we are just looking for friend of ours and want to surprise him:"

They split up and each took one of the shops. Minutes later they were back out in the parking lot. Jim and Ivan had drawn a blank, but Geordie walked towards them with a broad smile on his face.

Jim waited and then said, "Well?"

"That place we are booked to stay tonight, boss, the Golden Mile. It's just south of town and it seems Verstegen's place is a little way beyond it. It used to be a quite big farm, but he just has the farmhouse now. Apparently we drive past the hotel until we see a track on the left with a red sign by it. We take that and then after a bit we come to the farmhouse. The butcher said it's a good job we got the Land Rover; the track is rough as hell."

"Sounds like that's a job for first thing in the morning then. Before it gets too hot. Right now I reckon we head off and find the hotel and a few cold beers."

Ivan smiled. "Good plan, boss. I wonder what the local brew is like."

"So do we call and tell him we are coming?" Geordie asked, as he started the car.

"No, Geordie, we don't. This character is sitting with a nuclear bomb somewhere. If he knows we are coming we may panic him so that he sets it off or takes it away to hide it."

"That could happen when we roll into his front yard, too."

"That's true, but I'm counting on him having hidden it somewhere nearby, and we need to be there as a surprise so he can't get to it before we stop him, at least, that is my working plan."

Chapter 14

As the sun just crested the horizon Jim drove into Verstegen's farm and slid the Land Rover to a halt right outside the front door in a cloud of dust. He stepped out of the cab and looked around, spitting the dust out of his mouth. There was no sign of movement. He walked across to the door and knocked. There was no reply, but he heard another door slam somewhere at the back of the low bungalow.

He waited until he heard the scuffle and then walked along to the corner of the building and turned left. There was Ivan with a very firm grip on the arm of a paunchy red faced man who was struggling to no effect against the power of the Welshman's arm.

"Ah, Mr. Verstegen. Sorry to barge in like this. I see you've already met Ivan and no doubt Geordie will be here in a moment."

"Right behind you, boss," said Geordie, appearing from behind a battered looking tractor. "Looks like you were right to send us in early to wait for you."

Jim grinned at his Staff Sergeant then turned back to the farmer. "Now, Mr. Verstegen, we missed our breakfast to be with you this early, so how do you feel about offering us a cup of tea?"

The red-faced man found his voice. "You can go to hell and get off my land anyway!"

Jim shook his head slowly. "I'm afraid I can't do that. We have some rather important business to discuss with you. Ivan, would you take Mr. Verstegen inside, please?"

"You're wasting your time trying to do business here. The bloody government thugs have already taken my farm. All that's left is what you see right here."

Ivan encouraged Verstegen inside and sat him down in the chair next to the empty stone fireplace, then stood behind him. Geordie wandered off to the kitchen to make the tea. Jim sat down opposite the old man, noting his unhealthy looking flushed face.

"Now, sir, you weren't quite truthful with us outside now, were you? You do have at least one valuable thing left. Unfortunately, it was originally stolen from the British government and we want it back."

"I don't know what you mean. I've got nothing belonging to the British."

"Not even that nuclear bomb you bought from Niklas Christophides a short while ago? We need to take that back into safe keeping. We especially don't want it to fall into the hands of an unstable regime such as the one you have here. A nuclear device in the hands of your government would be something of a nightmare."

"How could I have a nuclear weapon? That's just ..."

Ivan leaned forward and poked Verstegen in the back with his large index finger. Jim had forgotten just how intimidating his Sergeant Major could be when he wanted.

"Don't waste our time, Mr. Verstegen. Mr. Christophides was very helpful and we know damn fine that you've got it," said Ivan in a low menacing voice.

Verstegen's shoulders slumped and he sat down into his chair with his head back, looking at the ceiling. He didn't react as Geordie clattered in with a tray bearing steaming tea cups. Geordie set the tray down on the low table and then quietly found himself a chair.

Verstegen's head came up and he looked at Jim with tears rolling down his florid cheeks. "You don't understand. None of you Europeans understand what has been happening here This was my last chance for payback on these bastards before I die."

Jim looked at the broken man opposite him. "Well, why don't you tell us about it?"

The old man wiped the tears from his cheeks and drew a long shuddering breath. "Have you ever heard about Flight RH825? No, of course not. It was a war crime during our long Bush War and nobody said a word about it. Even before most of the white people left this country, or were driven out by government thugs, we were only a small population, so we knew each other well. I knew people on Flight 825 and one of them went to school with me. She was a lovely girl and what was done to those people was terrible. Another friend of mine was one of the few survivors."

Chapter 15

3 September 1978. Flight RH825 from Kariba Rhodesia.

The late afternoon sun was dipping down to what would almost certainly be yet another glorious Kariba sunset as he walked across the hot tarmac to the waiting aircraft. The four-engine Viscount stood waiting for him with almost all the passengers already aboard. They were just waiting for him and the Danish guy with his wife. He waited as the couple climbed the aircraft steps and then followed them.

The plane was almost full with just a couple of seats left, right at the back. He walked down the aisle between the mixture of families and businessmen returning to Salisbury. He hoped there weren't going to be too many squealing babies this trip. He was tired and a short nap would be welcome.

The forward door was shut and the four engines rumbled into life in turn. With no other traffic at that time of day there was no delay as they lined up on the runway and accelerated forward for take-off. He was pushed back in his seat as the nose of the aircraft came up and they soared into the air. He looked out of his window to see the wide expanse of the lake moving away behind them with the sun reflecting and turning the water to bronze.

He was about to settle back into his seat when he saw the trail of smoke rising from the ground. He had no time to wonder what had caused it when there was an explosion from the port inner engine and flames started to gush backwards in the airflow. The aircraft seemed to stagger in the air as the nose dropped. His mind refused to process what had happened for a moment or two and then he realised what he had seen. A missile fired from the ground must have hit them. Why the hell would a civilian flight be targeted?

The Fasten Seat Belt signs flickered on and the calm voice from the cockpit came over the loudspeakers. It assured the passengers that everything was under control and that he was going to make a crash landing. Then came the command, "Empty your pockets, take shoes off and grab your ankles."

Before he bent over to obey he looked out of the window at the intensely burning gout of flame that now reached back as far as the tail fin. The landing would have to be soon if it was to be accomplished before the wing melted and fell away. The aircraft banked into what felt like a tight circle. Evidently the pilot had spotted a safe landing site.

The captain's voice echoed around the passenger cabin again. "Brace for impact, heads down!"

He cringed and gritted his teeth. A quick glance through the window at the tree branches flashing by, then there was an almighty crash and everything turned black. He could hear nothing. Then the smoke started and he came back to himself, coughing violently. The Danish guy and his wife, in the seats across the aisle, were moving slowly. He raised himself up gingerly and looked forward. Flames were licking around the front end of the passenger cabin and there were people screaming and calling for help from God. The luxurious red hair of the woman seated in front of him was on fire, but she never moved.

He tried to stand, but some force held him down. He fell back into the seat and looked down in a half stupor. The belt was still fastened across his lap. He flipped the catch open and staggered into the aisle. The smoke from the ever-building fire was choking him and making it difficult to see. He blundered forward two steps looking for a way out. There was a crack in the side wall of the fuselage and the Danish man was tearing at it with his bare hands. He moved to join him and together they ripped a hole just wide enough to climb through. The Dane picked up a little girl and lifted her out of the plane. Both men were screaming at the other passengers to move and get outside.

He climbed through the ragged hole and started to help other dazed and injured passengers as they made it out. Both men lifted more children out through the hole and carried them clear of the wreckage. The Dane's wife was inside the cabin holding yet another child. They reached in and got them both out.

She turned with tears streaming down her face. "It's too late for the rest. They are all on fire."

They picked up the air hostess, who had a crushed leg, and carried her away from the carnage. Her only concern was whether they had got the rest of the passengers out. The small group of thirteen survivors gathered away from the aircraft, which then exploded in a huge mushroom-shaped fireball.

The night was growing chilly so they searched around the crash site for anything to keep the injured warm and prevent them going into shock. As he walked among the scattered suitcases he found a pretty Asian girl lying dead on the ground. She was unmarked and must have been thrown from the crash on impact.

He walked on and stared at the remains of the huge anthill behind the plane. Hitting this must have been what ruined the crash landing. Beyond it, he could see the tail section of the aircraft that had snapped off and now stood alone in the gloom.

The pressing need now was for water and help. He joined the small group of uninjured passengers who volunteered to go to the village that must be nearby. They could smell the cooking fires on the breeze. They set off, stumbling through the darkness.

Some hours later, as they were making their way back to the crash site carrying what water they could in improvised containers, they heard gunfire ahead of them. Bursts of automatic fire, screams and laughter echoed through the flat bush land. They slowed and considered what to do.

Eventually the sounds stopped and they carried on, reaching the burned area around the wreckage just as dawn was breaking. As he walked past the remains of the aircraft he came across the Asian girl again. He stared at the bayonet hole in her head. He brushed the tear from his cheek and walked onto where the others in his party were standing looking down at the jumbled remains of the people they had left behind.

The Dane and his wife climbed from their hiding place and walked across to look down at the pathetic corpses: children, an old woman, the old man he had helped from the wreck and the injured air hostess. All shot and bayoneted to death. Their clothes wrenched roughly to one side in the search for valuables. Suitcases ripped open and scattered around.

"They came out of the bush. They shouted to us that they were our friends. Then when they had them all in the same place they started killing. The old woman pleaded for the childrens' lives, but they shot her and them anyway." The wife of the Danish man was crying as she told them.

He looked up, misty-eyed. A Dakota from the Rhodesian Air Force passed over, then turned and came back towards them. He saw the paratroopers dropping from it to try and help them. He looked down again. Too late for these poor souls.

Chapter 16

Jim sat quietly for a moment after listening to the story. "That was pretty bloody awful. I can see why you wanted payback, but a nuke? Really? What were you planning to do with it? And where the hell did you get the money?"

"Yeah. I guess I wasn't thinking straight when I bought it. Once I'd got the damn thing I realised that the only way I could get at the bastards who were in charge when 825 went down would kill an awful lot of ordinary people as well. And most Zimbabweans are decent people who just want to get on with their lives. This farm used to turn a handsome profit before the thugs stole it from me. Luckily I had seen the writing on the wall and got the money out before inflation sent it into free fall. So all a bit of a waste of time and money really."

Jim nodded. "So how about you just hand the damned thing over and we get the hell out of here with it?"

Verstegen shook his head. "I can't do that. There's no way you could transport it without getting stopped at an army checkpoint on the road. Those people always search every car to see if there's anything they can steal."

"Yes, we met them on the way down here," said Geordie, with a beaming smile. "But we reckon the boss here has a cunning plan that he hasn't told us about yet."

Jim nodded, then looked at Verstegen. "Listen, if we can get it out of here safely, with no chance of it falling into government hands, would you give it back to us?"

"I may still get my opportunity to get at these bastards. I just need to wait for a chance."

Jim shook his head sadly. "I'm sorry, Mr. Verstegen, but I really can't allow that. We daren't let it fall into the hands of your government and we can't have the UK blamed for a nuclear blast in an African country either."

"So what are you going to do if I refuse?"

"I'm pretty sure you must have it hidden close by so while you and I sit here Ivan and Geordie will systematically demolish your farmhouse until we find it."

Verstegen gave Jim a sad smile. "At least that would stop the local police chief stealing this house from me."

"Is that a real possibility?" Geordie asked.

"Oh God yes. Any thug with a bit of power steals what he wants and claims it is reparation for years of colonial oppression. They took the farm, but left me here in this house. Now the Inspector has decided he can't wait for me to die and he wants me out."

"So if he succeeds, he will find the bomb. Can you risk that?"

Verstegen looked at Jim, then at Ivan and Geordie. "I don't suppose you'd like to buy it back?"

"Not really, no. It was stolen from a British airbase and we need to recover it before innocent people suffer. So how about it? Are you going to hand it over?"

The old man sighed and stood up. He pointed towards the back door and started to walk that way. Jim and Ivan followed him closely while Geordie cleared away the teacups and then left the house by the front door. The three men walked across the dusty yard behind the house to a decrepit shed sitting beneath the shade of a huge baobab tree.

Verstegen reached into his pocket and produced the key for the brass padlock securing the door. He handed it to Ivan and stood back while the big man opened it and then pulled the door wide. The two soldiers looked in and saw a large, canvas covered lump resting on a wooden packing case. They walked into the shady shed and went to lift the canvas.

At that moment the door of the shed slammed behind them and they heard the padlock being inserted and locked. Ivan looked at Jim and shrugged. They turned back and lifted the dusty canvas sheet. The bomb was there, mounted on a green metal sledge with two grab handles each side. A timing device had been connected to the firing mechanism to replace the barometric trigger.

"Bloody hell, boss, up to now I don't think I really believed this and here we are standing at ground zero. Shouldn't you say something profound at this point?"

"I probably should, but my scriptwriter has let me down. Wonder what Geordie's up to?"

"Right here, boss," said Geordie's voice from behind the locked door. "Mr. Verstegen here is just unlocking the padlock for you."

The light flooded in as the door swung open to reveal Verstegen standing there with Geordie, who had one large hand gripping the back of the farmer's neck. Geordie whistled softy as he saw the bomb on the packing case.

"I think Mr. Verstegen here had forgotten an appointment by the way he was running away from here. Looking at that thing, I can see why he'd want to leave."

"You didn't have to hit me," snivelled the red faced farmer, rubbing his head.

Ivan smiled slightly. "If Geordie had hit you properly you'd be sleeping it off right now. He just had to get your attention."

Jim stepped out of the shed and looked around. "Do you have any sort of cart for moving this damned thing?"

Verstegen sniffed loudly. "Over there, behind the house." He pointed at a ramshackle four-wheeled handcart. Geordie let go of his neck and walked across to the cart. He pulled it back across to the shed and stopped just by the door.

Jim walked a few yards away from the small group, pulling a satellite phone out of his pocket as he did so. He checked around to make sure there was nothing likely to block the signal and then switched it on. He waited until the screen told him that he had connected with one of the orbiting telecommunications satellites, then selected a speed dial number.

He waited until it connected, then spoke into the device. "Do you have a clear signal from me? Good. Right then, home on my signal, maximum speed and maintain a stealthy approach as much as you can. ETA?"

Jim turned back towards the shed where Geordie and Ivan were manhandling the bomb on its sledge down onto the handcart. Despite their considerable strength, both men were struggling and sweating. He moved quickly to help them, but they managed it before he got there.

Ivan straightened up and eased his back. "I don't know what your cunning plan is, boss, but I hope it's able to carry this weight."

Jim smiled. "You'll see in about three hours. Can you two mark out an area that's clear enough to land on?"

Geordie looked at Ivan and then Jim in surprise. "A helicopter?"

"Good guess. They are prepping it now and should be here, as I said, in about three hours."

"Hang on, though. What kind of helicopter can make a six hour flight? I assume we aren't going to pop into the local airfield for a top up?"

"Quite right. The range is way too much for any British helicopter. That's why we had to spend a day in London while I set this up. We've hired one from a company in South Africa. It's been sitting just south of the border waiting for my call. Once it gets here, we load up and get the hell out of Dodge."

Ivan shook his head. "How does that work? The Zimbabwe Air Force is going to be waiting for us on the way back, aren't they?"

"They might be." Jim smiled. "If we were going back out the same way, but we're not. Wait and see. Now, Mr. Verstegen, since we missed out breakfast on the way here, how do you fancy letting Geordie rustle something up while we wait?"

Chapter 17

Three hours later Jim's phone rang. He pressed the button to connect and listened. Without speaking, he stood up and motioned his two men to the door.

"We'll be leaving you, Mr. Verstegen. Thank you for breakfast and I hope we haven't put you to too much trouble."

"Don't worry about it. According to the doctor I'm on borrowed time already, so a bit of excitement is quite welcome. Sorry about your bomb, by the way. It was a dumb idea in the first place. I would probably be better off just shooting one or two of the bastards. I've got my two AK47s if they ever come within range."

Jim nodded and followed his men. As he stepped out of the door he saw them heaving on the steering arm of the low cart and went to the back of it to push. They reached the edge of the area they had cleared ready for the aircraft and stopped in the shade of a small tree.

"We're in trouble, boss," said Geordie, pointing.

Jim and Ivan stood up to look and saw two billowing clouds of dust following a pair of police Land Rovers that were heading towards them as fast as they could, on the rough farm track.

"So close," said Jim. "The aircraft reports it's about five minutes out. In fact, listen, you can hear its blades thumping."

"So what do we do, boss?" said Ivan looking around. "They're going to be armed and all we got is the rocks we can pick up."

Geordie smiled and patted the bomb. "Or we could nuke 'em."

Jim chuckled. "Not my favourite option, I have to say."

The sound of automatic gunfire from behind them made them all spin round. There was Verstegen standing in the doorway of his farmhouse with an AK47 at his shoulder. A second one leaned against the doorpost. Jim looked for the two police vehicles and saw they had pulled off the road in a swirling cloud of dust. He turned back and ran towards the old man.

Reaching the farmhouse he grabbed the rifle from the doorway and checked that it was loaded. Without a word, the old farmer handed him two full magazines.

"Unusual to have these sorts of weapons lying about the place."

Verstegen smiled. "Not here it isn't. This is lion country and you can buy these anywhere for next to nothing."

"Do you know why the police are here?"

"Just one of their regular visits to try and drive me out of the house so the Inspector can take it. A bit different this time, with you and the bomb in the open."

Jim nodded, then pointed towards his men. "Can't stay here. You'll have to come with us after this. Come on, we'll try and keep them back from the edge of the field."

As they started back towards the landing area Jim saw the first of the policemen appear from behind a thorn bush alongside the road. A short burst over his head convinced him to get back under cover.

Jim and Verstegen dropped down alongside Ivan and Geordie. The dust from the police vehicles was subsiding and the pounding of the helicopter blades was coming rapidly closer. Jim opened up his phone again and dialled the number. He waited for the reply.

"Be advised you are coming in to a hot LZ. Enemies to the north of our position about 200 meters."

The first shots from the police rifles cracked overhead and then the huge roaring beast of a helicopter was above them, blasting dust and small pebbles in all directions. The four men grabbed the cart and heaved it towards the side door of the aircraft as it touched down.

A crewman jumped to the ground and between the five of them they lifted the bomb and heaved it into the cargo bay of the helicopter as gently as possible. Then they all piled in after it with the crewman sliding the doors shut as they lifted off.

Shafts of light appeared in the door and fuselage side as the rounds from the police rifles passed through the aluminium skin. Jim looked down out of the Perspex window and saw that the huge downdraft of their take-off was blasting the officers on the ground so that they were unable to aim properly. He smiled to himself and turned back to the people in the cabin.

Ivan was kneeling next to Verstegen with an arm around his shoulder, supporting him. A trickle of blood ran from the corner of the old man's mouth. He coughed and the splatter of foam and bright red blood told its own story. Ivan looked at Jim and shook his head.

"Two through the lungs. Not much we can do unless we land and get him to a medic."

The old farmer opened his eyes and looked at Jim. "Don't do that. This is better than dying of cancer over the next few weeks. At least I did something to make up for getting the bomb."

"You did, sir, you did, and thank you for your help."

Verstegen nodded and tried to smile, but the coughing fit stopped him. A few more shuddering breaths and it was over.

Chapter 18

Jim walked forward and stood between the two pilots. They were flying low over the flat, open bush country and he did not want to distract them. The co-pilot noticed him and handed him a spare headset. Jim plugged it in and waited.

"Right, Major, what can we do for you?"

"Just wondering how long we are going to be in Zimbabwean airspace?"

"Frankly, too bloody long. Those policemen we blew over are going to be contacting everyone they can think of to get after us. The big problem is that our direct route takes us way too close to the main airbase in Harare."

"Will we get any warning that they are onto us?"

"We don't have any fancy electronic kit to warn us of radar locks, if that's what you mean, but we do have one small advantage. The airbase shares a runway with Harare International, so they have to contact the tower to clear civilian traffic out of the way when they scramble. We are monitoring the ground control and tower radio frequencies."

"Anything to worry about?"

"Not yet. Just the normal civilian chatter so far. We'll let you know when that changes."

Jim took the headset off and returned to the massive cargo compartment. Geordie and Ivan had moved Verstegen's body to the rear of the cabin and covered him up with the canvas that used to protect the bomb. Ivan looked up as Jim approached and sat down next to him.

"So tell me something, boss, what the hell is this thing? It's like a flying garbage truck in here."

"Ah, Ivan, you don't appreciate the simpler things in life. This is an MI-26, a fine example of Russian aeronautical engineering. No bells and whistles; as you can see, everything is purely functional. She's not very fast, either, but she does have a remarkably long range, which is what we needed."

"So where are we going if not back to South Africa?"

Jim smiled. "We needed a sympathetic government who wouldn't ask too many questions, so we are on our way to Malawi, to Blantyre airport, to be precise."

"And what happens when we get there?"

"And then, if everything goes to plan, we drop this beast down next to an RAF C130. Whip the bomb across and get the hell out of there. These guys then get a refuel and return to South Africa tomorrow, carefully avoiding the Zimbabwean border on the way."

Ivan looked across at Geordie who had been listening. "Sounds way too simple. There has to be a catch?"

Jim smiled. "Oh there is. Because of the distance and the range of this machine we have to go on as direct a route as we can. That takes us way too close to the main Zimbabwean airbase."

"So are the Zimbabwean pilots any good?"

"Unless we are incredibly lucky we may find out first hand. Having those policemen spot us was rotten luck and has probably poked a stick in the ants' nest."

Jim looked forward to see one of the pilots leaning out of his seat and waving him forward. He stood up, walked into the cockpit and put on the headset.

The pilot's voice boomed in his ear and he turned down the volume. "Sorry, say that again."

The pilot spoke again. "I said, we are in trouble. The tower is clearing the airspace to give the fighters room to take off. On the upside, they have just said we are not on their radar, so we are going to stay low."

"What are we up against?"

"I checked up on that before we crossed the border. On paper they've got seven Chinese F7 fighters and three MIG 23s from Russia. That's worst case. Some will be unserviceable and some will be getting routine servicing. How many, we don't know. The other good thing is that we are not being picked up by ground radar, so they are going to have to spread out to look for us. I'm hoping they think we are heading south, which is why I flew that way to start with after we picked you up."

"So we could be OK?"

Jim was dismayed to see the pilot shake his head. "Don't count on it. These Zimbabwean pilots are combat veterans. They have been involved in a couple of wars and they did a lot of damage. Plus, they must know we have a limited range of options and they're not stupid."

"So what now?"

"So now we increase to our maximum speed, which is not very exciting, but it will rattle your teeth. Get your guys to keep a watch behind us and sing out if they see anything. Then we just hope we can move out of the way of any cannon shells."

Chapter 19

The extra speed set the two cabin side doors rattling as Geordie and Ivan slid them open and took a position to watch to their rear. They had each taken one of the AK47 rifles and the two spare magazines for them. They were both fully aware how useless their weapons were against a fighter aircraft, but there was just the possibility of distracting the pilot for the couple of vital seconds during an attack.

Jim stood between the two pilots and scanned ahead anxiously. They skimmed low over a slow-moving cargo train as the tracks gave them useful navigational clues at this low altitude. Thirty minutes into the flight he could see Harare off to the right and the pilots eased the helicopter into a gentle turn to the left to gain some distance between them and any likely watching eyes in the city.

The thud of bullets striking the underside of the aircraft was a violent reality check. They had passed over an alert army patrol who had managed to loose off a couple of magazines before the aircraft was out of range. More worryingly, they would now be radioing in their location and course. Jim keyed the 'talk' button on his headset.

"Anything we can do about that?"

He saw the pilot shake his head. "Not much unless you want to make a dramatic course change and risk running out of fuel short of the destination. We just have to hope the fighters are too far away to get here in time."

Jim went back into the cargo cabin. Both his men gave him a thumbs-up and returned to watching behind them. Ordinary conversation was not possible without headsets, with the aircraft vibrating and the wind rushing through the open doorways.

Geordie slapped his leg and pointed. Jim moved to the starboard doorway and looked out. For a moment or two he could see nothing, but then the glint of sunlight on a windscreen high in the sky caught his attention and he saw the fighter lining up for a strafing run. Jim plugged in his headset and told the pilots what he had seen.

He heard the co-pilot's voice. "OK, we're as ready as we're going to be. Tell us when he's lined up and diving and whatever you do, hang on tight."

Jim passed the word to his two men who tightened the safety harnesses they were wearing. Jim grabbed a harness for himself and strapped it on, then hooked it to a tie-down ring in the floor before leaning out of the door. It took him a couple of seconds to locate the chasing aircraft as it lined up on them and then nosed down towards them. The closing speed was rapid and he realised the pilot would only have to be distracted slightly to miss them completely. He had no idea how many rounds these aircraft carried, but he knew the rate of fire would be fast.

The aircraft was powering towards them in a shallow dive and Jim took a guess about when he would fire. "Now! Firing now!" he yelled into his boom microphone.

As the helicopter was heaved round to the left Jim saw the flickering fire from the barrel of the cannon mounted under the nose of the fighter. The heavy-duty tracer rounds flew past the helicopter's tail rotor as Jim clung on for his life to the doorframe The fighter was past and gone in an instant and the helicopter returned to an even keel and continued skimming across the bush land

All the men in the helicopter were scanning the sky, trying to keep track of their attacker Ivan saw his wings as he rolled over at the top of his climb away from them. He pointed at the Zimbabwean and kept pointing so they could all keep an eye on him. The fighter turned against the clear blue sky and lined up on his target again. This time it was to be a head on attack. Nerve-wracking for the pilots, but it meant their closing speed would be increased and make them even more of a fleeting target.

Jim looked forward into the cockpit and could see the pilot's white knuckles clenched around his cyclic control column. Both men were leaning forward, staring up through the windscreen and judging their moment. The pilot saw his chance and jinked the heavy helicopter to the right. The men in the rear cabin were thrown into their safety harnesses, but the second burst of cannon fire from the MIG 23 passed safely down their port side.

The Zimbabwean pilot was a fast learner and this time he lined up to attack them beam on. He chose Ivan's side and the Welshman could do nothing but sit in the doorway and watch the approach. As the cannon fired for the third time the helicopter pilots heaved back on their controls, causing the aircraft to rear up in an emergency stop. The fighter pilot seemed to have anticipated this and swung the nose of his aircraft just slightly to his left. The stream of cannon shells swung with him and closer to their target. As he lined up on the now stationary target, his firing stopped; he had run through his ammunition.

The MIG passed directly over them, causing the helicopter to sway in the violent wind of his passing. Then the nose of the heavy helicopter dropped as they flew forward and rapidly regained their maximum forward speed. The three soldiers watched as the fighter circled them high in the air.

Jim moved swiftly back into the cockpit and plugged in his headset again. "Nicely done, guys. Now what?"

"About now he is screaming into his radio trying to get his pals here before we cross the border. It all depends on how far away they are in their search patterns."

"How far to the border now?"

The co-pilot checked his chart and his watch. "Best guess we should be over the Mozambique border in about twenty minutes at this speed."

"Are they going to give us any trouble?"

"Ah, Major, now there you have the big question. The Mozambique Air Force is having serious problems keeping its aircraft serviceable, so I don't think they are a direct threat. It depends whether the Zimbabweans will cross the border after us. They may not want to irritate their neighbours, or they could be welcomed with open arms. We don't know, is the short answer."

Chapter 20

Jim remained kneeling between the pilots' seats scanning the sky from left to right and back again. Every few moments he saw the MIG pass across their path as it circled them, marking their position.

He thumbed the talk button on his headset. "So tell me, how come he didn't use a missile on us? At this speed we would have been a sitting duck."

The co-pilot turned to Jim and smiled. "This is Africa. Those missiles are damned expensive and if they are left on the wings of the fighters as a matter of course they deteriorate. So they only install them when there is a known threat. We haven't given them time for that."

"Did you know that before you took this job?" Jim asked.

"Yeah, that one was a pretty safe bet. Running into the police and having them raise the alarm was just damned bad luck. You have any idea why they were there?"

"Maybe. Verstegen was telling us that the authorities had confiscated his farm a while ago, but he managed to keep the house. Then it seems the local police chief decided he wanted it, so there has been harassment and regular threats ever since."

"Just bad luck then. So when do we find out what is so bloody important about your cargo?"

Jim paused and looked out through the left-hand windscreen. He waited. There it was again. He wasn't imagining it.

"No time to discuss that now. We've got company. There's a helicopter heading our way out to the port side and he's closing fast."

Both pilots stared out towards the aircraft Jim had spotted until they saw the flicker of the main rotor blades through the trees. The pilot altered course slightly to starboard to slow down its approach, but still get them over the border in the minimum time.

Jim returned to the cargo area and moved both of his men to the port doorway. The two AK47s would be a poor defense if the Zimbabwean helicopter was fully armed, but maybe they would discourage the pilot from coming too close.

Ivan and Geordie checked their weapons were loaded and the spare magazines were in easy reach. They watched as the approaching helicopter became clearer above the tree tops. Jim knew they could be trusted to fire only when they had a chance of hitting something and returned to the cockpit. He plugged his headset back in and thumbed the talk button again.

"Any chance we can outrun him?"

Both pilots shook their heads. "Not in this old lady and he's got too damned close before we saw him. We'll just have to see if we get over the border before him."

"And if he follows us over?"

"Well then we've got some serious trouble. Those things are a leftover from the Rhodesian Air Force and they usually carry a waist-mounted machine gun. If he gets close enough he can do us a lot of damage."

Geordie and Ivan sat in the doorway watching the lighter and more manoeuvrable Alouette III aircraft get closer and closer. Ivan raised his hand and signalled Geordie to get ready. Both men cocked their weapons and set them to automatic fire. They were fully aware that the AK47 on automatic is not an accurate weapon and fired from a vibrating helicopter is even less so, but they had nothing else.

They judged when the approaching machine was within range and Ivan raised his weapon to fire. They had agreed that only one of them would fire at one time to conserve their limited supply of ammunition. The Welshman took aim and fired a series of short bursts whenever he thought he had a faint chance of hitting their enemy.

As Ivan emptied his first magazine, he ripped it off the rifle and picked up the second. Geordie lifted his weapon as the Alouette slewed round to give the gunner in the rear area a clear shot with the ugly machine gun mounted there. Geordie fired first and was rewarded by the Perspex in front of the pilot fracturing as a round hit it. The pilot reacted instinctively and swung the aircraft rapidly away from the incoming fire. The gunner was thrown onto his weapon by the sudden movement and the stream of heavy-calibre rounds flew upwards through the rotor blades of his own helicopter. The first few flew between the rapidly rotating blades, then the next blade was pierced and a violent vibration shook the airframe.

The pilot realising what had happened struggled to control the bucking machine as the ground came up to meet him. He nearly made it. The tail rotor struck a Mopani tree and was ripped to shreds. Without the control from his tail end the pilot was helpless to control the helicopter as it went into a rapid ground spin, until the main rotor blades struck the ground and the stricken machine thrashed to a stop, on its port side, in a cloud of dust and debris. Geordie and Ivan watched in horror as the small helicopter flew apart in its death throes. They were cheered that there was no ball of fire, so the crew at least had a chance of getting out of it alive.

Jim had watched the short battle from the cockpit windows with the pilots and now he heaved a sigh of relief. "Well, with luck, that's the last of them," he said.

"Don't speak too soon. It looks like our friend in the MIG wants another go," said the pilot, pointing forward.

As Jim looked the Russian built fighter was just pulling out at the bottom of its dive and heading towards them, low and fast. He grabbed the seat backs and braced himself as the jet aircraft skimmed just above them. The turbulence from the fighter's passing flung the big helicopter around in a spin and the pilot struggled to control. As he brought it back upright and back on course Jim stepped back into the cargo area.

He looked around and could only see Ivan, who was hanging out of the door hatch. He crossed quickly over to see Geordie outside the aircraft, held by his safety strap and being buffeted alongside the fuselage. Ivan had a firm grip on the black man's hand and, using the massive strength in his shoulders and arms, was pulling the Staff Sergeant to safety. Jim joined him and together they pulled Geordie back into the aircraft where he lay, panting, on the gray metal floor.

The noise inside the helicopter from the engines, the blades and the rushing wind made conversation impossible without headsets, but Geordie mouthed his thanks and gave the thumbs-up sign to show he was no worse for the experience. Jim patted his shoulder and then stood up and walked back into the cockpit to plug in his headset once more.

"How far to the border now?"

"We've just passed it. Unless the Zimbabweans want to cross over we should be in the clear all the way to Blantyre."

Jim nodded. "OK, that's good, but tell me what happens to you after this? The Zimbabweans must have your tail number by now and a description of your aircraft. Won't they want to get hold of you?"

The two pilots looked at each other and smiled. "You remember that big red stripe the length of the fuselage?" the co-pilot said. Jim nodded. "Well, once we leave Blantyre we find a nice quiet spot to land and peel that off the side. We are then back to our usual paint job of two thin blue lines. The registration number will come off at the same time. The one they can see now is the number of the South African President's personal

Boeing 737. That should cause enough confusion for this all to go away. And anyway we are presently on a job in the far south of Mozambique as far as anybody knows."

"Can you deal with Verstegen's body for me?"

"Not a problem as long as he doesn't need the full memorial service."

Chapter 21

The flight continued and they made a normal approach to Blantyre airport. The big helicopter landed and taxied around the perimeter track towards the refuelling area. Just short of the dispersal area they paused alongside a Royal Air Force C130 that was standing on the side of the runway with its engines running and the rear cargo ramp down.

The three men jumped down onto the baking hot tarmac and dragged the nuclear device out of the helicopter. They walked quickly across to the C130 and straight up the rear ramp. Just before the ramp closed Jim leaned out and waved his thanks to the two helicopter pilots who were already moving their aircraft away. As he turned back into the huge cargo area of the RAF Hercules the loadmaster was already strapping down the bomb and Ivan and Geordie were settling themselves into the red canvas seats and fastening their seat belts.

Before Jim could reach his seat he felt the pilot release the brakes and the big aircraft rumbled forward towards the runway. Jim sat and strapped in as the engine noise increased and the fuselage started to vibrate. They all leaned towards the rear of the aircraft as the take-off acceleration began. Seconds later the noise dropped as they cleared the ground and powered into the sky. He leaned back in his seat and sighed.

The loadmaster came back down the centre of the cargo area and handed each of them a plastic bottle of cold water, which disappeared down parched throats in short order. As he felt the aircraft level off to a gentle climb, Jim unfastened his safety belt and climbed out of his seat. He walked forward and climbed up into the considerably quieter cockpit area. He tapped the aircraft captain on the shoulder and she turned around and smiled at him.

"Had an exciting trip, Major?"

"We certainly have. Where are we headed for?"

"First stop is Akrotiri in Cyprus for a refuel and to pick up a new crew, then you are straight on to the UK. They've got you scheduled for landing at RAF Marham to unload you and your cargo, then the aircraft is off home to Brize Norton."

"How long are we on the ground in Cyprus? There's a call I would like to make."

"It's only going to be about twenty minutes, I'm afraid. We have strict instructions to get you back as soon as possible."

"Right then. Next order of business is to get some sleep. I'll see you in Cyprus to say goodbye."

Jim turned and walked back down into the cargo bay. His two men had already made themselves as comfortable as possible in this noisy space and were both either asleep or nearly so. Jim shrugged and joined them, making a nest of the canvas covers he found on the cargo floor.

Chapter 22

The sunlight blazing through the window of the American Airways Boeing 757 as they made the turn to line up with the Belize City airport woke Jim from a fitful sleep. His planning for this phase of their task was damned thin and he knew it. He would have to wing it once he had a chance to see what they were up against.

Geordie came awake as the stewardess moved through the cabin and touched him on the shoulder to make sure his seat belt was fastened. Ivan was already alert and scanning through the window to get an idea of conditions. None of them had been to Belize before, so they were heavily reliant on the contact who should be waiting for them.

The aircraft touched down heavily and rumbled along the tired runway onto an even rougher taxiway. The heat inside the cabin rose markedly as the cabin door was opened and the steamy heat of this tropical country rushed in. They were all starting to sweat before they managed to disembark.

With the normal tedious immigration formalities out of the way, Jim led the way through to the front of the terminal where they were supposed to find their contact. They stood looking around as the arriving passengers found their taxis and buses and the crowd thinned.

The voice from behind them had a distinct Scottish burr and they turned in unison to see the speaker leaning against the wall behind them. The over long hair and beard, both streaked with grey gave no indication that this man was ex-Special Forces. The well-developed body and the piercing green eyes were the only slight giveaway.

He spoke again. "I said, are you waiting for a lift to Belize City?"

"We are," said Jim. "But we are meeting someone, so we don't need a taxi."

"That'll be me, Major Wilson. Danny Magee, ex-Sergeant in the SAS. Follow me. The truck is parked round the corner."

Without another word Magee turned on his heel and started walking to the left of the terminal building. As they followed him around the corner Jim spotted a battered Land Rover waiting for them in the shade.

"Fling your bags in the back, gents, then we'll get going and get you outside a cold beer as soon as we get to my place."

They did as they were told and climbed into the retired army vehicle. Magee slammed it into gear and accelerated out of the airport grounds and along the highway towards the city. His hair blew all over the place as he drove, giving him a slightly insane look. He turned and looked at Jim as he drove.

"So then, lots of mystery here. I was told to meet you and give you whatever support you need. What's going on?"

"We need to find a particular individual who has something that belongs to the British government and then we need to get it from him and get it back into safe keeping."

Magee looked at Jim again, waiting for more detail. "Well, is that it? Nothing else to tell me?"

Jim looked the man over as he drove. "Tell me some more about you first. We know nothing about you, except we were told you would be our guide."

Magee nodded forward to indicate the house set back at the side of the road. He slowed the Land Rover and swung in through the gateway before parking in the shade, under the branches of a large tree. He climbed out.

"Come on in. I've got beer on ice and we might as well be comfortable while we tell each other stories."

The four men made their way around the side of the house, and then climbed up the wooden staircase that led to a wide shady veranda. Magee waved them to the rattan chairs that were scattered about and went inside the house. He returned as they sat down, carrying four bottles of beer already streaming with condensation. He took a chair and handed the beer round.

"Well, since I'm the host, should I start?"

Jim took a long pull on the icy cold beer and nodded. "Please do."

"Right then, as you know, I'm Danny Magee. I'm ex-SAS. I was stationed out here when we had a permanent army presence, running the jungle warfare training school. When the army pulled out I decided to stay and married a local girl. There are still jungle training courses and I'm employed as a civilian contractor to run them.

Plus, I do some guiding when the courses aren't running."

Geordie put his empty bottle down. "What sort of guiding?"

"In the jungle mostly, but with the odd bit of diving round the offshore islands. The towns can be a bit run down, but the country itself is stunning and the islands look like something from one of those adverts you see on TV."

"Where's your wife now?" Ivan asked.

"Away visiting her mother. I wasn't sure how classified this was going to be."

Jim cleared his throat. "That sounds like my cue." First he introduced his two men, then said, "We know you have a serious level of security clearance, but this is heavy-duty material, so not a word to anyone." He waited until Magee nodded before he continued. "We've lost a nuclear bomb, or more accurately, two of them were stolen from an RAF secure facility and have been sold to two individuals for rather a lot of money. We got one back from a guy who was deluded about using it and was more or less happy to hand it back. The other one is somewhere here, according to the arms dealer who sold it."

There was a silence, broken only by the screeching of birds in the trees, while Magee absorbed what he had been told. He looked carefully at the three men to make sure this wasn't some kind of joke.

"Bloody hell! So who is this nut job?"

Jim withdrew a notebook from his pocket and flipped it open. "According to our information, he is Mark Frobisher, an Englishman. Apart from that, we know nothing about him, except he is obviously well off financially and he lives here somewhere. Any ideas?"

Magee shook his head. "I've never heard of him, but he shouldn't be too hard to find."

"You have the contacts to do that? Maybe we could Google him?"

Magee smiled. "I probably do and we probably could, but this isn't that big a country. We could just look him up in the phone book."

Jim was shaking his head as the smiling Magee stood and went back into the house. He returned carrying a thick book and four more beers.

He stopped and looked at Geordie. "Peters? Royal Engineers? Are you the madman who pulled that stunt with the bulldozer in Afghanistan a while back?"

Geordie smiled and nodded. "That was me."

Magee shook his head and sat down. "So I'm working with crazy men then?"

The beers were passed around and Magee opened the phone book and started to search.

"Here he is, Mark Frobisher. The address given is not very specific. Looks like he lives in the back country, well away from town. I know someone who lives out that way. I'll give him a call after dinner."

Ivan grinned at Jim. "Well, that was easy. So do we just drive up and ask for the bomb back?"

"I can't see that working again. We were incredibly lucky with Verstegen. Let's see what Danny comes back with after he calls his mate."

Chapter 23

An hour into the journey Magee pulled the Land Rover off the highway outside a down-at-heel roadside shop backed up to the jungle, in the middle of nowhere. He parked outside the door and got out of the vehicle.

"Come on, guys, we need to kit you up for this jaunt while I talk to my mate Prakash."

They walked into the darkened interior of the small building, ducking under the myriad of things hanging from the rafters and dodging around the teetering piles on the sagging shelves. They found Magee by the wide plywood board that did duty as a counter. Facing him was a small dark skinned man with a broad smile.

"Guys, this is Prakash. He knows everybody out this way and he also sells the fiercest bug repellent on the planet. Believe me, you want to buy some if we have to go into the deep jungle. More urgently, he's also got a fridge back there with cold drinks."

The man Magee had named as Prakash bobbed his head in acknowledgment and pointed behind them. "The fridge is over there, gentlemen. Help yourself and we will settle up later."

The three engineers walked over to the large rusty fridge and opened it up. Each made a selection and cracked open the can. They sipped at the cold liquid while they wandered round this hot and dusty Aladdin's cave. Magee stayed by the counter talking quietly to the Indian shopkeeper.

After a few minutes Magee walked across to them, picking up four small cans on the way. "We'll need these. Apparently Frobisher lives way back in the country and a long way off the paved highway. It seems he doesn't like visitors either. He has a gang of armed men who keep people away and aren't afraid to open fire. Prakash tells me he is what they used to call a Remittance Man back in the nineteenth century."

Geordie put his empty drink can in the nearly full bin by the door. "I'll bite. What the hell is a remittance man?"

Jim answered. "Back in the day, if a wealthy family had a relative who was an embarrassment to them they sometimes sent them to live abroad where they wouldn't run into anyone that knew them. They used to remit money to them, as long as they stayed away and didn't make a fuss, so they were called Remittance Men."

Ivan grunted. "So we already know he's a bloody nuisance to somebody. I wonder if the guards are there to keep him in control as well?"

Magee smiled. "Guess we'll find out when we meet him, eh?"

"So, Danny, how have you planned to arrange our meeting?" Jim asked.

"Carefully." Magee indicated the shopkeeper with a nod of his head. "My mate Prakash tells me that there are rumours of people who have strayed onto his place, who have never come home again. No bodies have been found, so there is no evidence the police can act on, but the locals are pretty sure he's a wrong 'un."

"Bloody hell!"

Jim and Magee swung around to look at Geordie, who had opened one of the cans by the doorway and was holding it at arm's length. "This stuff stinks like a sewer. You can't want us to put it on, can you?"

Magee nodded. "It stinks, right enough. It's fierce stuff, I told you, but the bugs here can be a serious problem and the gentler branded stuff does nothing to ward them off, especially at night. Don't worry, I'll find you a nice place to wash it off before we try and join polite society again."

Jim grinned at Geordie and turned to Magee. "Is that all we are going to need for this walk in the park?"

"Not quite. Some of this jungle can be pretty thick, so we'll need to take machetes. I've got mine, but you three will need one each."

"Surely we just take turns using yours, don't we?" Ivan said.

Magee shook his head. "There's more needs cutting than foliage, mate. Now, how do you feel about firearms?"

Geordie looked surprised. "I don't think anyone is going to come within rifle range if we are wearing this sewer water in a tin."

"You never know. I think we'd better hire a couple from Prakash."

Chapter 24

Geordie stood looking between two trees at the strange sight of a carefully trimmed expanse of green lawn in front of the sprawling bungalow, with the wild jungle as a backdrop. His dark skin let him fade into the deep shadow cast by the tree canopy above him. Howler monkeys screamed out all around him, but he had yet to see one. What he could see was the enormous beetle walking slowly down the trunk of the tree in front of him. It ignored him, so he let it alone.

The disgusting stench of the insect repellent seemed to be working, since nothing had bitten him yet, despite the clouds of insects that seemed to erupt around him as he pushed through the undergrowth. He settled down to watch the house and wondered if Ivan was in position on the far side yet.

There was nothing moving around the bungalow until a guard came around the far corner with a rifle slung over his shoulder. He watched as the man stopped and unclipped a radio from his belt. He was too far away to hear the conversation, but the guard turned to look along the wide driveway towards the entrance gate. Geordie looked in the same direction and saw the battered Land Rover clatter around the bend and approach the house.

The guard slipped the rifle from his shoulder and held it down by his side, ready to be brought up to use if necessary. The Land Rover stopped and Jim and Magee got out, then walked towards the house. Geordie noticed that they kept their hands in sight and well away from their bodies. With the trigger-happy reputation of the security men on this estate, they were taking no chances.

Geordie heard the slithering movement by his feet before he saw it. He looked down at the large snake sliding across his right foot. Of all the things in this world, a snake raised the most primeval of fears in this tough soldier. He swung the machete that he had been holding and the razor sharp blade sliced the head from the reptile. The body curled and writhed as the animal died in front of him. As it stilled he looked back towards the house. His two companions and the guard were gone, just the Land Rover sat drooping in the driveway on its punished suspension.

Inside the house, Jim could feel the sweat on his back being cooled by the air conditioning that blew gently through the impressive hallway he was being led along. The paintings on the walls looked old and expensive; presumably the cool air prevented the jungle climate from rotting them away. The guard tapped gently on a broad mahogany door and then turned the brass handle to swing the door wide. Jim and Magee walked forward into a large book lined study. The bookshelves covered every inch of wall from floor to ceiling with just the two windows that gave a view across the incongruous croquet lawn they had driven past.

The massive desk also seemed to be made of mahogany with a green leather inlay offsetting the highly polished wood. The man behind it stood and stretched out his hand. He was slim, of medium height, and had a full head of dark hair. His only distinguishing feature was the short, ragged scar that curled his mouth downwards at the left side. When he spoke it was with a cultured English accent.

"Good morning, do sit down. Would you care for some tea? I was just about to call for some."

Jim shook the outstretched hand, which was withdrawn before Magee could do the same. They both sat in the chairs in front of the desk.

Jim spoke. "Good morning to you, too. I assume you are Mr. Frobisher? My name is Major Jim Wilson and I have come from London to speak to you."

"And how is London these days? I haven't been back there for, oh, it must be twelve years or more. Still rainy and cold, I take it?"

Jim nodded and smiled. "It's certainly a lot colder than here, though by the look of the jungle you must get a fair dose of rain here as well."

"That's true." Frobisher turned and pressed a button set into the bookcase behind him. Almost immediately the library door swung open and a tall cadaverous man entered, dressed in a formal black suit. "Tea for three, please, Jenkins."

The man nodded silently and withdrew.

"A butler?" Jim asked.

"Indeed. One must maintain standards, even here in the tropics. By the way, please don't mention his resemblance to Lurch. He is a little over sensitive about it."

"I'm sorry?" said Jim. "Who is Lurch?"

"Never watched the Addams Family on TV? Lurch is the family butler."

Jim shook his head. "I'm not a great one for TV. I prefer to find things to do myself rather than watch others doing them."

"Good for you. Unfortunately, I have rather too much time for watching old TV shows here." Frobisher smiled. "But tell me now, why have you come all this way to see me? This is certainly not the easiest place to find, so it can't be a social call. A message from my dear family, perhaps?"

"I'm afraid I don't know your family."

"Don't feel the need to regret that. We don't get on terribly well since they banished me to this place."

"Banished?"

Frobisher leaned back in his chair and raised a mirthless smile. "Oh yes. Dreadfully old-fashioned, but they decided I was an embarrassment, so I was sent here with a nice generous financial allowance as long as I stayed away and did not become more of an annoyance to them. In the old days they called it being a Remittance Man. A nice cultured term, but I prefer banishment as being nearer the truth."

Jim absorbed that while contemplating the obviously bitter man across the desk. His face had changed to one of fury as he was speaking and his eyes almost blazed with indignation. Jim noted that the hands on the arms of his chair had balled into fists while speaking about his family.

Jim drew a breath. "Well, not wishing to add to your woes, I have come to ask you about a weapon you recently purchased."

Frobisher stood and walked to the window. He stared across the immaculate lawn to the riotous jungle beyond. "And what weapon would that be? One of my guards' new rifles, perhaps?"

"No, sir. I'm talking about the modified bomb you bought from Mr. Christophides of Cyprus. The British government has just discovered it has been stolen from one of our bases and obviously we want it back."

Frobisher paused, then turned around slowly and walked back to his desk. He went to the bookcase and pressed another button mounted there. In a heartbeat, the library door swung open to reveal one of the guards with his automatic rifle pointed squarely at Jim. No more than ten seconds later he was joined by two more men with their rifles at the ready.

Jim looked from the guards to Frobisher, who smiled back at him. "You see, Major, I have no wish to discuss my private affairs with you or anybody else. That device is mine and will be used at my discretion. You and the British government can go to hell as far as I am concerned. But out of courtesy I will give you some advice. Don't go to Guatemala anytime soon." He looked over Jim's shoulder at the waiting guards. "Escort these two gentlemen back to their car and see that they leave the estate. If you see them again, shoot them."

Jim was startled at the sudden turn of events, but recovered quickly. "I think you are being unwise, Mr. Frobisher."

"Think what you like. Now get out of my house and don't come back. My men will obey me if they see you here again, have no doubt."

Chapter 25

Ivan was waiting outside the gates to the estate as Magee drove the Land Rover back towards the road. The vehicle pulled over next to the big Welshman, who looked carefully at Jim.

"I take it that didn't go well then, boss?"

"What makes you say that, Ivan?"

"I've seen that expression on your face before and Magee over there has a face like a mile of unpaved road. So what happened?"

Jim forced himself to calm down. A fit of temper would serve no one. "Frobisher didn't deny having the weapon, but threw us out and issued a death warrant for us if we ever go back."

"So you're off the Christmas Card list then, boss?" said Geordie walking up to the Land Rover from the other side. Jim turned round to see his dark smiling face and the large snake he carried in his left hand.

"What the hell are you intending to do with that?"

Geordie grinned. "Our guide here was telling me that snake tastes like chicken and I wanted to see if he was right, since it's nearly lunchtime. What do you say, Danny? Fancy cooking this up for us?"

Danny Magee looked down at the bloodied snake that was dripping onto Geordie's boot. "If we go back to Prakash's place he has a barbecue pit round the back. He can sell us a few cold ones while I cook that and you lot can decide what you want to do next."

The trip back to the jungle shop run by Prakash was completed in silence, which gave Jim time to think. They sat and watched as Magee skinned and gutted the snake, then slid it onto skewers to roast it over the barbecue. The icy cold bottles of beer, beaded with condensation, eased their parched throats as they sat around him.

Jim looked up from the doodle he was making with a stick in the sand between his feet. "Danny, what's the story with Guatemala? Why would Frobisher have an issue with them?"

Magee turned the skewers and took a drink from his beer bottle. "Back in the day, the Guatemalans claimed Belize should be theirs. There was a fair amount of sabre rattling about it, which is why we had a military garrison here for about twenty years. But those days are gone. Maybe Frobisher is just a bit of a nutcase?"

Jim nodded slowly. "That would explain some things. Only a bloody madman would want to actually use a nuke:"

Geordie took a swallow of his beer then said, "So what else is good to eat round here, Danny?"

"Depends, mate. If you want to take your life in your hands, ask Prakash to get his wife to make you a 'Fire Down Below'."

"I'll bite. What's that when it's at home?"

"That, my friend, is the fiercest curry you have ever tasted. The jungle training groups use it as a test of manhood on three levels. First, it is bloody hot when you eat it, feels like your throat is going to melt. Next day it is a challenge as well, which is where it gets the name from, and thirdly there is no guarantee what meat she has floating around in it."

As he spoke Prakash came out of his shop carrying four more of his icy cold beers. He was followed by a small smiling woman in the brightest blue sari. She regarded the four men.

"Does anybody want a proper meal after that awful thing?" she said, pointing at the snake. "I can do a nice curry for you. All the boys like it, when they come through here."

Danny glanced at the other three, who were hesitating. "We'll give that a miss this time, Chandra. Maybe on the way back to the airport."

The Indian shopkeeper and his wife both shrugged as they turned away and went back inside. Danny decided the snake was properly cooked now, so served a decent sized portion to each of them on the metal plates they had borrowed from Prakash.

The three friends bit into the meat gingerly, not sure what to expect. They brightened up after the first bite on finding that it was quite a pleasant taste and texture.

Ivan, obviously enjoying the strange meat, licked his fingers. "So what's our next move, boss?"

Jim swallowed the lump of snake meat he had been chewing. "Not sure yet. It depends whether you two saw anything of interest when you were creeping about in the forest. Geordie?"

"Nothing much about the house itself. There are metal bars over the windows, as you probably saw, and at least one guard patrolling around it.

Behind the house, over to the right side, there is a boathouse."

Danny looked up from his food. "The river doesn't run there. How can he have a boathouse?"

"It looked to me as if he has had the diggers in and made a channel through the forest which joins the river. The trees overhang it, so it's probably not visible from the air."

"Anything unusual about it, other than that?" asked Jim.

"Nothing I could see, but I didn't get right up close to it."

"Ivan, how about on your side?"

Ivan put down his plate and wiped his greasy fingers. "A bit more interesting my side, I think. Tucked under the trees there is a small aircraft hangar and an airstrip. There was a guard on the hangar, but after you arrived two more came out of the house in a hurry and joined him."

"Sounds like there is something in there that they value."

"That was my guess. They looked alert as well, moving quickly and scanning the area."

"Anything else there of interest?"

"There was a fuel truck parked back into the trees, clear of the hangar, and it looked like they had cans set alongside the landing strip. Probably for night landings. Then alongside the house there's a big shed of some kind. No idea what it's used for, though."

"OK." Jim absorbed the information. "Can you get us back there on foot, Danny, after dark?"

Chapter 26

The tiny luminous green markers clipped onto the back of their collars were the only things keeping them together as they slipped silently through the jungle to the edge of Frobisher's estate. How Danny Magee was finding his way was a mystery to Jim and he began to doubt that they were on course, until the lights from the bungalow appeared through the vegetation.

Magee stopped and Jim walked into the back of him in the dark. "Sorry, didn't see your brake lights."

"Shh," Danny whispered. "Sound carries at night, even amongst these trees."

He dropped down behind a bush and Jim joined him. Ivan and Geordie crouched down where they were and stayed still and silent.

Danny moved slowly to his right and studied the clear area across the ridiculous lawn. "There is still a guard patrolling round the house. Just saw him pass in front of a lighted window."

He stood up and started moving slowly through the trees again. Jim and the others stood and then followed him carefully. Apart from the dim light from the bungalow windows, the only illumination came from the fireflies that fluttered around them, but still Danny seemed to be able to find his way.

Ten minutes of slow, careful walking brought them to the edge of a clear area and Jim could see the starlight reflecting off the waterway that led to the boatshed. They walked across and flattened themselves against the wooden wall, waiting for a cry of alarm. There was nothing, so they started to move again.

They moved around to the side of the boathouse away from Frobisher's house where the door to the waterway was. The sliding door was secured by a large brass padlock that stood out against the dark wood.

Jim tapped Geordie on the arm and whispered, "Time for your party trick again."

Geordie's broad smile showed through the dark as he stepped around Jim, pulling a small packet from his pocket. He knelt down in front of the lock and inserted the two lock picks he had in his hand. He was silent as he worked, then he grunted and then sighed.

"Got it. That was a bit stiff. I don't think it's been oiled in a while."

"When did the army start teaching that skill?" Danny asked.

Geordie grinned. "We did a job a while ago that needed a burglar. He showed me how to do that one night when he was bored. It's come in useful before."

The big Staff Sergeant removed the padlock from the hasp and slowly pushed the door to one side. Ivan moved past him and switched on a tiny hooded flashlight. In the dim light they could see two boats parked in the small dock with their bows facing the door and the waterway. Jim climbed down off the small platform and into the first boat. He inspected it using Ivan's flashlight.

"The keys are here and the fuel tank is full. It's a jet boat, so no propeller to catch on the river bottom. Looks like the other one is the same. This could be a quick way out of here when we find the bomb."

Danny Magee grunted. "Not much use, though: the river bends away from where we want to be, if we are heading back to Belize City."

"We are, but I seem to recall we passed over a bridge on the way to see Prakash this afternoon. If you park the Land Rover there we can come to you, cross load the cargo and then get the hell out of here. How does that sound?"

In the dim light Jim could see Danny nod. "It could work out all right. Provided you three are OK here on your own? I don't want you getting lost in the jungle."

Jim smiled. "We'll be fine, and just in case we're not, we can use the radios and you can ride in to save the day if it all goes wrong."

Chapter 27

Jim watched Danny slip back into the trees as Geordie was relocking the boathouse door. They didn't want one of the guards to find it open if they patrolled this way. Geordie came to join him and Ivan and they turned to the path they could just see in the faint moonlight.

"Lead the way, Ivan. You're the only one of us who's seen the hangar."

"OK, boss, but I've only seen it in daylight, so this could be slow."

"Slow is good. We don't want to make any noise in case that guard you saw is still there."

"Do you think he still might be?" Geordie asked.

"We'll soon find out, but I'm hoping they go down to minimum numbers at night. There can't be much of a threat normally."

Jim followed the dim marker that showed Ivan's position. For a big man, Ivan moved surprisingly quietly. The marker on his collar dropped as the Welshman knelt down on the path. Low down, they had more chance of seeing a silhouette against the marginally paler star-studded sky. Ivan stood again, having seen nothing untoward, and moved forward.

Over the big man's shoulder Jim could now make out the shape that could only be the aircraft hangar Ivan had seen earlier in the day. They came alongside it and Jim could feel the heat of the day radiating back out from its metal side. Geordie waited alongside him as Ivan slipped around to the front of the building. He was back inside a minute, coming from behind them having circled the whole structure.

"OK, we seem to be in the clear. No sign of a guard and no lights inside. As far as I can see, there are no alarms, but we need to be careful."

The three men walked to the front of the hangar where the doors were mounted ready to swing open wide to allow the aircraft to move in and out. This door, too, was secured by a large brass padlock. Jim looked to his left across the airstrip. He could see a shape not far in front of him.

"Hang on with the door, Geordie. I just want to check something."

Geordie paused as Jim walked quietly towards the shape he had seen. After no more than ten paces he could see that he was approaching a light aircraft, sitting on its tricycle undercarriage. He walked closer until he could see it was a high-wing monoplane with a single propeller. He recognised the type, it was a Cessna 172. He walked quietly back to his two companions.

"There's a Cessna parked just over there on the end of the runway. Looks like they are planning to fly at first light."

"It certainly wasn't there earlier on," Ivan said. "They must have wheeled it out after your visit. Do you think Frobisher is making a run for it?"

"Could be. In any case I might as well search that while you two check the hangar."

Geordie turned back to the padlock and, with his lock picks, he turned the mechanism and opened it. Ivan and he slipped inside through a slightly opened door while Jim walked back to the aircraft he had found.

Once inside, Ivan flicked on his shrouded flashlight and shone it forward to find another light aircraft sitting there. Around the walls he could dimly make out what appeared to be work benches and tool racks. Boxes and crates were stacked on pallets at the rear. He guessed they must be a stock of spare parts for the two aircraft.

Outside, Jim carefully opened the door of the aircraft he was inspecting and leaned in. The pilot's seat seemed normal, but the co-pilot's seat had been removed and replaced by a square box connected to the flight controls by pierced metal levers. On top of the box he could make out a laptop computer and a wireless receiver that seemed to be linked. He retrieved his own shrouded flashlight from a leg pocket and carefully shone it over the strange contraption. Then he shone the dim light back into the passenger area. The seats were gone and bolted to the floor he could see the prize he had been looking for. He reached in and tried to turn the bolts by hand, but they were far too tight. He would need tools.

Jim withdrew from the doorway and walked back to the hangar. Ivan was running the flashlight across the boxes to make sure the bomb had not been stored there.

"Ivan, Geordie," Jim hissed. "I've found it. They've got it fitted to the floor of the other aircraft, behind some kind of improvised auto pilot. It looks to me as though they've turned the Cessna into a poor man's cruise missile. I'll need tools to get it out."

Ivan looked at Geordie, then back to Jim. "Can we do it before dawn? It's getting a bit close. The sun comes up early round here."

"Shouldn't be too much of a problem. It looks like four big bolts set into the floor. They shouldn't take too long. Help me find the tools, then you two stay under cover until I've got it free. Then we grab it and get it back to the boathouse and away downriver."

Chapter 28

Jim opened the starboard side door of the aircraft and put his handful of tools on the floor before climbing behind the co-pilot's seat into the passenger area. He knelt over the bomb that was bolted to the floor and examined the fittings. As well as the four bolts mounting it to the floor, a cable led from the bomb to the laptop computer on top of the autopilot contraption. He decided to deal with that last.

He reached behind him and picked up the adjustable wrench he had brought with him. Adjusting the jaws, he fitted it to the first bolt and started to turn. It was stiff, but he managed to get it turning and gradually unscrewed it. As he laid the bolt down on the deck beside him he realised that he could now see a lot better. Ivan had been right: dawn was breaking.

He checked around the aircraft to make sure nobody was approaching and then bent to undo the second bolt. This one seemed even stiffer than the first and he was adjusting his position to get better leverage when he heard the starter motor whine and the engine kick over. He looked up to see that the instrument panel lights had come on and then the engine coughed into life. This was getting urgent, but he should have time to get the bomb out while the engine was warming up.

He braced his back against the co-pilot's seat back and pushed on the wrench with his foot. It moved, so he returned to kneeling over the bomb, removing the bolt as quickly as he was able. He pulled it free and threw it to one side before bending over the bomb to reach the third bolt. As he did so the brakes released and the aircraft lurched forwards, flinging him over the bomb and into the bulkhead at the back of the passenger area. The hammer he had carefully placed beside him was flung backwards with him and struck him hard on the forehead. Disorientated and dizzy, he felt the aircraft accelerate and then the unmistakable feel of take-off as the machine lifted into the air.

Jim sat up and shook his head to clear his blurred vision. As the world swam back into focus he noticed that in falling over he had ripped out the cable between the laptop and the bomb. He would not have chosen to do it that way, but at least he could now be fairly confident that the small computer was unable to trigger the nuclear device. He scrambled to his knees and looked at the instrument panel. The compass told him they were on a steady heading to the south west and he could see they were climbing gently.

Jim called to mind the map that had been hanging on the wall of the shabby jungle shop. Flying south west would take them straight to Guatemala City which he knew was about 600 kilometers away. If the bomb landed there it would be a disaster and the Cessna had more than enough range to get there without refuelling. He sat down on the metal deck to work out his priorities.

First he needed to get the bomb unbolted from the floor. If all else failed, he could drop it in the jungle, before they arrived at the target city. Even if the computer could not trigger the device, a crashing aircraft would make a very effective dirty bomb and spread radiation to thousands of people. Then he would have to see if he could stop the aircraft reaching the city in the first place.

He retrieved his tools from the back of the passenger compartment and turned back to the bomb. After appreciable effort, he removed the third bolt and then started on the last one. Without the others distorting the mounting, this bolt was easier and he wound it back until there were just a few threads holding the bomb in place. He could whip that out in seconds when the time came, but for now he did not want the device sliding around the floor.

Taking his handful of tools with him, he struggled his way over the back of the pilot's seat and sat down to contemplate the situation. The improvised autopilot was linked to the flight controls by a series of flat metal rods that pulled and pushed to adjust the course and height and were driven by three small servo motors connected to the computer. Jim was surprised at how effective such a crude apparatus was proving to be. Clearly the Cessna had been chosen for its simplicity of operation, to allow it to work with this odd device.

Jim leaned across and started to undo the nuts that held the bolts in place that linked the metal rods together. As he took the nuts off he tossed them into the back of the plane, but he did not remove the bolts themselves. The last thing he wanted was to be fighting a half disabled autopilot while trying to disassemble it.

Eventually he had all the required nuts removed. He strapped himself into the pilot's seat, checked the aircraft heading and took hold of the control wheel. Leaning across the cabin, he pulled the unsecured bolts out of their mounting holes and tossed them over his shoulder. In seconds the autopilot was disconnected and Jim was flying the aircraft himself. He blessed the Army Air Corps flying instructors who had taught him at Middle Wallop and then put the aircraft into a gentle turn back the way he had come.

Chapter 29

As Jim settled the aircraft on the opposite course the small VHF radio in his pocket crackled to life. "Boss, this is Ivan. Are you receiving?"

Jim pulled the radio out and thumbed the transmit button. "Receiving. Thought you might have called before now."

"We would have, but we've had company. Been lying under a bush with all sorts of fun creepy crawlies for entertainment."

"What's the situation now?"

"The second aircraft has been pushed out of the hangar and refuelled. It's just sitting there at the moment and the guards have gone back to the main house. I'm guessing it's breakfast time. What the hell happened to you? What are you doing?"

"The bloody plane took off faster than I anticipated. I've gained control and I'm on the way back in, but all this damned jungle looks the same. I'm going to have a hell of a job finding the airstrip."

"How about flying straight to Belize City and putting down there? We'll push off and join you later."

Jim looked down at the instrument console to confirm his fears and then thumbed the transmit button again. "Nice idea, but I've used way too much fuel for that. It's going to be find the airstrip or drop it into the jungle."

"Leave it with me. I've got an idea. Look for smoke and the airstrip should be nearby. Out."

Jim continued scanning the jungle ahead of him and checking the fuel gauge more and more nervously. An aircraft this small crashing into the jungle would be hard, if not impossible, to find and it would not be a comfortable landing.

Twenty minutes later, still with no sign of the airstrip, he was scanning all around him hoping for a jungle clearing, a road or a river to put down on. He could see nothing that looked promising. The jungle canopy seemed solid from up here and the fuel gauge was not helping to keep him calm.

He turned his head again and there was a column of dark grey smoke billowing up from the trees away to his right. He turned towards it and a few moments later he could just pick out the roof of Frobisher's bungalow through the trees. Just short of it he could now see the airstrip and then he saw the other Cessna sitting outside the hangar that had been hidden by overhanging branches. As he got closer he could see that the large garage next to the bungalow was burning fiercely. A distraction and a marker; perfect.

Jim flew the Cessna round in a wide arc away from the house and the fire to line it up with the airstrip. He throttled back the engine and began the approach that should lead to a gentle landing. They would then need to remove the bomb, get it to the boatshed and away down river before Frobisher and his people could stop them. It was going to be tight.

Jim tightened the safety harness and prepared to touch down. At the end of the runway he could see Geordie and Ivan standing beside the small hangar. Flying towards the morning sun was dazzling, but then a shadow passed across the windscreen. He looked up to see a large bird of prey diving straight at him with its claws extended. The confused bird smashed into the whirling propeller and the windscreen was instantly plastered with blood and bird entrails. Jim could see nothing ahead of him.

The aircraft smacked down onto the rough jungle airstrip and Jim tried desperately to keep it on track by looking through the side windows. He cut the engine and watched the airspeed indicator start to drop. He applied the brakes and felt the aircraft start to swerve to one side. He heard the port wing starting to strike the smaller branches at the side of the airstrip and tried to swing the aircraft back the other way. He was just too slow to stop the wing hitting a more substantial tree trunk.

The impact ripped a large piece out of the wing and spun the aircraft around violently. The nose plowed between two trees, bending the propeller blades back and bringing the out of control machine to a shuddering stop. Before he had chance to move, the door was wrenched open and Geordie's smiling face appeared.

"Coconut Airways welcomes you to our jungle airfield. Please ensure you take all your belongings with you when you disembark."

Jim was shaken up by the unplanned nature of the landing so Geordie helped him to climb out. "Ignore me, but get that damned bomb out of there."

"Don't worry, boss, Ivan's already in there getting it loose. You head for the boathouse and we'll be right behind you."

Jim looked around him as Geordie moved quickly to help Ivan. The starboard wing had swung round and impacted the refuelling truck that was now leaking aviation gasoline. The smoke from the fire in the garage seemed to be increasing and he could hear shouting from that direction. He pulled himself together and set off towards the boathouse. As he passed the hangar he looked back and could see his two big men carrying the bomb between them on its mounting frame. Despite their strength, they were struggling with the weight.

Jim reached the boathouse and slipped the padlock out of the hasp, then slid the door wide open. He walked along the narrow wooden dock inside the hut and dropped down into the first boat. As he started the engine Geordie and Ivan came through the door, sweating and panting. Jim helped them lower the bomb into the back of the boat and then Ivan climbed in to secure it with a length of rope he grabbed from a hook on the wall. Geordie untied the mooring ropes and jumped down into the boat.

"Hang on. Here we go!" Jim said.

Slowly, he pushed the throttle forward and the boat moved out of the boathouse with a throaty burble from the water jet exhausts. As soon as they were clear Jim heard shouting from behind them. He turned to see three armed men running towards them. The first one slid to a stop and took aim. The burst of automatic fire passed just behind them as

Jim slammed the throttle forward to its maximum stop. The boat responded instantly and accelerated rapidly along the artificial creek towards the main river.

Chapter 30

Frobisher woke, bleary-eyed and confused, to the sound of the alarm. He pushed the girl's arm off him and reached out to slap the top of the alarm clock. The alarm continued so he slapped again. He looked at the digital green numbers on the clock and swore loudly. He had missed the programmed take-off time for his gift to the Guatemalans.

He forgave himself; last night the girl had been inventive and enthusiastic. For what he was paying her she damned well should be. He lay back on the rumpled pillow and smiled. The alarm continued and the realisation dawned that it wasn't the clock. He pushed the girl violently away from him and leapt out of the tangled bed as she hit the floor.

He ignored her cry of protest as he grabbed his clothes and dragged them on. He ran from the bedroom and down the wide curving staircase. Flinging the front door open, he ran out into the early morning sunlight. The black smoke pouring from the windows of the garage increased even as he watched. His security guards were fighting the fire and losing. He called the nearest one to him.

"What the hell happened?" he asked, looking at the man's blackened face and burn marked shirt.

"We don't know, sir. It started after we heard the plane take off, but nobody was near the building so we don't know what caused it."

Frobisher stood and stared at the building that blazed so fiercely. There could be no hope for his collection of fine cars. Nothing could have survived that. Over the roar of the flames and the exploding fuel cans he heard the sound of an engine. Had one of the cars been saved? He looked around.

His mind cleared as he recognised that this was not the sound of a car engine. He looked past the smoke and saw the glint of sunlight on the windscreen of the Cessna, just as it touched down. It vanished behind the building and fury flushed his face and held him in place for a second or two as he realised what was happening.

He ran towards the fire, screaming at the security men. "Leave that! Let it burn! Get my bloody bomb back! It's that damned army officer, I'm sure of it. Stop him and stop him permanently."

The nearest security guard turned. "Permanently?"

"Kill the bastard and anyone with him, but get my bomb back."

The man in the smoke stained uniform nodded once and ran to assemble the rest of the security team. They hesitated, looking at the fire, then ran to collect their weapons, before running around the other side of the house, towards the airstrip.

Frobisher walked stiffly back towards his front door. He stopped when four of the men ran back into sight.

"What the hell are you doing?"

"Sorry, sir. They've taken one of the boats. Marco and two others are going to go after them down the river while we try and cut them off by road."

"Don't just stand there," Frobisher hissed. "Get a bloody move on and make sure of them at any cost!"

Chapter 31

As he swung the boat round into the main river at the end of Frobisher's canal, Jim eased back on the throttle. The boat slowed and sank a little lower in the water, giving improved directional control. Ahead the river seemed fairly tranquil, but with rocks here and there that would need to be avoided.

Jim relaxed into driving the boat and turned to look at his two companions. "What the hell did you do to Frobisher's garage?"

Both men smiled happily and Ivan said, "Oh, that was fun. They'd left a side door open and we found the cars covered in big white sheets to keep the dust off. There were barrels of fuel stored in there and cans of engine oil just waiting for us. We soaked the first dustsheet in fuel and oil and set it on fire just outside the door. It looks like we might have been careless and the fire caught some of the stuff inside. At least it got all the security guards to run that way."

"Well, it certainly made a hell of a blaze. It saved me from having to put down in the jungle and it distracted them long enough for us to get away."

"We're not away yet!" Geordie yelled over the noise of the engine. "The other boat is right behind us."

Jim looked back to see the second jet boat powering up behind them. He smacked the throttle to its furthest stop and spun the wheel to one side to avoid a large boulder. The boat responded beautifully, sliding into the turn and just grazing the stone face of the boulder. He swung the boat back in line with the river and at maximum speed it skipped along on the small ripples shooting a curtain of water behind it.

Ivan moved forward to sit beside Jim, but facing backwards to observe the following boat. "He's going to be a bit faster than us, I guess, since he doesn't have a bloody great bomb weighing down his boat."

Jim nodded, but concentrated on getting every ounce of speed out of their boat and keeping it on course. The burst of automatic fire passed over their heads and Jim slid the boat left and then right to make the aiming more difficult for their pursuers. He looked across at Ivan, who was watching the other boat intently.

"Swerve, boss!"

Jim turned the boat rapidly to the right and then back left to keep on course. The burst of fire passed harmlessly down their left side.

Ivan looked across at Jim. "They're gaining. We need a new plan."

Jim swung the boat around a tight bend in the river. Just past it there was another bend in the other direction and he took it at an uncomfortably high speed. The boat behind them slowed marginally in the turns and the distance between them increased just a little, but not enough to make them safe.

Jim swung the boat round a third tight bend and managed to control the craft as it skipped sideways in a skid across the water. After the bend

Jim was looking at a long straight stretch of river with no chance to avoid the pursuing boat, unless the driver made a mistake. Jim pressed the throttle arm against the stop to make sure they were getting every tiny bit of power they could. It was not enough.

The boat behind them was closing the distance and Ivan reported two men were getting ready to fire. The chances of avoiding the rounds from two automatic weapons at this distance were slight at best.

Ahead, Jim saw the water was marked by small, white-capped waves and there was spray in the air. He puzzled for a second or two before he realised what he was approaching.

"Hang on! Waterfalls!"

The high speed jet boat bounced and vibrated as it hit the first patch of disturbed water then suddenly became still as they flew off the front of the waterfall and headed for the water six feet below them. The boat hit the water with an almighty, teeth-jarring crash, but the screaming engine kept on going and the boat shot forward. Jim just managed to steer it between two large and jagged boulders and away into the clear river beyond.

Ivan's jaw dropped as he stared backwards and Jim turned round in time to see the pursuing boat leave the waterfall and fly through the air, as they had. The boat crashed down into the water, but they were a few feet to one side of where Jim had landed and the boulder just below the surface punched through the hull of the boat, throwing one of the men cartwheeling into the water and rupturing the fuel tank.

Jim pulled back on the throttle and turned the boat slowly back towards the waterfall.

"Where are we going, boss?" said Ivan, looking at him strangely.

"Back to see if there are any survivors. We can't just leave them."

"I bloody well could," Geordie said as he scrambled back up from the floor of the boat, where he had taken cover.

Jim hung back at the edge of the disturbed water and scanned across the river. He could see nobody. The leak from the ruptured fuel tank reached the hot engine at that moment and the pursuers' boat exploded in a sheet of bright yellow flame, sending a dark cloud boiling into the sky.

"That looked pretty final," Ivan said. "Anybody near that is beyond any help from us."

"Sadly true," said Jim, as he turned his boat away and continued down the river.

They drove on for another ten minutes at a more reasonable speed before they came in sight of the road bridge where Danny Magee was waiting for them with his Land Rover. Jim ran the boat ashore and the four of them manhandled the bomb up the river bank and into the waiting vehicle.

Danny climbed into the driver's seat and started the engine. "Where to now then, Jim?"

"Belize City airport, as quick as you can. I doubt if that was the only group chasing us."

Chapter 32

The Land Rover barrelled along the winding road between the banks of high trees. Jim couldn't see any wildlife except the insects that smacked off his face, but he could certainly hear the howler monkeys all around them. They passed the occasional car driving the other way and there was always a friendly raising of the hand from the steering wheel.

Jim's head was still throbbing from the impact of the hammer against his forehead, but the throaty drone of the engine and the gathering warmth of the day were lulling him into a doze. His head came up quickly when Geordie tapped him on the shoulder.

"Ivan thinks we have company."

The big Welshman turned to face forward. "I'm pretty sure I heard an engine behind us working hard and there was a flash of light from a windscreen through the trees on the last bend."

Jim turned around, then looked at the driver. "A little faster, if you please, Mr. Magee."

He pulled the satellite phone from his pocket as the vehicle accelerated. He was pleased to see it seemed intact after all the battering he had been through in the last few hours. He keyed the number and then looked over the back of the truck as he waited for the connection to be made.

"How long to the airport, Danny?"

"From here, maybe thirty minutes, give or take a couple."

"Which way do we approach it?"

"This road comes out just about at the end of the main runway and then we skirt round to the terminal building."

Jim heard the phone ringing and then a voice at the other end. Ivan and Geordie listened to Jim's end of the conversation.

"Get your crew into the aircraft and get her warmed up."

He paused, listening. "I don't care about that. I want you on the end of the main runway turning and burning with the ramp down in thirty minutes."

He paused again. "Squadron Leader, your problems do not concern me. It's up to you to adapt and overcome them and then be where I need you. Without fail!"

"Problems, boss?" Geordie said.

"I hope not. Before we came over here I organised an RAF C130 to be here on standby to take us home with the cargo. The pilot seems to think his crew finishing breakfast is more important than being ready for us and he is trotting out some garbage about air traffic control."

Danny Magee looked in his rear view mirror and jerked his thumb over his shoulder. "Company's arrived. Their truck looks newer than this one, but they don't know about my new engine."

"New engine?"

"Yes. Didn't I mention it? I put a new engine in a couple of months ago. It should be nicely bedded in by now and ready for a proper test run."

Jim looked across at the smiling driver. "Are you sure the suspension is up to it? You seem to be hanging over to one side a bit."

"Never you worry, that's all cosmetic. If the truck looks like crap there's less chance of it being stolen."

Jim looked back at the large green pickup truck behind them in time to see two men stand up in the bed of the vehicle and lean forward over the cab roof to steady their automatic rifles. He watched them take aim as best they could on the swaying, speeding truck.

Danny checked his mirror again. "Time to go, I think. Hold on!"

He mashed the accelerator to the floor and the roar from the engine heralded a surprising leap forward. The Land Rover picked up speed quickly, even as Danny swung it from side to side of the road to throw off the gunmens' aim. The distance between the two vehicles increased, then steadied as the big pickup increased speed, too.

Ivan leaned forward and shouted over the wind noise. "He's matching us!"

Danny nodded. "That's OK as long as he can't catch us. At this range and speed he would have to be bloody lucky to get a shot on target."

"From your mouth to God's ears," Ivan said.

Chapter 33

The gunmen in the pursuing pickup truck held their fire, a sure sign of a professional not wanting to waste ammunition. Despite Danny Magee's best efforts and new engine, the distance was very steadily closing between the two speeding vehicles. Danny checked his mirrors constantly.

"In about a mile we come to a long straight stretch," he said. "We daren't risk that with two assault rifles behind us and it looks like they're guys who know their business."

"Do you have an alternative?" Jim asked.

"I do, but if I screw it up at this speed we are probably all going to be dead with a Land Rover on top of us. You game for a try?"

Jim looked back quickly. The pickup was gaining on them slowly but surely. He nodded at Danny.

"Go for it. What do you need from us?"

"Get down as low as you can and hold on for grim death."

Jim turned to pass the instruction on to his men, but they had heard and were already down on the floor of the cargo area next to the bomb. They both nodded in answer to Jim's unspoken question. Jim turned back to the front and hunkered down in his seat, gripping the hand rail in front of him as he did so.

Danny tightened his seat belt and allowed the speed to fall off just slightly. He needed the pickup to be just a little closer. In the mirror he saw the gunmen bracing themselves as they saw the distance narrow. As the first one raised his weapon to the aim Danny swung the wheel over and took the Land Rover in a tire squealing turn into a small track to the left of the road. Through the cloud of dust they kicked up as they hit the start of the track they could see the big pickup slamming on its brakes to avoid crashing into the jungle.

Danny floored the accelerator again and the pickup vanished from view behind them as they cannoned along the jungle track. The track wandered through the trees until it reached a fork where Danny took the right hand track. Seconds later, the roaring engine pulled them back off the track and onto the main road again. Danny accelerated away towards Belize City once more.

His passengers eased themselves back into their seats, rubbing the bruises the high speed run down the rough track had caused. Ivan patted Danny on the shoulder.

"Nice one, mate. A bit more warning of what to expect would have been nice."

"Nah. Where's the fun in that?"

Jim checked his watch and opened up the satellite phone again. He dialled the number and waited for the connection.

"Right then, Squadron Leader, where are you?"

He paused, listening to the reply. "Good! We should be there in about ten minutes. Are you able to get onto the end of the runway by then? Good. Now remember, I want the ramp down and clear your people out of the cargo bay."

Jim closed the phone as the first round passed through the windscreen. He spun round to look behind them. The green pickup was back. At this range it had been a lucky shot; he guessed the gunmen were irritated and had fired in frustration.

Once again Danny floored the accelerator. "I thought it would take him longer than that. He's good. How do you want to play this?"

Jim looked back at the pickup that was creeping closer. "Keep ahead of him as far as you can. I'm hoping it's just the usual type of wire fence around the airport?"

"Yeah, about eight feet high. No barbed wire on top. Steel fence posts holding it up. Are you going to tell me what you want?"

Jim grinned. "Nah. Where's the fun in that?"

Ivan and Geordie got down as low as they could in the back of the Land Rover, thought they knew the metal tailgate would give them scant protection from rifle rounds. Jim watched the pickup closing the distance behind them. Another burst of fire flew low over them and then another just to one side. The gunmen clearly knew they were running out of chances to stop the fleeing truck.

The Land Rover seemed to lift as they howled over the brow of a slight rise. In front of them Jim could see the airport and there was the dull gray bulk of the C130 on the end of the runway, with its engines running. The main ramp was down and he could see that the vehicle wedges were in place.

"Right, Danny, straight through the fence and into the Hercules, if you please!"

Danny looked across at him and grinned. "And I thought the SAS were supposed to be the crazy bastards. Hang on, there's a ditch this side of the fence that might be fun."

The Land Rover ignored the turn and drove straight off the road, aiming for the fence. The slight bump before the ditch gave them just enough lift at this high speed to fly across the narrow gap and crash to earth on the other side. Danny fought to control the wildly bucking truck and, without slowing, aimed between the two nearest steel posts. He hit the fence in a scream of tortured metal and powered through.

Once through the fence, he swung the Land Rover left and then right to line it up with the back of the waiting aircraft. The truck bounced onto the concrete runway and settled down. Danny allowed the power to drop away, but they were still doing at least thirty miles an hour as they hit the ramp and bounced into the aircraft's cavernous cargo bay. Danny stood on the brake pedal and the truck skidded to a halt inches from the forward bulkhead. A shocked loadmaster stood to one side with his mouth hanging open.

Jim sat up and yelled at him. "Shut the ramp and tell the pilot to get the hell out of here!"

The loadmaster pressed the control panel by his side and spoke into the headset he wore. Jim heard the ramp whining closed and then the brakes released and the aircraft started to make its take-off run.

They all heard the thudding against the metal at the back of the aircraft. The loadmaster turned to Jim. "What the hell is that?"

"Woodpeckers."

Chapter 34

Jim sat by the window in the aircrew briefing room looking out across the aircraft dispersal area at RAF Marham in Norfolk. He could see the C130 they had arrived in, with the crowd of ground crew and the aircraft's crew clustered around the tail end discussing the bullet holes and how they had got there. Ivan and Geordie had gone with the detachment of RAF Police to put the nuclear device into safe storage and Danny Magee had gone to the base shop to get himself some warmer clothes. The cold drizzle of an English summer across the airfield was a challenge for someone used to the steamy heat of Belize.

Jim sat back and opened up his private mobile phone to check for any messages that had come in while they were out of range of the cell towers. There were five messages from Megan assuring him she was well and asking how he was and when he would be back home. Then there was the sixth that just said, "Call Me!" He smiled at that and carried on to look for his missed calls. There was just one and it appeared to be a Scottish area number. He pressed the button to call back.

He waited for the call to be answered and when a woman's voice said "Hello?" he said, "Good morning, I'm Jim Wilson and I have a missed call from this number."

"Oh! Major, thank you for calling back. It's Dolly Hesketh-Brown. You asked me to call you if Arthur remembered anything useful."

"Thank you for calling me, Dolly. What has Arthur recalled?"

He heard a sigh from the other end of the call. "Well, nothing, I'm afraid. He has been having a poorly time, but I did find something that might help."

Jim's felt his heart sink. Without the information from Hesketh-Brown things were going to be much more difficult.

He tried to be upbeat for Dolly. "And what was it that you found?"

"Well, you see, my husband was always very particular about sending Christmas Cards to everyone he knew. He kept a very detailed list of everyone who was to get a card, what the card was to be and why."

"That's interesting, Dolly, but I don't see how …"

"You didn't let me finish. I was going through the list when I noticed a name at the back of the book that I had never seen before. There was the name and address, but no reason for why they should get a card. That's most unlike him."

Jim shook his head as he listened this was damned thin, but he had nothing else. "OK, Dolly, can you read it to me please?"

"Certainly. Are you ready?"

She read out the strange address and Jim wrote it on the back of an envelope he had in his pocket. He thanked Dolly for her help and broke the connection. The address was in Norway, in a place he had never heard of. He put the envelope away and dialled the number for Megan.

He could hear the phone ringing as he pictured the cabin in British Columbia. The snow must be almost gone from the cabin by now and the season would be in full swing as the groups of students came up from Vancouver.

"Hello?"

"Megan. It's me. I got your message to call. How are you?"

"I'm fine. I need to know when you are coming home."

"To be honest, I'm not sure. This job is still going on. It could be a while yet. Why do you need to know?"

He listened as she gave him the news that put a broad smile on his face. He was still smiling as Ivan and Geordie walked in with Danny right behind them, in his new clothes.

"Something's cheered you up, boss. Going to share?" Geordie said.

"Two things. First we have a lead on one of the locations we need for more of these devices and, more importantly, Megan just told me I'm going to be a daddy."

"Congratulations, boss. Does she know what caused it?"

Jim just grinned happily. "But now we have to get ourselves over to Norway to look up an old friend of Arthur Hesketh-Brown."

Ivan looked at Danny and then back at Jim. "I think we need to get this hot house flower back home as well before he freezes to death."

"Already arranged. Danny, your Land Rover is going to be cross-loaded onto an aircraft taking supplies out to the Caribbean guard ship. It should drop in here in a couple of hours to pick you up. You should be on your way home first thing in the morning and if I haven't said it enough already, thanks for everything."

Chapter 35

Ivan put down the map he was studying and looked across the room at Jim and Geordie. "Do we have any idea who and what this person is that we are going to visit?"

"In what way?" Jim asked.

"Well, is he sanctioned by the Norwegian government? Is he a crook that we are paying? I'm just wondering what we are walking into and how sure are we that Dolly's information is any good. This all seems a bit thin for a jaunt to the top end of Norway."

Jim nodded and put down his own map. "Not quite as thin as it was. I looked at the address Dolly gave me again. There was a word in there that made no sense to start with, 'Milorg'. I did a bit of research and it turns out that was the name for the Norwegian Resistance organisation during the Second World War."

Geordie looked up. "Hang on, boss, I was watching a movie not long ago about the raid on the heavy water plant in Norway. They called the resistance guys 'Company Linge'."

Jim nodded. "Yes I found them, too. Company Linge was a part of the Special Operations Executive that eventually gave birth to the CIA, so it was directly under allied control and operated out of one of the Scottish Islands. Milorg was set up and run by the Norwegians themselves. Apparently they were quite a large force by the end of the war."

Ivan smiled. "So do we think we are going to see some geriatric old guy left over from the war?"

Jim shook his head. "Not likely. My guess is that the Milorg people didn't close down after the war. Norway was taken by surprise when the Germans marched in. They're not a militaristic nation, even though their army is pretty good, but in their position I would leave the Milorg in place in case it all happened again. After all, they are right next to Russia and we all thought those lads were going to come over the border one day."

Ivan nodded slowly. "That makes sense, and if we have prepositioned nukes there, they would be the ideal sort of people to keep an eye on them."

"Then let's go and find out. Geordie, can you book us a flight to Norway for tomorrow, please? And I think we need to take those cold weather coats the Russians gave us if you still have yours. It will still be winter that far north."

Chapter 36

The three men stood in front of the main building of Kirkenes airport in the far north of Norway, well above the Arctic Circle. The thirteen hour journey, changing aircraft in Stockholm and Oslo, had taken its toll and all three men were tired and short-tempered. Even Geordie had stopped smiling.

The taxi pulled up and they loaded their bags into the trunk for the short drive to the port to catch the red and white Hurtigruten coastal ferry to their destination. Once aboard, the warmth of the bar cheered them up as the ferry pulled away from the dock.

Ivan sipped his beer. "At these prices I'm damned glad we're not on this tub for very long."

"Beer's expensive all over Norway. It's the same in Denmark even though they brew it there," Geordie agreed.

Jim studied the ship's itinerary on the card on the bar. "Looks like we are only in port for minutes, while they drop off the mail. So we'd better stay awake or it could be a bloody long walk from the next stop."

They settled themselves in the corner of the large bar room that stretched from side to side of the ship and watched the coastal lights slip by them. Vadso came and went, as did Vardo, with the ship pulling into the dock for a very short stop while mail was dropped off and picked up, with just one or two passengers disembarking.

"Next stop is the one for us," Jim said. "Batsfjord, here we come."

"So how do we find this guy when we get there, boss?"

"Shouldn't be too hard, Ivan. There's only about two thousand people in town, so we should be able to just ask someone."

"A bit bothered we couldn't find a hotel in town when we did the Internet search. What happens if our guy is away?"

"Trust you to worry about the basics, Geordie," Jim said. "My thinking is that there has to be someone in the town that will rent out a room if our guy isn't there. If not, well, we'll have a story to tell when we get home, eh?"

Ivan nodded towards the wide picture window. "Looks like we are coming into port now. Guess we'd better go and get freezing cold again."

The ferry slid gently into the small dock and the hatch in the ship's side swung open to reveal one man standing there holding a sack. He threw the sack into the ship and caught the one that was thrown to him. He seemed quite startled when the three men stepped onto his dock. They all stood and watched the ferry pull backwards into the fjord and head back towards the Arctic Ocean.

Geordie turned towards the postman. "Hello, mate. Do you speak English?"

The man nodded slowly. "Little. Not lot."

"OK. We are looking for Per Haugen. Per Haugen, you know him?"

"Per Haugen. I am knowing him. I show you where."

The man turned and walked away, gesturing for them to follow. With the small mail sack over his shoulder, he walked them along the dock. Under the streetlights they could see they were walking past a raft of moored inshore fishing boats. After about two hundred yards the man stopped and pointed.

"That blue house. Red door. That is Per."

They thanked him and watched him walk away. There were lights on in the house with the red door, so Jim climbed the short flight of wooden stairs and knocked. He could hear movement inside as someone walked across wooden floorboards and then the light flooded out as the door opened.

A short, but powerfully built man wearing a brightly colored Norwegian wool jersey stood in the doorway. "Mister Haugen? Per Haugen?"

"That is me."

"We are friends of Arthur Hesketh-Brown and we need to talk to you."

The man stepped back and gestured for them to come in. They each paused at the doorway to kick their boots on the step to shake off the snow before they walked in. They found themselves in a wood lined sitting room being warmed by a black cast iron stove. There were two women who rose to greet them. One was white haired and rosy cheeked from sitting too close to the fire. The younger one was something quite different; tall, slim and with long blonde hair that fell to her shoulders. Both women smiled a greeting, but didn't speak.

"My wife, Ingeborg," said Haugen, "and my daughter, Solveig. My son is away at college."

"Very nice to meet you all," said Jim as he undid his heavy coat and slipped it off. "Is it possible to speak to you privately, Mr. Haugen?"

The Norwegian nodded and turned to speak to the two women, who left the room and closed the door behind them. He waved the three visitors to chairs around the heavy wooden dining table and sat down himself.

"It has been a long time since Arthur sent anybody to check on his stores. Is something wrong?"

Jim cleared his throat. "Very wrong, I'm afraid, Mr. Haugen."

"Call me Per, and you are?"

"I'm Jim, the big one here is Ivan and the black one is Geordie."

"Good to meet you all. So what is wrong? I checked on the stores and equipment three weeks ago and everything was in order."

"I'm glad to hear it. What is wrong is that British Government policy has changed and we have been sent to recover the stores you have been looking after."

"Good. That is good. With the Cold War over it never made sense to me to keep that material here in Norway. If the Norwegian government had ever found it, I would have been in much trouble, I think."

"The thing is, Per, this material was put here a long time ago and we are not really sure what it is. Just what have you been looking after?"

Per moved slowly back from the table. He looked at each of the three men in turn and Jim could feel the atmosphere in the room change. The door swung open and the lovely blonde girl stood there covering them with a very unlovely sub-machine gun.

Haugen stood up and backed away. He half turned and when he turned back his fist held a large automatic pistol that had been secreted in the bookcase by the fire. He steadied the weapon, pointing directly at Jim.

"If you are friends of Arthur, how can you not know what is being kept here? How do I not know you are spies or thieves?"

Jim kept very still. "If you let me go into my pocket I can show you my identity card and a letter from the British Prime Minister giving me authority to retrieve the devices."

Per nodded and Jim took the documents out and put them on the table. Per stepped forward and picked up the two documents, then read them carefully

"And how do I know these are not forgeries?"

"Ah. A good question. I could ask you to telephone Arthur, but that would do no good. He is an old man and his memory has gone, I'm afraid. There is a phone number for the Prime Minister's office on the letter and they will confirm who we are."

"Father," said the girl from the doorway, in unaccented English. "That is meaningless. The phone number could be anywhere and the people who answer could also be spies."

"Solveig is correct. I have not a way of knowing if the number is true. One at a time, stand up and turn to face the window. Put your hands behind you and keep very still. Ingeborg!"

Jim was the first to stand and do as he was told. He heard Per's wife bustle through from the kitchen and he watched her reflection in the window as she tied his hands behind his back.

"Now sit down again. You next," he said, swinging the pistol around to Ivan.

Ivan stood slowly and turned to the window. "I bloody hope you know how to handle those weapons."

"We do," said Solveig. "Now put your hands behind you:"

With his hands tightly tied, Ivan sat down again and watched as Geordie was quickly tied, too. With all three of them with their hands behind them, Per visibly relaxed.

"Solveig, you keep watching them while I phone the emergency number."

Per walked to the other side of the wood burning stove to where the telephone sat on a cloth covered side table. He removed a small black notebook from the drawer of the table and thumbed through it. Finding the number he wanted, he lifted the receiver and dialled.

The room was silent as he waited for the phone to be answered. Per contemplated Jim and his companions. Solveig stood very still and never took her eyes off them with the gun held on them very steadily.

"Ah, at last!" said Per into the phone. "Codename Aegir. Password Bylgja."

He paused, listening intently. He turned to Jim. "It has been a long time. They are having to look up the codename and password."

"Who are you phoning, Per?"

"The duty officer at the British Ministry of Defense. I was told only to ring here if there was a serious threat to the material."

"Are you able to put that phone onto speaker so we can all hear?"

Per nodded and pressed the button. The hum of an open line came through into the silent room. They waited. Then the phone came to life.

"Codename and password correct. What is your emergency?"

"May I speak, Per?"

The Norwegian nodded and waved for Jim to come closer to the telephone. Jim stood and walked slowly so as not to alarm Solveig.

"This is Major James Wilson, Royal Engineers. I need to have my name and mission verified for the owner of the codename."

"Very well, sir, and how would you like me to do that?"

"I am going to give you a telephone number and I want you to confirm that it is the number for the duty officer at Number Ten, Downing Street. Can you do that?"

"Yes, sir, I can compare it with the emergency number I have here for that office."

Jim recited the phone number from memory and Per checked that it was the same one written in the letter. There was a pause and then the Ministry of Defense official confirmed that the numbers matched. Per thanked the man and put down the phone.

"Sit down again, Major. We haven't finished checking yet."

Chapter 37

The four men sat around the table again. This time nobody had their hands tied behind them. Solveig had put down her weapon and joined them while Ingeborg busied herself in the kitchen making coffee and a meal.

Jim looked at Per and his daughter. "So now that you know we are not spies, can we talk about our mission?"

"I would like to. I never thought that I would speak directly to the Prime Minster of England. He spoke very highly of you and asked for my full cooperation. We are ready to help you in any way we can."

"He's the Prime Minister of the United Kingdom, not just England," Ivan grumbled, his Welsh pride pricked by the Norwegian's words.

Per looked at him in some puzzlement, the distinction making no sense to him. He turned back to Jim who smiled.

"Per, tell me exactly what we are dealing with here. We know that nuclear devices were prepositioned here during the cold war, but we don't know what type and we don't know what the intention for them was."

Per gave the group a small smile. "Ah yes. They were very special devices, as you call them. The people who brought them here called them 'backpack nukes'. Does that mean anything to you?"

Geordie gave a low whistle. "I always thought they were a myth. I could never imagine that anybody would be mad enough to use them."

Per nodded. "It is difficult to imagine but it was not intended to be a suicide mission."

"So what was the plan?" Jim asked.

"When the time came, the idea was that your special forces would arrive here and pick up the backpacks. They would then take them across the border into Russia to place them around the naval bases near Murmansk. They would set the timers and leave. The Red Banner Northern Fleet would be damaged greatly. If they were detected and captured they were only then to detonate the device they carried."

Geordie whistled again. "Bloody hell! I knew Special Forces were somewhere just south of crazy, but that sounds insane."

"Not really. It is rough country up here and the border is almost impossible to secure. A man walking alone could slip across with ease. If he timed his approach well he could walk through the blizzards and never be seen. Remember, with a bomb of this size they only had to get close to their target, not right into the naval base." Per sat back and looked at them as they absorbed all this.

Jim cleared his throat. "So how did you get involved in all this?"

"My grandfather was part of the Milorg resistance movement during the German occupation. They realised after the war that they were still needed, so they were never fully disbanded. My father was a fisherman here and he used to report on the movements of the Russian Navy ships as they went around the North Cape. I helped him and when he died I took his place. The British knew about us and one day Arthur Hesketh-Brown came to see me and asked me to help them prepare a surprise for the Russians, if they ever invaded Norway. We found a place to conceal his stores and we got it ready. Then one night a small submarine came into the fjord and unloaded everything in secret. It has been here ever since."

Jim looked at Ivan and then back to Per. "We have come to take it back. There is no longer a need for it to be here now that the cold war is over."

"That is good. I think if the Norwegian government ever found out what we were doing we would have been in much trouble."

"OK then, Per. So where is this weapons hide and when can we go there?"

Per stood up from the table and opened a drawer in the cabinet behind him. He drew out a map and placed it on the table facing Jim. He placed his scarred and stubby finger on a spot at the head of the fjord.

"Just here there is an old house that my family lived in, many years ago. We still own it. It looks like it is abandoned, but inside it has been made good. There is a small room inside with the four backpacks in it and below there is a place for the four snowmobiles. Inside the small room there is also a rack of weapons and ammunition as well as food and warm clothing for the men who were to come."

Geordie perked up. "Snowmobiles? Do we get a go on them? I've always wanted to try one."

Per nodded. "There is no reason why not. They are ready to go. Every month I go and check them over and start the engines."

Jim grinned at Geordie and then turned to Per. "And how do we get there?"

"At this time of year the only easy way there is by boat. We will take my boat up the fjord tomorrow and I will row you ashore." Per looked towards the kitchen. "But now we eat and then I find you places to sleep. In the morning you can decide how to remove these things from Norway."

Chapter 38

The fishing boat chugged slowly up the fjord in the dim light of an Arctic morning with Per steering in the small wheelhouse. Ivan and Jim sheltered from the chill wind of their movement sitting on the fishing nets behind the wheelhouse. Solveig and Geordie sat at the rear of the boat on the transom rail chatting quietly.

"Young Solveig seems quite taken with our Geordie," Ivan said watching the couple.

"Well, why not? Geordie is a free agent now that Sam is out of the picture and he must seem quite exotic to a girl from a remote village this far north."

"True. A shame we won't be here long enough for them to get properly acquainted."

Jim nodded and stood up. He walked around to the side of the wheelhouse and called up to Per.

"How much further?"

The wind-burned face of the Norwegian appeared through the small window. "Not far. If you look over there, to the left, the house is just appearing around the small headland."

Jim looked where Per had indicated and could just make out a roof and a shabby wall appearing through the gloom. As they got closer Jim could see that this was a small ruined house with a rocky beach in front of it. The hills rose behind it before becoming quite steep cliffs that would shield the house from the worst of the Arctic wind.

The engine note changed as Per throttled back, then dropped the engine into reverse to bring the boat to a halt, fifty yards from the rocky shore. The wooden rowing boat they had been towing bumped against the stern and Solveig dropped lightly into it over the transom. Jim and the others watched as she quickly put the oars into the rowlocks and brought the graceful boat alongside the larger one.

The anchor chain at the bow of the fishing boat rattled down into the icy water of the fjord and, once he was convinced the anchor had a firm hold, Per cut the engine and walked back to where they all stood.

"If you climb down into the boat we will go ashore and see your stores."

The three soldiers climbed over the side of the fishing boat and into the dinghy that Solveig held alongside for them. Per followed them and they pushed off towards the beach in front of the wind-battered house. The Norwegian girl was clearly well used to handling boats as she rowed them skilfully and swiftly to the shore. The boat ran up onto the pebbles of the beach and Per hopped, remarkably nimbly, over the bow. Jim, Ivan and Geordie and Solveig followed, once she had stowed the oars. Per made the mooring line fast to a rusty metal pole that protruded from a boulder a little way up the beach and then led the way to the house.

As they walked Jim took stock of the building. The roof was sagging badly with holes showing where there had been a collapse. The walls were far from vertical and the glass in the windows was dirty and opaque. The door seemed ready to collapse at a touch, but the two clean, modern locks gave the lie to the illusion.

Per unlocked the door and swung it inwards. He stepped back and gestured for Jim and his companions to enter. As he walked through, the layout took Jim by surprise. Inside the building was a concrete block held off the floor by stone pillars. Below it were parked the four white snowmobiles, each one connected by a cable to the electrical socket behind them. To the right a staircase led up to the block and, as he walked towards it, Jim could see that it ended in a door that allowed access to the material stored within the concrete structure. There was a pipe leading into the concrete wall from a machine of some description that sat on top of the block that was in turn connected to a small windmill that was mounted so that the wind blowing through the ruined roof could turn it.

Jim turned to Per. "So what is that contraption for?"

"That is a clever machine that blows warm dry air into the storeroom to protect the devices from deterioration in the cold. I think you call it a dehumidifier. It protects electrical circuits from corrosion, or so they told me when they put it here."

"All driven by wind power?"

"Yes. So there is no reason for the electricity company to ever come here. It also puts current down below to keep the snowmobile batteries charged and the engines warmed so they do not freeze solid."

"Clever. Can we look inside?"

Per sorted through his bunch of keys and climbed the short set of stairs to the doorway. Unlocking it, he pulled it open and again stood to one side for Jim to enter. As he did so he found himself in an insulated room, with racks against the walls. To his right were four large white backpacks with wide shoulder straps. To the left were sets of cold weather clothing, dried Arctic rations, small tents and hand held radios resting in charger units. At the end of the room was a weapon rack holding four assault rifles, four automatic pistols and the ammunition to go with them. There was even a small box of grenades and four 66mm anti-tank rockets.

Jim returned to the door and looked down at his two men. "Come on up and have a look. We have everything you might need to start a small nuclear war."

Geordie and Ivan walked into the small room and looked around. Ivan went up to the weapon rack at the end of the room and inspected the firearms. He turned to Jim and nodded. If they had passed the Sergeant Major's inspection they must be in perfect condition, thought Jim. Geordie meanwhile had lifted one of the nuclear weapons up to test its weight. He looked at Jim and shrugged.

"Heavy, but not unmanageable. The lads who marched across the Falklands were carrying more than this. So do we know how powerful these things are?"

Per spoke from outside the store room. "They told me they were six kilotons each."

"Bloody hell!" Geordie said, putting the backpack down carefully. "That could really ruin your day, if you were nearby when one of these went off."

Jim nodded agreement. "But now we need to get them out of here and back into safe custody. What do you think, Per? If we took them back to your house, could we store them there until I can get a Royal Navy ship in to pick them up?"

Per was still considering that when Solveig came into the building. She whispered to her father, who looked up at Jim before sending her back outside.

"There is another boat coming along the fjord and heading this way."

"Is that a problem?" Jim asked.

"It might be. It is not a local boat and there are no fish worth catching, this far from the sea. There is no reason for it to be here."

Chapter 39

Jim turned back into the storeroom and took the binoculars that Ivan handed to him. He moved rapidly down the staircase with Ivan close behind. As they walked out of the doorway in the front of the house they looked to where Solveig pointed silently. Jim trained the powerful binoculars on the approaching boat. He adjusted the focus wheel and as the image cleared he could see that there were armed men on the deck waiting to land.

Jim handed the glasses to Ivan. "That's not good," he said turning to the girl who stood beside him. "Call your father, please. We have a problem and not long to solve it."

As he spoke Per came through the door and looked along the fjord. "Solveig is right. That is not a boat from our village. This is not fishing."

Ivan lowered the binoculars. "You're right there. These guys are armed to the teeth. Most of them seem to have assault rifles and I've seen at least one machine gun."

Jim took another look at the boat. "If we start a gunfight here," he said to Per, "we are going to end up trapped and probably dead. There are way too many of them for that sort of heroics. We need to get the hell out of here, right now."

Per nodded. "Come."

They went back inside quickly and, following Per's instructions, they grabbed clothing and weapons from the storeroom. Geordie and Ivan carried the nuclear devices down the staircase while Jim and Per started the engines on the snowmobiles.

Per took another quick look out of the doorway. "No time to waste. Solveig will show you where to go. She knows these mountains well. You should take a radio each in case you are forced to scatter."

Jim looked at the older man. "What about you? If we each take a bomb behind us on the snowmobile there is no room for you."

The Norwegian smiled. "Me and my brother played here for many summers when we were younger. I know every rock and gully. They will never come close to me and I need to make sure they do not take my boat. Do not worry about me."

Jim looked into his eyes and saw only quiet confidence. He nodded and turned to take the weapons that Geordie handed to him. Ivan passed him one of the VHF radios which he was about to put into his pocket when the Welshman spoke.

"Better test these quickly before we go, boss."

The four of them who were to take the bombs to safety switched on the small radios and in turn pressed the transmit button and tapped the receiver. All were fine, except for the one being used by Geordie. As he pressed the button they were rewarded with a high-pitched electronic squeal from the one he held.

"Can't worry about that one now. Let's go. Looks like you get your wish for a snowmobile ride, Geordie."

"Yes, boss. A few minutes' practice before we head off into the mountains might have been nice, though."

Solveig smiled and patted his arm. "Stay with me. I will take you the easy ways until you are used to it."

Per spoke quickly to his daughter in Norwegian, then slipped out of the building carrying one of the assault rifles and a handful of spare magazines.

"What did he say?" Jim asked.

"He wished us Godspeed and told me to take you to one of the cabins in the high pastures. The Sami sometimes use them when they come through here following their herds of reindeer."

"Sami?"

"Nomads who live up here and still live a lot like their ancestors did. Although they use snowmobiles sometimes and mobile phones when they get a signal. But now we must go. Are you ready? Then follow me."

They pushed the snowmobiles out through the door and, at a nod from Solveig, they set off up the slope and away from the oncoming group of armed men.

Chapter 40

Geordie paused his snowmobile at the corner of the building and looked back. He saw Per vanish behind a fold in the ground as the old man headed around the small bay. He turned to look at the approaching boat and could see that at least three rifles were aimed in his direction. He twisted the throttle and the snowmobile leapt forward as the burst of automatic rifle fire spattered the snow around him and howled off the wall of the building. No mistaking the intentions of the people on the boat then, he thought.

Careful now to keep the building between himself and the gunmen, while he was in range, Geordie accelerated up the slope to catch up with the rest of the party. The white snowmobiles and the white cold-weather clothing would make them difficult to pick out against the snow covered hillside, but the tracks of the vehicles in the virgin snow were all too easy to follow.

He followed the tracks up a narrow defile between two outcroppings of rock and emerged on the other side to find the three snowmobiles and their riders waiting for him.

"We heard firing," Jim said. "What happened?"

"The guys on the boat saw me and let rip. Not bad shooting from a rocking boat deck; they came close."

Ivan looked behind Geordie to make sure the defile was clear. "No doubt they are unfriendly, but if we keep going they should be no problem. They can't have snowmobiles on that boat."

"That's true, but I did see they had skis with them and the tracks we are leaving are pretty clear."

Jim looked back down the slope. He could see that Geordie was right about the tracks. Even if they pulled something behind them to cover the imprint of the snowmobiles, that would still leave a trail to follow.

"You're the local expert, Solveig. Is there anything we can do to stop them following our trail in the snow?"

She thought for a moment or two and then gave them a slow smile. "There is. Did you bring any grenades?"

"Yes. We've got two each. What's your plan?"

She threw her leg over the snowmobile and started the engine. "Follow me and I'll show you."

They all restarted the vehicles and set off after the girl's snowmobile. She led them further up the slope and then angled away to the left until they were passing below a steeper slope with overhanging windblown snowdrifts at the top of it. Once past it, she pulled her tracked vehicle to one side and waited until they had all joined her.

She pointed back at the steep slope. "That drifting at the top is ready to fall and make an avalanche. If you throw your grenades up that way we could trigger the fall. The snow should fill that valley at the bottom and cover up our tracks "

"What stops them crossing the fall and finding our tracks again the other side?" Ivan asked.

Solveig smiled. "The snow at the bottom of the avalanche will be rough and dangerous to cross and a lot of the lighter snow will blow around and drop to fill our trail. If we follow one behind the other to make less of a trail it should be difficult for them and we can be a long way away before they find the route we have taken."

Jim looked across at Ivan, who shrugged. "Worth a try, boss."

Jim nodded. "All right then. Geordie, Ivan, one grenade each and we'll spread them along the bottom of the ridge. As soon as they are thrown get onto the snowmobile and get moving out of here."

Ivan took the grenade from the pocket of his parka and looked at the others. "I'll take the far end, Geordie you aim for around the middle, and boss, could you drop yours somewhere at this end of the line?"

Jim grinned. "So you think I'm the worst grenade thrower then, do you?"

"Maybe not, boss. Would you like to throw for the far end?"

"Thank you, Ivan. I'll take this end. You give the word."

The big Welshman hid his smile and turned to size up the length of throw he needed to achieve. It was a long heave, but he thought he could do it.

"All ready? Pull the pin and keep hold of the striker arm. Ready to throw? Throw! Now let's go!"

The three men swung their arms and the grenades arced away down the short valley. As one, they spun round and jumped onto the already running snowmobiles, accelerating away from the narrow valley behind them and chasing after Solveig who had already gone ahead to show the way.

The white, tracked vehicles responded rapidly and ran smoothly up the hillside towards the notch in the ridge line ahead of them. Jim counted down under his breath as they went and as he reached zero he heard the triple thump of the grenades exploding behind him. He risked a quick look over his shoulder and could see the three small clouds of dark gray smoke at the foot of the steep slope. He looked upwards in time to see the overhang of snow start to move.

As he swung his head forward he heard the roar of the avalanche beginning, as the snow mounds cracked apart and dragged more and more material down the hill. Despite the speed he was travelling, the cloud of loose snow caught up and overtook him, blanking out his forward vision in a veil of white. Seconds later, as he crested the ridge, he was out of it and could see the other three snowmobiles moving rapidly ahead of him down the back side of the ridge.

Jim stopped his vehicle and trudged slowly back to the crest of the ridge. Below him he could see the tumbled mass of snow and rock that had cascaded down the hillside and filled the bottom of the narrow valley. More importantly, he could see that the cloud of light blown snow had filled in any tracks they might have left. They could relax and drive on to the Sami cabin for a well-earned rest.

Chapter 41

The cabin was small, but strongly built and set in the shelter of a large outcropping of rock to shield it from the worst of the winter storms. Fuel for the fire was stacked below it in a shielded enclosure to keep it dry. With the snowmobiles parked out of sight between the cabin and the rock, they shouldered the nuclear backpacks and took them inside for safe keeping. Geordie went back to carry the load for Solveig, but found her entering the door with the heavy pack over one shoulder. He said nothing, but looked at her in admiration.

While Ivan made up the fire, Jim and Geordie took a look round. There were no separate bedrooms, but sleeping areas were set to one side so they could enjoy the warmth from the fire. The walls were hung with animal hides for insulation and the beds had the same hides on them.

Solveig saw them looking at the skins. "Reindeer," she said. "The Sami use them for all sorts of things. The antlers make tools, the meat to eat and the skins for warmth."

"Do all the Sami herd reindeer?" Geordie asked.

"Not all. There are many who live on the coast and fish. Others work as fur trappers and some herd sheep. I think about a tenth of the Sami herd the reindeer."

"Are they all in Norway?" Jim asked as he admired the carving along the wall.

"No. They were originally nomads and some still are. They live all across the north of

Scandinavia and into Russia. They were not always treated well by the governments, but things are better now. The people of villages like ours always worked together with the Sami. We help each other in times of trouble."

"That's good to know," said Ivan, walking towards them wiping his hands. "The fire's going. It should warm up in here quickly."

Jim looked across at the fire burning in the hearth. "Should we be worried about the smoke showing these bloody people where we are?"

"Probably not, boss. The fuel is very dry, so it won't make much smoke and the wind blowing across the mountains should disperse it as soon as it leaves the chimney."

"That's good. So as long as they don't pick up our tracks again we should be in the clear." Jim sat down on a three-legged stool by the fire and warmed his hands. "I wonder who the hell these people are. It's obvious what they are after, but why now? Why not come before now and take these damned things?"

Ivan sat across the fire with his elbows resting on his knees. "Just a coincidence maybe?"

Jim gazed at the leaping flames. "Maybe, but it seems odd. Are we missing something? And where do they want to take these weapons anyway?"

"All good questions, boss," said Geordie sitting down on another stool. "But more immediately Solveig has found us some food. I think we are about to find out what preserved reindeer meat and dried fish taste like."

Jim smiled at his ever-hungry soldier. "How about you help her? Ivan, come and talk to me."

The two men left the comfort of the fire and walked across to the only window. It was still cold on that side of the cabin, but they could feel the heat building up slowly.

"What's bugging you, boss?"

"These people who followed us up the fjord to the weapons store. There are too many unanswered questions. Per didn't know the boat they were on, so they didn't get it from the village. That means they sailed round on it from elsewhere. They are heavily armed, so they were expecting trouble. They have cross-country skis. And they opened fire on Geordie without any hesitation. Just who the hell are they?"

"All puzzling, boss, but do we need to worry? We've lost them after that avalanche. With the snow drifting in this wind, our tracks will be gone by now and if they don't come from round here they won't know about this cabin. I guess we can relax and wait for Per to call us back down after they leave."

Jim stared through the window as he thought. The short daylight was ending and the dark was returning quickly. The temperature would be dropping rapidly outside. He turned back to Ivan.

"I may be being over-cautious," he said, "but I think we'll mount a watch tonight. It's too cold outside, so we'll take it in turns to watch from here."

Ivan looked at Jim quizzically. "You still think they are a danger?"

"I would be very surprised if they are the sort of people who give up at the first obstacle. We need to be extra careful while we have these damned bombs."

Chapter 42

Jim came awake as soon as Geordie shook his arm. The fire was burning low now, but it gave enough light to show Geordie's grinning face and Ivan just climbing out from under the reindeer hide of his bed.

"What is it?"

"Come on, boss," said Geordie. "This is a once in a lifetime thing. You have to see it."

Jim climbed off the bed and walked to the window with the reindeer hide around his shoulders. He stepped between Ivan and Geordie and bent down to look through the glass. He saw moving shapes in the darkness and he could hear the tinkling of bells. He peered harder to try and make it out, then he realised what he was seeing. Reindeer, dozens of them, all walking through the snow to the cabin.

Geordie looked at his companions with a broad smile. "Isn't that amazing? I saw them coming over the pass and thought it was the scumbags, but instead it's this. I never thought I would be in a Santa Claus scene."

As the animals reached the cabin they milled about and almost immediately started to cluster in the lee of the building to avoid the icy wind that Jim could hear moaning over the rocks. He heard footsteps coming to the door and it swung open to reveal a man in reindeer-hide clothing with big boots and a red woollen hat with massive ear flaps. His dark face broke into a smile as he saw Solveig and he crossed the room to hug her after first closing the door to conserve heat.

The two of them walked across to the fire and added more fuel as they talked. The language sounded nothing like the Norwegian they had heard between Per and his daughter. Jim assumed this was the Sami tongue. Solveig turned to Jim with a worried look on her face.

"My friend Bede says there are people coming. He saw them moving up the next valley over. They are on cross-country skis and they have weapons on their backs. He thought maybe they were hunters on their way here."

Jim controlled his surprise. "Does he know how many? And how long will they take to get here?"

Solveig spoke to Bede and then turned back to Jim. "He says he saw five and he thinks it will be less than an hour before they arrive."

Ivan stepped forward to the fire and warmed his hands. "How the hell are they tracking us? Did your friend see our tracks on his way here?"

Again the girl spoke to the stout Sami herder. "He says he saw no tracks. He thinks the wind will have filled them with snow. He did say they are coming directly towards us, so they are not following the curving route we used."

Jim looked at Ivan and then Geordie. "Not a good place for a gunfight, guys. If it all goes wrong we would end up trapped here. And if there are only five of them the rest are probably on the way."

"Agreed," Ivan said. "Time to go, then, but if they are that close they will be able to see our tracks before the snow fills them."

Jim gave a slow smile. "Solveig, would your friend be willing to help us before he and his people settle down for their rest?"

The Norwegian girl spoke again to her friend who nodded almost immediately and took her hand. "He will do it for me, but we have to do it now. His family are tired."

"Right then! Grab your gear, folks and let's get these bombs back on the snowmobiles. It's time we were on the move."

Chapter 43

They drove slowly, one behind the other, following Solveig along the valley and then up the ridge in a wide arc. The herd of reindeer kept pace with them, urged on by the Sami herders. The hooves of the animals churned the snow and obscured the tracks of the fleeing vehicles. Once they reached the top of the ridge they felt the full bite of the icy wind that scoured the top layer of snow and sent glistening crystals of blown ice into the ruts they left behind them.

The Sami had the herd mill around for a while, then sent them back towards the relative warmth of the cabin tucked into the rock outcrop they had left. They took the beasts downhill to left and right of the route they had come up the hillside, causing a wide swathe of disturbed and camouflaging snow.

Jim and his companions rode along the flat expanse behind the ridge, then he called a halt. "Ivan, come with me and you two stay down here. We won't be long."

"Where are you going?" Solveig asked through the thick scarf she had wrapped around her face.

"Back up to the ridgeline over there." Jim pointed. "There should be enough moonlight by now to see across the valley and watch what our friends are up to."

Ivan and Jim wheeled their snowmobiles round in a half circle and drove towards the peak of the ridge. They stopped just short of it and walked up to the top, careful to not walk too far and show themselves. They stopped behind one of the sharp outcroppings of rock that pushed through the snow and watched.

Ivan pointed. "There! Skiing down the valley like they don't have a care in the world."

"That's strange."

"What is?"

"They aren't even trying to find tracks. The route we came up is off to the right, but they are heading directly for us. How the hell are they doing that? Have they got a drone up or something?"

Ivan stared down at their pursuers. "You're right. In any case we need to get on the move or they are going to be on top of us. Taking direct routes is letting them catch up way too quickly."

"Right then. Back to the others and let's get out of here fast. If they don't need our tracks, then we don't have to worry about them so much."

They retreated from the ridge and remounted their snowmobiles. They drove rapidly back down the hill to where the other two were sitting chatting. Geordie looked up and Jim saw the smile drop from his face.

"What's the matter, boss?"

"That obvious, eh?" Jim tried to look calm. "They are over the ridge, heading directly for us. We need to go now. Where to, Solveig?"

"There is another cabin, that way." The young woman pointed. "It is bigger than the first one and they store fuel for the snowmobiles there. We will need to fill up the tanks shortly."

"That sounds good, bonny lass," said Geordie with a silly grin on his face. "But don't call me shorty."

The other two men groaned at Geordie's favourite joke, but the Norwegian girl just looked puzzled. She shook her head and started the engine beneath her. Without another word she set off in the direction she had pointed and the three men followed her.

Chapter 44

As Solveig had promised, the cabin was bigger, but not as cosy as the one they had left. The fuel cans were dragged out and the snowmobile tanks were filled while Solveig started the fire in the main living area. Jim climbed up the hillside behind the cabin and took a long slow look around through the binoculars. Seeing nothing to cause him any worry, he returned to the cabin to find Ivan and Geordie stripping off their heavy coats and warming themselves by the fire.

He walked across to where Solveig was rummaging through the store cupboards in the small kitchen area. He tapped her on the shoulder and she turned to face him.

"What is it, Jim? You look worried."

"I am. I'm worried about your father and also about these people following us. Is there a way down from here to your village, without going back the way we came?"

The girl shook her head and the blonde hair tumbled around her shoulders. "Not really. There is a range of cliffs in front of us that cuts us off from the village. We could go around, but the snowmobiles do not have the range without a refuel."

Jim nodded slowly as his mind worked on the problem. "And with the backpacks on the bikes behind us we have no way of carrying extra fuel. So what other options do we have from here?"

"I am waiting for my father to call. When he says it is safe, we can go back down to the head of the fjord and get back on the boat. There is a valley over that way that cuts down to almost where we started from. But if we go there before the boat is ready we could get trapped if they are behind us."

"How will he call? These small VHF sets are no good at this range in the mountains."

She smiled at him. "We may be a long way from the city, but we still use modern technology. I have a satellite phone in my coat and he has another."

"Fine, so we'll wait for his call. Anything to eat here?"

Solveig pointed into the cupboard. "There are many things in cans, if that will do?"

Jim smiled at her. "Anything warm and filling will do nicely and I'll buy you and your parents a good dinner when we get rid of those backpacks."

He returned to the fire to warm up and leave the young woman to her cooking. He looked across at Ivan who was now sitting by the window using the binoculars to keep a watch.

"Boss, quick! Look at this."

Jim moved swiftly to Ivan's side and took the binoculars he offered. He saw where Ivan was pointing and brought the glasses up to his eyes. He focussed and then saw it. There were men coming around the edge of a rock outcrop and heading straight for them.

"That's impossible! No way could they have made it this far by now."

Ivan touched his arm. "Look back the way we came."

Jim did so and there in the distance he saw the five men who had been following them. He swung back to the first group and counted. There were six of them, so definitely a different group. How the devil were they being found? Both groups were heading arrow-straight for their position. It made no sense. He made his decision.

"Geordie! Solveig! We're leaving."

The girl turned looking shocked. "But your food ..."

"Now!"

Geordie and Ivan grabbed two of the heavy backpacks each and headed out of the door, while Jim grabbed the startled girl and hurried her out as well. By the time Jim had got her to the snowmobiles the backpacks had been lashed in place. They leapt into the saddles and started the engines, remembering to rock the small vehicles to break them free of the ice that had formed while they were parked.

"Solveig, we need to get down to where the boat is and we need to do it fast."

To her credit, the girl recovered quickly and, gulping a little, she nodded at Jim. "Follow me."

She twisted the throttle and her snowmobile leapt forward from under the cabin, where it had been parked. The three men were right behind her. Traveling as rapidly as the small vehicles would go, she led them in a wide arc away from the cabin and around the nearest group.

Jim looked over his shoulder and saw the muzzle flashes from the assault rifles the men carried. One man had flung himself to the ground and his reason became clear as the machine gun opened fire. Mounted on its bipod it was likely to be much more of a danger than the rifles. The bullets splashed the snow all around them, but at this speed they were a difficult and receding target.

Solveig angled the snowmobile to the right and they raced after her, down a slope and into a narrow valley between two rugged cliffs. From his position at the back of the group Jim saw Ivan and Geordie pull off to one side and stop at the end of the gorge. He pulled up alongside them.

"What are you doing?"

Ivan heaved the backpack off his snowmobile and placed it on top of the backpack lashed behind Geordie. As he was strapping it down he glanced at Jim.

"These buggers are running us ragged. Time to make them a bit more cautious. Looking at the ridgeline above us, this valley is going to be their best way to come after us. If you three carry on I'll snuggle down into the snow over there and give them a welcome as they appear. Once they've gone to ground, I'll follow you."

Jim looked around at the position Ivan had chosen. The big man was right, as usual.

"OK, but don't leave it too long and get yourself pinned down here."

Ivan grinned. "I won't. Now go before they get here."

Jim and Geordie set off after their guide again while Ivan moved his vehicle into the cover of a fallen boulder and then found himself a useful sniper nest. He unslung the assault rifle from his back and settled down to wait.

Chapter 45

Jim pulled his snowmobile to a halt between Geordie and Solveig, out of sight of Ivan's position. Geordie was re-strapping the extra load to make it more secure.

"Solveig," Jim said, "anything from your father yet?"

"Nothing so far."

"We are going to have to call him. With these people somehow able to follow us directly we are running out of room. Can you call him and tell him we are on our way back to the boat? Make sure he knows that these people are shooting to kill. He shouldn't take any chances."

Solveig fumbled the satellite phone out of the pocket of her parka and removed her glove to be able to press the small buttons. She held the phone to her ear and then spoke in fast Norwegian. She looked at Jim as she was speaking and nodded to him. As she closed the phone down she smiled happily.

"He is safe and he tells me we should drive down to the beach a little further down the fjord. He has a plan."

From behind them they heard the sharp crack of rifle fire. Single shots, a second or two apart. Geordie looked at Jim, who nodded his confirmation. The Staff Sergeant unslung his rifle and walked to take up a position from where he could see across the flat area between them and the gorge where Ivan had set up his nest. He settled down in the snow with his weapon at the ready.

Back in the gorge Ivan had lain quietly waiting. His white cold-weather clothing against the field of white snow had made him virtually invisible. He scanned the area in front of him patiently until the first of the pursuers appeared.

The man curved into the top of the gorge in a graceful arc, controlling his skis precisely so he lost no speed. Ivan waited for his moment as the second and third men appeared close behind. Ivan controlled his breathing and took aim. His first shot struck against the stone wall and whined off into the distance. His second hit the leading man in the thigh and brought him crashing into a heap of tangled limbs in the snow.

The second man, with no time to react, crashed into his fallen comrade at full speed. Ivan saw the tip of the right ski smash into the fallen man's head, ripping a large strip of skin off the skull before the skier was thrown over him and struck his own head violently against the rock wall of the canyon.

The third man slid to a rapid stop and started to unsling his rifle while scanning for their attacker. Ivan's third shot struck him high in the shoulder and flung him into a snowdrift, with his rifle spinning away from him through the air. The remaining three men in this party had time to dive for cover at the upper mouth of the gorge. Still Ivan waited.

The first two injured men lay still, though the third was crawling painfully into cover behind one of the jagged rocks near him. He slid out of sight and then there was nothing but stillness. Ivan waited.

The second half of this group was invisible to Ivan until one of them decided to put his head up to observe what was happening below them. Ivan waited. The man raised himself further to get a clearer view of the full length of the gorge and Ivan took his fourth shot. The round passed through the attacker's throat, throwing him backwards in a cartwheel of spouting blood from the severed carotid artery. He was dead in seconds.

Ivan prepared to slither back from his position to reach his snowmobile that was hidden behind him. Before he moved he took a scan around him. There, coming over the ridge to his left and angling towards where the rest of his group had gone, was the other party of five skiers. At this range and at that speed single shots would be ineffective so Ivan thumbed the fire selector to automatic and took aim.

His first burst of fire sent seven rounds through the group, causing them to dive into the snow, but hitting none of them. His second burst was more successful. He fired off five rounds and two of the high-speed projectiles found their mark. One man had a bullet smash through the palm of his hand as he waved a signal to the rest, and another took a savage wound to the back of his right calf muscle as he lay in the snow.

Ivan continued to move back to his snowmobile, assessing the situation as he did so. Driving across the open space now would open him up to fire from the second party, and maybe from the first if their courage returned. He was left with the uninviting option of driving up a steep slope away from his companions, with no certainty he could find his way back to them later.

The first round from the second group of skiers cracked past his head and pinged off a rock that jutted out of the snow. If he stood and tried to mount his vehicle he was finished. He looked around for an alternative and found none.

The burst of fire from his left dismayed him until he realised it was aimed at his attackers. He raised his head to see Geordie taking aim from behind a rock across the open area. He could see Jim was moving up to support him with his rifle already coming up into the aim. Behind him the young Norwegian woman was also moving forward carrying her own rifle.

As the three of them opened fire Ivan dived onto the snowmobile, started it and accelerated away as fast as possible. He streaked past his rescuers and brought the vehicle to a halt alongside the three that were parked there. He was about to dismount and go back to help when the others ran clumsily back through the snow and jumped onto their own snowmobiles. Geordie paused long enough to give Ivan a beaming smile and then they were off down towards the fjord, following their guide.

Chapter 46

The Norwegian girl led them quickly down the hillside in a swerving path through valleys, over ridges and around rocks. She never slowed for any obstruction and never looked back. The extra weight on Geordie's machine started to tell and he dropped slowly further behind. Ivan realised what was happening and eased off on the throttle to let him catch up.

He looked around behind them as Geordie came up alongside him. "No time to cross-load, mate. That looks like another lot of them coming in from over there."

Geordie turned and looked where Ivan had pointed. Coming hard down the slope was yet another group of skiers. He could see them pushing hard with their ski poles to increase their speed. He took a look back the way they had come and, some way off, he could see that the original two chasing groups had combined and they, too, were on the way.

Ivan leaned across and tapped Geordie on the shoulder. "Enough sight-seeing. Time we weren't here."

The two men throttled up and set off after their guide at the best speed they could manage. Coming round one of the bends, they found Jim waiting for them, rifle in hand. Ivan signalled Geordie to keep going and then brought his machine to a stop beside his team leader.

"Another group has appeared and the remainder of the first two groups are behind us as well."

"Both groups heading directly for us again?"

"Yeah. I'm damned if I can see how they are doing that."

Jim scanned the hill behind them. "We'll worry about it later. For now, we need to get down to the shore and hope Per knows what he is doing. We'll set up a defense position and keep these beggars at a distance. Let's go."

The two men set off chasing Geordie down the hill, As they swung into a shallow valley they could see the water of the fjord below them. Just that, just water. There was no boat waiting for them. At the end of the valley the snow petered out and became a rocky beach with the icy water lapping gently between the stones.

The group made a small wall with the snowmobiles and laid the backpacks behind them for protection from random bullets. Then the four of them spread out to where they could cover the valley that sloped down towards them. The sharp ridges of stone at either end of the small curving beach should shield them from attack from those directions, but Jim and Ivan kept a wary eye on them in case the attackers did manage to scale them.

The first group of skiers were not long in arriving. They swept into the head of the valley and slid to a rapid halt. Apparently they were surprised that the shoreline was so near. They shed their skis and took cover in the rocks at either side of the gorge. Jim could see one of the group waving to the second group, to stop them before they, too, skied into view.

Lying in a fold in the ground, Jim could feel the cold seeping through his clothing. Moving now would be fatal, so he ignored the creeping discomfort and eased his rifle forwards, ready to fire. Geordie had found a position slightly higher up and so was the first to see one of the attackers moving. He took the shot. The man spun round with a loud scream. Geordie couldn't see where he had hit him, but he could see the blood splattered across the virgin snow.

There was silence as Jim's team waited and the attackers considered their options. Jim saw the two dark balls flying upwards and then dipping back down to the ground. The grenades exploded, sending up two clouds of black smoke, but the shrapnel was contained to a great extent by the snowdrifts the weapons had landed in.

Jim turned his head as he heard the metallic sound to his right. Ivan was extending the tube of the 66mm anti-tank rocket he had picked up back at the weapon store. He watched as the Welshman spotted his target and drew his knee under him. Ivan looked at Jim and nodded. Jim fired a burst up the valley towards the men on the right, then swung and sent another burst to the left. With their heads down, the attackers did not see Ivan rise to his knees, aim and fire.

The rocket projectile shot out of the short dull green tube and flew straight and fast to strike a low cliff face behind the group to the left. The explosion of the warhead sent shards of metal and rock flying out behind the cover the attackers had found. Ivan smiled as he dropped back into cover; the screams and curses had told him all he needed to know about his success.

Beyond Ivan, Jim heard the incongruous sound of a telephone ringing. He realised it must be the satellite phone that Solveig carried, although he couldn't see her. There was a pause and then he heard her voice over the small hand-held VHF radio in his pocket.

"Jim? Jim? Are you there?"

"I'm here," Jim answered. "What was the call about?"

"My father he says to wait no more than ten minutes. He will be here."

Jim looked around. He could see no help coming, just the mist and the water behind him and a group of angry enemies in front. There was no way to leave this beach safely.

Chapter 47

Geordie turned on the small hand held VHF radio to report to Jim about the movements he could see in front of him. As soon as the radio came on all he heard was an electronic screech. The radio was unusable. He switched it off with a vehement curse and shoved the useless piece of garbage back in his pocket. He returned to watching for a decent target to appear in front of him.

Ivan lay further to the right and eased himself forward to get a better firing position up the valley. As he did so a high-speed round cracked over his head. He rolled to one side, keeping low, and looked behind him. The boat that had followed them down the fjord had appeared out of the mist to the right of the beach and he could see there was a man on the foredeck. The man raised his rifle again and Ivan could see that he was the target again. The Welshman rolled rapidly into cover and swung his own rifle around to return fire. Before he could do so there was a pounding of automatic fire from his left. He cringed down into cover before he realized that the rifleman had vanished from the foredeck. He looked left and saw that another fishing boat had appeared from the bank of mist. It wasn't Per's boat, but he could see Per standing at the wheel.

Per saw him looking and waved from the wheelhouse of the boat. The man lying on top of the cabin with a bipod mounted machine gun in front of him fired another burst at the enemy boat, which turned rapidly away and headed for the bank of mist. The boat with Per at the wheel angled in to the beach at the left side and slid in next to a ramp of jumbled stone where there was obviously a deeper channel.

Ivan watched Per for a second or two then realized what the Norwegian intended. He thumbed his VHF set and called to Jim. "Boss, I need covering fire for about four minutes."

Jim acknowledged and fired two bursts of automatic fire up the valley. Solveig did the same a second later and Geordie joined in as soon as he realised what was going on. Ivan raised himself from his hiding place and ran across the stony beach to where the backpacks lay behind the snowmobiles. With a grunt he lifted two of them and slung one over each shoulder. Weighed down, he could not run, but walked as quickly as he could towards the boat where Per waited.

He waded into the icy cold water up to his thighs and then he heaved one pack and then the other up to Per, who was leaning over the side of the boat. He forced his way back out of the water and across the beach with the freezing cold water sloshing inside his boots. He grabbed the last two packs and once more waded into the water of the fjord to deliver them to the boat. Turning away from the boat, he assessed the situation. He turned back and grabbed the side of the boat, then heaved himself over the gunwale and onto the foredeck.

Unslinging the rifle from his back, Ivan knelt down behind the heavy wooden side of the boat and took aim up the valley. "Ready, all of you! Withdraw now!"

Geordie, Jim and Solveig all jumped to their feet and ran back across the stony beach and into the water. As soon as they moved, the assailants in the valley rose up to take aim. Bursts of automatic fire from Ivan and from the machine gun on the cabin roof sent them diving back into cover as Per helped the three wet people over the boat side and onto the deck.

The last one into the boat was Jim and as soon as he hit the deck Per ran to the steering position and put the boat into reverse away from the beach. Spinning the wheel, he turned the boat to face down the fjord and then took the engine out of gear. After a pause to let the prop shaft stop spinning, he thrust the throttle lever forward and the boat started to gain way forward.

As the boat left the beach and turned, Ivan ran to the aft end to maintain covering fire and as he passed the small wheelhouse he saw that the machine gunner was turning around as well. Once again, bursts of fire from the two of them discouraged their attackers from causing difficulty. Within a minute or two the beach had disappeared in the mist behind them and they could breathe more easily.

Jim walked to the back of the boat and stood beside Ivan looking behind them over the churning wake. "That was a bit too close."

"Certainly was, boss, but at least we shook them up a bit."

Geordie joined them. "My legs are bloody freezing after that paddle. Any chance we can do any more of these things in Africa again?"

Jim grinned at him. "Wherever we find the next one, it has to be warmer than this, so that should suit you a bit better."

The big staff sergeant nodded happily. "Oh yes. Somewhere with a nice sandy beach and palm trees, please. Just what the doctor ordered."

Ever practical, Ivan said, "But while we are still here we should get out of the wind before we get frostbite with these wet clothes."

Jim led the way to the back of the wheelhouse where they were sheltered from the worst of the biting wind. As they were sheltering Solveig came out on deck with mugs of steaming cocoa that she passed to them. The machine gunner on the cabin roof called down to them and passed down his weapon to Ivan before climbing down himself.

Ivan looked at the curved magazine on top of the weapon and the flared barrel mouth. "Damn me, it's a World War Two vintage Bren Gun. No wonder they kept their heads down."

Solveig pointed at the newcomer. "And this is our friend, Aldor. It's his boat, but he let my father drive it because he is the better shot with the Bren."

They all shook hands with Aldor, who spoke no English.

Jim looked at Solveig and said, "Good of him to risk his neck coming to get us."

"Aldor is part of the Milorg as well," Solveig replied. "We are all prepared for the risk."

"So how many of you are there?" Geordie asked, over the rim of his cocoa mug.

"Enough to make anybody who invades Norway feel the pain of loss. We could not throw the Germans out during the big war, but we tied down a lot of their troops who could have been used elsewhere and they had to work hard to combat our people."

Aldor quietly handed his mug back to the girl and then pointed over the stern. As they turned they could see that the other boat was following them and it seemed to be closing the distance. Jim whipped up his binoculars and could clearly see the armed men positioning themselves in the bow of the boat ready to open fire.

Aldor tapped Ivan on the arm and beckoned him to follow with a crooked finger. They walked around to the side of the wheelhouse and the Norwegian opened a hatch panel in the side. He reached in and pulled out another Bren gun that he handed to Ivan. He reached in again and there was yet another that he gave to Geordie. Pushing his head inside the hatch, he grabbed a green metal box from the back of the locker and pulled it out. He opened it on the deck to reveal twenty of the curved magazines for the weapons. He took six himself and pushed the box back towards the two soldiers, who picked it up and headed for the stern of the boat to find firing positions.

Aldor called to Solveig, who took Jim by the arm and led him to where the old man was kneeling by the hatch. She listened to what the kneeling man said and then relayed it to Jim.

"He asks if you can use an anti-tank weapon."

Jim was surprised, but recovered quickly. "I can certainly try. What type is it?"

Solveig asked and then turned back to Jim. "He says it is called a PIAT. Do you know this thing?"

"Only from one I saw in a museum. How many of the bombs does he have?"

"He says only two, but he says we only need one to hit."

"Funny guy. Well, let's give it a try, but first we need to get those backpacks below decks, in case any stray rounds hit them."

Chapter 48

Jim walked to the back of the boat carrying the PIAT and the spare bomb, all the while keeping a careful eye on the pursuing fishing boat. He laid the weapon down on the deck between his two men and hunkered down behind the heavy wooden transom rail.

Geordie looked at the PIAT curiously. "What in the name of hell is that thing? It looks like something out of a steam punk fantasy."

Jim patted the ungainly weapon. "That, gentlemen, is a PIAT, or Projector Infantry Anti-Tank, one of the most useless weapons of the Second World War. If I recall its reputation correctly, it's hard to use, unreliable and inaccurate, plus it was pretty useless against the enemy tanks by the end of the war, even if you hit one with it."

"So what's the point?"

"The difference is that boat over there is not built of armour plate and if we do manage to land one of these bombs on it we could just about ruin their day. Even if we miss, seeing one of these big lumps heading towards them has got to worry the hell out of them and put them off their stride."

Geordie grinned. "Well, rather you than me, boss. Ivan has just given me a crash course in using the Bren and, if it's as good as he says, we should be ruining their day anytime soon."

The throbbing rumble through the deck as the fishing boat reached its top speed was comforting until they realised that the boat behind was still gaining on them. Slowly but surely the enemy boat crept closer. The first few speculative rounds flew past them and then the firing stopped as the pursuers decided to wait until they were close enough to be more sure of success.

Geordie took a quick look over the stern bulkhead and dropped down out of sight again. "So what's the range of one of these Brens, Ivan?"

"If I remember correctly, the .303 round had achieved hits at a thousand yards, so the bullet carries a long way. With the bipod this should be accurate to about six hundred yards so call that five hundred meters for cash. With the boat moving, I reckon we should be pretty sure of hits at three hundred meters."

Geordie grinned. "Time for a rest then? No point sticking our heads up until we have to." He jerked his thumb forward. "And Aldor up there on the cabin roof is probably going to fire first anyway."

Jim looked up at the Norwegian lying calmly on the cabin top. He had placed two boxes of fish up there as improvised sandbags and the barrel of his weapon stuck out between them on its bipod mount. The glass window at the back of the cabin was smashed where one of the ranging rounds had struck it and passed through. Jim could just see the top of Per's hat as he steered the boat from where he was kneeling behind the bulkhead. There was no sign of Solveig.

Ivan risked a quick look over the stern and dropped quickly back down. "They're getting closer. Do we wait for them to open fire or give them a surprise now?"

"Are they in range for the Bren?" Jim asked.

"I would say so. I reckon they are about 500 meters back. If we go for it now we can give them something to think about."

Jim nodded and pulled his rifle closer to him. "No point in trying the PIAT at that range, but I might as well join in the fun."

Ivan and Geordie both cocked the old machine guns and looked at Jim. "Right, keep the bipods folded, just rest the gun on the stern so you are more in cover. Ready? Right then, on my count. Three, two, one. Now!"

The three men rose up together and rested their weapons on the wooden stern rail. The two Bren guns began their chatter together, with the two men putting precise five round bursts into the following boat. Jim joined in with his rifle, taking what he hoped were carefully aimed single shots.

They could see that the enemy riflemen had taken cover behind the high wooden bow, but the man in the steering position was too slow and the first burst from one of the machine guns threw him to the back of the cabin with blood spraying onto the shattered glass windscreen. The curved thirty round magazines emptied quickly and both men slapped them forward off the top of the weapons and clipped a second magazine in place. As they did so they heard the welcome sound of the third Bren firing from the cabin roof as Aldor protected them during the reload.

Ivan looked up from the reload to see the following boat bearing off to one side. Through the smashed windscreen he could see the spokes of the unmanned steering wheel spinning as it did so. He held his fire and waited for a target. One man appeared from the deck and dived into the wheelhouse, but he was too quick to give Ivan a shot. Seconds later, the bloodied body of the original helmsman tumbled out of the cabin doorway and the wheel stopped spinning. The pursuing craft steadied and then turned to follow them once again.

Jim ran forward and crouched down next to the wheelhouse and looked up at Per. "How far to the village?"

The grizzled Norwegian looked down at him calmly. "Is too far. Unless you stop them they will pass us and then we have much trouble, I think."

Jim nodded and ran back to the stern in a crouch before diving to the deck between his two men. "According to Per, they are going to catch us well before we get to the village unless we stop them. If they manage to come alongside they will board us and we will surely be outnumbered."

Jim looked at Geordie and waited for the inevitable joke. It didn't come. Now things must be serious if Geordie would let one of his favourite jokes go by.

Ivan risked a look over the stern and was rewarded with a burst of automatic fire that splintered the wood near his head. He dropped down and picked splinters from his hair. He looked at Jim and nodded to the PIAT.

"They are catching us again, boss. I think it's time you got that drainpipe ready to use."

Jim looked down at the PIAT lying next to him. Using it should be fairly simple, but to aim it he would have to raise himself above the stern bulkhead and that prospect did not thrill him at all.

"How close are they, Ivan?" he asked.

"About two hundred and fifty meters, I would guess."

"Fine, let's try it. I need covering fire while I aim this damned thing so, when I give the word, you are going to have to be quick to get their heads down."

Chapter 49

Jim checked the PIAT was properly loaded and drew his legs up under him, ready to rise and fire. Geordie and Ivan did the same and checked that the spare magazines were lying near them, ready to be grabbed. Jim looked back to see Aldor peer around one of his fish boxes and wave. He had clearly worked out what was about to happen.

"Same as before, guys, on my count," Jim said. "But this time take it in turns so we keep them down longer while I aim. Three, two, one, go!"

All three men rose and saw that the enemy were ready for them until Aldor put a long burst of fire into the bow of their boat, sending them diving for cover. Jim lifted the heavy PIAT and steadied it against his shoulder. He was thrown back by the force of the recoil as the old weapon fired. He watched fascinated as the projectile arched over the water straight at the enemy boat. It plunged down and smacked into the water just feet from its target. The three men dropped down into cover again.

"Not bad for a first try, boss. A couple more and you should be right on target." Geordie smiled.

Jim smiled back. "All good, with just one drawback. We only have one more round for this thing."

Ivan popped up, took a look and dropped down again. "She's closer this time. Aim the same way and we should get a hit, if there's any justice."

"From your mouth to God's ears. Stay down while I reload."

Jim picked up the heavy anti-tank projectile and slid it into place, making sure it was properly seated. He braced himself again and looked to his two men for confirmation that they were ready. His mouth was dry. At this range, the enemy gunmen could hardly miss him if the Brens did not keep their heads down.

"Ready? Now then!"

The three men rose once more and again Aldor opened fire as they did so. Geordie and Ivan put down a withering barrage of fire, one after the other, taking it in turn to reload. Jim took his time, trying to make sure this time. As he fired the boat hit a wave and he staggered. The PIAT fired high and he watched in dismay as the round climbed away from him. He saw it reach the top of its arc and angle downwards, a certain miss.

But he was wrong, and the projectile smashed into the aft deck of the following boat. The shaped charge exploded as it hit the deck, sending splinters and red hot metal into the engine compartment of the old fishing boat. Small leaks over the years had splashed fuel oil onto the wooden hull around the engine bay and that had soaked into the fibres of the planks. The fuel tank was mounted close to the engine to allow more room in the hold for fish and poor maintenance had left oily rags scattered around the throbbing engine.

The splinters ruptured the fuel tank as the red hot metal ignited the rags and the hull planking.

The fire caught hold in seconds and worked back up the stream of fuel to the main tank. It seemed to pause for a heartbeat or two before the tank exploded with a roar that sent an enormous gout of flame and black oily smoke up into the air. The bottom was ripped out of the boat and the ever waiting sea boiled in to claim its prize.

With the hull smashed open, the fishing boat foundered quickly as the fish hold filled with water through the shattered aft bulkhead. The icy water poured over the sides and covered the decks. The gunmen waiting on the bow had no time to do anything but throw their weapons to the deck and dive over the side to try and save themselves. Their heavy winter clothing and boots were soaked in seconds and, added to the extra ammunition most of them had in the pockets, dragged them rapidly down into the dark depths of the fjord.

Per slowed his boat and steered around in a circle coming back to where shattered wood floated between burning patches of fuel. They scanned the water for survivors for a long fifteen minutes, before finally acknowledging there was nothing they could do. Per restarted the engine and they slowly sailed back towards the village.

Chapter 50

Geordie looked around. "Where's Solveig? Is she all right?"

Jim smiled tiredly. "She's fine. I gave her a job down in the radio room where she was in cover, but don't tell her that's why."

Ivan looked up from where he was sitting with his back against a rolled up fishing net. "So what did you have her doing?"

"I arranged for a Royal Navy boat to be on standby to pick us up. I wasn't sure where the nukes were going to be, so they have been waiting offshore. She was calling them in to get us. I was hoping they might get here in time to catch those poor beggars so we could have a chat and find out who sent them."

Geordie grinned. "Better not let the Navy hear you calling their ships boats, boss. They get really touchy about that. They only call submarines boats."

Jim said nothing, but reached across and turned the big Staff Sergeant round so he was looking forward to where the black hull of an inshore submarine was heaving through the surface of the wide fjord. "And there's our boat."

Ivan stood and walked across the deck to stand by Jim. "So do you think they were Russian Special Forces?"

Jim shook his head. "If they were Spetsnaz we would be dead or on our way to the Gulag by now. My best guess is that this lot were mercenaries of some kind, but who hired them, I have no idea. More worrying is how the devil they found us and then followed us so easily."

Per brought the wooden fishing boat alongside the submarine with just the lightest kiss against the black hull. The captain up in the conning tower looked down and waved for his sailors to throw the mooring lines and Aldor and Solveig caught them and whipped them around mooring posts fore and aft.

Geordie and Ivan manhandled the heavy packs out of the fish hold where they had been placed for safe keeping and then passed them across to the sailors waiting on the pressure hull of the submarine. The three soldiers shook hands with the two fishermen and then each of them hugged Solveig to say goodbye. They climbed across onto the submarine and waited until the mooring lines were released. They waved as the fishing boat pulled slowly away and then stepped through the hatch in the side of the conning tower.

Geordie tapped Ivan on the shoulder as they reached the bottom the ladder into the control room. "I hope these guys have got some spare boots. My feet are bloody freezing."

Chapter 51

The submarine landed them on the east coast of Scotland at Rosyth Naval Dockyard in the Firth of Forth. There the nuclear backpacks were unloaded and taken by road with an escort of Royal Marines to the Atomic Warfare Establishment at Aldermaston. Once there, they could safely be decommissioned or stored for future use.

Jim watched the trucks pull away from the dock and turned to look across the water to the red ironwork of the Forth Bridge. "While we are here we might as well call in on Hesketh-Brown to see if he has remembered anything else," he said.

"I'll go and find us a car," Ivan offered. "The dockyard must have some available. If I get a driver to take us, we can take the train south out of Edinburgh later."

Queensferry looked just the same as they climbed out of the dockyard pool car. Jim sent the driver away and started up the path of the house they had come to visit. As he reached the bottom of the steps up to the front door it opened and Dolly stood there waiting for them with a small, sad smile.

"Hello, Major. I didn't expect to see you all so soon. Come in and sit down. I'll make you all some tea."

Ivan and Geordie walked into the pretty sitting room while Jim followed Dolly into the kitchen. "Dolly, something's wrong. What's the matter?"

She held onto the kitchen counter top and stared through the window into the small back garden. There was a catch in her voice as she spoke.

"You're too late to see Arthur. He passed away last week. We buried him on Friday." She turned to look up at Jim, her face streaked with tears. "Just before he went, he recognised me for the first time in months. It's a comfort that he knew I was there with him at the end."

Jim stepped forward and put his arms around the sobbing woman. "Dolly, I am so sorry. Are you going to be all right?"

She snuffled and nodded. "I'll be fine, thank you for asking. My daughters live just down the road and I'll get to see more of my grandchildren now. So it's not all bad, is it?"

"Dolly, my timing's awful, but since you called me, did Arthur mention anything else about his last job in the military?"

She shook her head sadly. "He never really spoke about anything much until that last day. So I'm afraid you've had a wasted journey. I'll get that tea now."

Jim walked back to the sitting room and looked at his men. "You heard?"

They both nodded. "So that means we could have another site out there in the world and no leads on how to find it." Ivan said.

"That's about the size of it."

"This is going to be a bit rough for Dolly, but do you think she would let us go through all his papers, to see if there are any clues in there?" Geordie asked.

"Of course I would, dear," said Dolly as she came through the door balancing the tea tray. "I'll show you where they all are after you've had your tea. Do you still like chocolate biscuits, Ivan?"

Having cleared the tea cups away, Dolly led them up the stairs to the top of the house and then showed them a pull down hatch in the ceiling. She handed Ivan a wooden rod with a metal hook on the end and pointed to the ring in the hatch. Ivan hooked on and pulled down, opening the hatch and exposing the set of folding stairs that dropped slowly down.

"It's a long time since Arthur was up there, so it may be a bit dusty. He couldn't manage those stairs once he became ill."

Jim climbed the rattling loft ladder and found himself coming into a neat study built in the attic, with a dormer window built into the roof. As he looked around, his two companions joined him and they looked at the stacked document boxes and wooden cases lining the walls. Beneath the window sat a very dusty computer on an oak kitchen table. Geordie switched it on and watched as it went through its start-up cycle.

"Seems like we need a password, boss."

"Fine, you go down again and see if Dolly knows what it is while Ivan and I start going through these papers. This could take a while."

Geordie disappeared down the ladder and Ivan said, "So where would you like to start? None of the labels on the boxes looks promising. It would have been nice if one said 'nuclear devices', but no luck there."

Jim studied the labels. "I'll take 'contacts' and you just pick any that take your fancy. We may have to do them all."

Ivan pulled down one of the cardboard boxes and gave a mighty sneeze as he was assailed by a cloud of dust. "Sorry, boss." He wiped his nose. "Looks like Dolly was right about the dust."

Geordie reappeared. "She doesn't know, but she says he liked to use the names of aircraft he had flown for other passwords. Any ideas?"

Jim put down his box and pointed at the aircraft pictures around the walls. "There are your clues. He seems to have flown quite a range of aircraft during his career."

Geordie settled himself in the office chair by the computer and looked at the first photograph. He typed 'Tornado' into the machine. Nothing. The next photograph along the wall gave him 'Canberra'. Nothing. He sighed and carried on without success until he got to the eighth picture.

"Does anybody know what the hell that one is? Arthur looks very young in the picture."

Jim looked at the aircraft and shook his head. "No idea. Looks quite a beast though. Any ideas, Ivan?"

The big Welshman heaved himself up from where he was sitting on the floor surrounded by boxes and walked across to peer at the fading photograph. "Yep, I know that one. That's a Buccaneer. Fantastic machine for low level work. They used to fly through the valleys of Wales when I was a boy. You could stand in our top pasture and look down on top of them as they went by."

Geordie turned back to the computer and typed in Buccaneer. "We're in. Now let's see if we can find anything on here." He clicked on the Internet icon and then opened up the email folder. "Hell's teeth! It looks like there are hundreds of unopened emails on here." He scanned the first page. "And a lot of them seem to be advertising Viagra or Penis Extensions."

Ivan grunted. "Just like the rubbish I get coming to me."

Geordie smiled and looked at Ivan. "I wonder how they know," he said, chuckling.

The Staff Sergeant turned back to the screen in front of him and started deleting the spam mail. It took quite a while, but once done he was left with considerably fewer emails to work through. There were messages from Arthur's children, but they stopped after a while. Then there were a few from friends and some from the RAF Pensions authority. Geordie eased his back and then opened up one that looked a little different to the rest. It was in fractured English and he was about to dismiss it as more spam when he saw that it was a report. He read through it slowly.

"Boss, I think we may have a winner here."

Jim came across and looked over the sergeant's shoulder. "What is it?"

"As far as I can see it is a condition report for something Arthur had left with this person. He doesn't say what, but look there; he says the hiding place is secure."

"Promising. Now, do we know who sent it and where he is?"

Geordie scanned through the document. "He signs it Manuel and the email address of the sender has a '.es' in it, so that looks like Spain to me. Where in Spain, I have no idea."

"Forward it to my email and we'll let the computer geeks in the MoD headquarters have a look at it. But for now, we need to go through the rest of these boxes to make sure there is nothing else."

Chapter 52

"Well, we are a bit closer," Geordie said as he came round the door into the office. "The IT guys in the MoD Main Building have narrowed it down. I was right about it being in Spain. They reckon it's in a town called Denia, or very nearby."

Ivan swivelled round in his chair and looked across the desks at Jim. "Denia? That's just down the road from that village we went to when we were chasing those gold coins, isn't it?"

Jim nodded. "It is, but that's quite a large town. They are going to have to do better than that."

Geordie smiled happily. "They reckon they can get it down to a street address, which will be fine unless it's an apartment block. But it does mean we can get over there and be on the ground when they finish doing their thing and give us the detail."

Ivan looked back at Jim. "He's right and a bit of time looking round might be useful. Jumping straight into it in Norway was a bit of a risk."

"Agreed. OK, Geordie, make the bookings. Flights and a decent hotel somewhere in Denia. Since the Prime Minister is paying we don't need to go too cheap."

"Outstanding! How do you fancy the centre of town? Lots of nice bars and restaurants while we are waiting."

"Whatever you like, but just get on with it. I'd like to be on the way this afternoon if we can."

♦ ♦ ♦ ♦

The British Airways flight from Gatwick to Alicante saw them land in Spain a little after one o'clock in the afternoon. Carrying just hand luggage, they were through arrival formalities within twenty minutes and walking across to the hire car offices. They booked in and crossed the road to the parking structure to collect the vehicle. Within minutes of leaving the airport they were on the almost empty motorway driving north.

After paying the toll fee as they left the motorway, Geordie drove through the winding streets of Denia until he reached the road that ran alongside the large port. He followed this and parked almost exactly opposite the *Posada del Mar* hotel. They crossed the road and booked in, then Geordie went to the hotel computer to check his emails.

"Bad news, boss," he said as he joined the other two in the bar. "They've worked out where it is and according to Google it's a house, so we should be able to walk up and knock on the door."

Ivan put his beer down. "How is that bad news?"

"Did you see all those bars and restaurants as we came through town? We could have had a great time while we were waiting."

Jim sipped his beer and grinned. "Better luck next time. So where is it we need to go?"

"I spoke to the lady on the desk and she tells me it's in an area called Les Rotes. Just along the bay and just before we reach the cliffs of El Montgo."

"And just what is El Montgo?" Ivan asked.

"You remember we saw that stuffing big mountain right on the coast, with the orange cliffs, as we were driving in? Well that's the Montgo. It's a *Parc Natural* so there are very few buildings inside it once you get past Les Rotes."

Jim sat forward in his chair. "That sounds like the ideal place to put a weapons hide if there are few people around to stumble across it. Can you find us a map, Geordie?"

"Already done, boss. They have them in a rack by the door we came in through."

Geordie handed the map over and they spread it out on the table between them. Les Rotes was clearly marked, as were the cliffs at the edge of the park that dropped down into the sea.

"Finish your beer, gents," Jim said. "We need to go and take a look round before it gets dark."

Chapter 53

Jim opened the black wrought iron gate of the white walled villa and walked slowly up the path to the front door. Ivan and Geordie waited in the car to avoid intimidating the householder. Jim reached the carved wooden door and knocked. He waited and then the door was swung open by a strikingly attractive woman. Her long dark hair framed a face of remarkable beauty with a flawless Mediterranean complexion and the kind of dark eyes that can steal a man's soul in a heartbeat

Jim hesitated and cleared his throat before he spoke. He noticed the small smile play across the perfect lips. She was obviously aware of the effect her appearance had and was amused by it.

"Hello, do you by any chance speak English?"

"I do. How can I help you?"

"I'm actually looking for Manuel. I'm afraid I don't know his last name."

"Then why would you want to see Manuel if you do not know him?"

"Could you tell him a friend of Arthur is here to see him, please?"

The smile vanished from her lips and the eyes widened just slightly. If Jim had not been staring he would have missed the definite signs of recognition. She started to swing the door closed.

"Wait in the garden. There is a seat by the tree. I will see if he is wanting to see you."

The door closed and Jim turned away to walk back down the three steps and across to the large tree the young woman had pointed at. He shrugged his shoulders to his men and then sat down to wait. He leaned back against the tree and looked around the garden. He could see orange and lemon trees, heavy with ripening fruit, and other trees and bushes he did not recognise.

The house door opened again and he saw the girl point him out. An older man came around the door and stood contemplating him for a moment before he walked down the steps, leaning heavily on an aluminium walking stick.

He stopped in front of Jim and looked down at him. "You are a friend of Arthur, my daughter tells me. Who is Arthur and why would I care about him?"

Jim stood up and looked the man in the eye. "Arthur Hesketh-Brown was a Royal Air Force officer and you sent him an email a little while ago that confirmed the hiding place was secure. I think we both know what is in that hiding place and my government wants to retrieve them."

The man sat down heavily on the bench and eased his right leg out in front of him with a small groan.

"What happened to your leg?" Jim asked.

"I fell off my motorbike two weeks ago. The doctor says it will mend, but it will take time. So tell me, friend of Arthur, if your government wants the packages, why do they not just go and get them?"

Jim sat down again and looked at the Spaniard. "It's a stupid story. Arthur was tasked with placing these packages, as you call them, in various places in secret. Very few people knew where they were and we do not know who those people are. Our only lead was Arthur, who died two weeks ago. We looked through his papers and his computer and we found the message from you. The items were put in place in different times and now we need to secure them and return them to the UK."

The man rested his chin on top of his walking stick and contemplated Jim. "I am sorry Arthur is gone. What happens if I tell you I know nothing about this and ask you to leave?"

"I wish you wouldn't do that, sir. I have just come back from meeting another person who was guarding things for Arthur. He had a phone number to call and code words to use to get confirmation from London that what I say is true. Maybe you have the same?"

"Maybe I do, maybe I don't. Do you have proof of who you are?"

Jim had expected this and handed over his military ID card, his passport and the Prime Minister's authority letter. The man took them and looked them over before he looked up at Jim. He groaned as he stood up and rested on his walking stick.

"You should stay here and your two men should stay in the car while I check these. My daughter is an accomplished shot and her rifle is very accurate."

As the older man turned to walk painfully back to the house, Jim looked at an upstairs window to see the daughter standing there with a hunting rifle in her hands. The weapon was not pointing at him or his two men, but she held it ready to swing into use and her hair was tied back so it did not get in her way. He sat quietly and waited.

He sat for fifteen minutes or more until the door opened again and the man beckoned him in. Jim stood and walked to the bottom of the steps.

"You should bring your men in as well, Major. We can sit on my terrace and look at the sea while we have a glass of some very excellent Spanish wine."

Jim waved to his two companions and they climbed out of the car and walked along the path to Jim. Ivan looked at him enquiringly.

"Yes, we've found Manuel and he has checked us out with the MoD duty officer. So now he would like to give us a glass of wine. Oh and Geordie, when you meet his daughter, try not to drool."

Chapter 54

Manuel led the three men through the house and out to a terrace where a cast iron table and four chairs stood. Between the trees and the neighbouring houses the azure blue Mediterranean reflected the sun. The Spaniard waved them to the chairs and sat down slowly himself, with a groan. He stretched his injured leg out to ease it.

"Well, sir, you have a lovely house," Jim began. "And it is a nice area you live in, but tell me, how did you get involved with Arthur and his project?"

"Arthur met my father when they were both boys. Years ago Denia used to be famous for its raisins and Arthur's father was in the raisin trade, as was my grandfather. Even after the disease came and wiped out the raisins in these valleys, they stayed in touch and Arthur came here for holidays, before he joined your air force."

Manuel paused as his daughter came out onto the terrace carrying a tray of glasses and two bottles of rich red wine. As she bent to lay the tray on the table Jim looked past her at his two men and tried not to smile at their expressions. She was a truly beautiful woman.

"Ah, you have not met my daughter properly. Gentlemen, this is Carmen, the light of my life."

The girl smiled fondly at her father and nodded to the three men before turning and walking back into the house. Jim watched her as she moved with a feline grace and turned back to Manuel.

"You were saying, sir?"

The Spaniard was filling their glasses. "I think you will like this wine. It is from our family vineyard. My brother Antonio runs that part of the business. I am in charge of our orange groves." He finished pouring the wine and lifted a glass. "*Salud.*"

They all took a sip and Manuel was right, they did like the deep fruity flavour of the wine. Geordie reached forward and took a small handful of the peanuts that Carmen had also left on the table. He ignored the dish of olives she had left.

"In fact, it was Arthur and my father who were the ones who discovered the cave on our land and that is why he came back here."

"What cave is that, sir?" Jim asked.

"We have drunk wine together, so now you should call me Manuel, no? You have seen the granite mountains all around us here. In them there are many caves, some big, some small. Some are well known and open to tourists; others are dangerous and others are kept secret so they are not disturbed. This family owns land on the lower slopes of the Montgo." Manuel said, pointing at the flat topped mountain that towered over them. "Arthur and my father were boys playing up there, when my father fell into a hole inside an old shepherd's hut. Arthur went to pull him out, but they found that beyond the hole it opened up into a long thin cave, tall enough for a man to stand."

He took another sip of his wine and eased his leg again. "The next day, without telling anybody, they took lights and ropes and everything they could think of and went back to explore the cave. A grand adventure for two young boys, no?"

Jim noticed that his men were leaning forward in their chairs, fascinated by the story. Even Geordie had stopped chewing the peanuts.

"And what did they find, Manuel?"

"Yes, they went up the hillside behind this house. There were few houses here in those days. They climbed down into the cave inside the ruined hut and started to follow it. It went into the hill a long, long way. After a while they came to a narrow passage and after that the floor of the cave sloped down. At the bottom of the slope they found they were in a chamber that was half full of water and had a way out to the sea. They tried to swim down through to the outside, but it was too far. So they had to go back the way they came in."

"It sounds amazing, Manuel," Jim said leaning back and sipping his wine again. "This really is good wine. But what was the outcome?"

The Spaniard looked puzzled. "The outcome? What is ... Oh yes, I understand. Many years later, Arthur appeared at our door one day to ask my father for his help. This was in the days of the Cold War, you understand? He needed to hide some things ready in case the Russians invaded Western Europe. He thought they would try and take the big ports like Barcelona, Valencia and Gibraltar. Then they could control the whole of the Mediterranean."

"I see. I guess your father agreed?"

"Of course. How can you deny a childhood friend who needs your help?"

"So what happened next?"

"Arthur brought some engineers. Quiet men who did not go out to the bars. They improved the cave a little bit to make it easier to walk through and then they made a dock in the sea cave. Not a big one, but one you could tie a boat up to if it is not too big. They brought in the four packages in the dead of night and put them down near the sea cave. Then they built a concrete floor in the ruin at the entrance so nobody else could find it."

"I'm still not sure we understand this. Why would they block the cave? What if they needed to use the things they had brought in? And anyway, what are these things?"

Manuel turned dark serious eyes on Jim. "I am surprised you do not know what is here:"

"The secrecy got a little out of hand. The project to put these weapons ready for use broke any number of international laws and treaties. It was all so secret that knowledge about it was lost."

"Foolish when dealing with things like this. There are four Nuclear Sea Mines down in the cave. A small submarine was going to come in through the sea cave when they were needed and they would then take them and explode them in the port entrances to deny the use of the harbours to the Russian navy."

Jim sat back, letting out a low whistle. The enormity of the plan and the number of civilians in Spain who would have suffered was incredible.

And now they had to get these weapons back without the Spanish government finding out they had ever been here.

Chapter 55

Jim and his team stood in the ruin on the lower slopes of the Montgo. The concrete slab had been well constructed; it was going to take a major effort to get through it. Jim walked outside and surveyed the area slowly. Less than a kilometer away, towards the town, was the first of the houses. Although not easy to see through the orange grove, that surrounded the ruin, the occupants would hear any explosives being used to shift the concrete.

He walked between the low trees, back to where they had left the hire car on the unusually straight, wide track that ran between the trees and straight up the gentle slope to a low cliff face in the mountain. Jim looked up and down it, but could see no reason for constructing such a path here.

He walked across to Carmen, who was leaning against the car enjoying the sunshine. "Your father was right. It will take quite some effort to shift that slab."

She smiled at him. "So maybe you and your friends will be here for a while longer?"

He nodded without thinking too deeply about what she had said. "But tell me, what is this track for? It seems a lot wider and smoother than the others around here and it seems to go nowhere."

She smiled again and pushed herself away from the car to look along the track. "Is a mystery. This land belongs to crazy Alberto. His father built it many years ago. He tells nobody why and nobody is allowed to use it."

"You used it."

"Is true, but Alberto, he likes me. He lets me come up here to watch the eagles that have nests on the mountain. Sometimes he sits with me."

"Will he let us use it to get to the ruin, when we try and open it up?"

"I think yes, if I ask him for you."

Jim looked down the gently sloping track towards the road in the bottom of the valley. "So is that your friend Alberto down there watching us?"

Carmen shielded her eyes with her hands and looked where Jim was pointing. "No. Is not Alberto. I do not know who it is. He is not from here, I think."

"Never mind," Jim said, as Geordie and Ivan walked out of the ruin towards him. "What do you think? Can we shift it?"

They both shook their heads. "That's a damn big slab and it's been laid well. We need pneumatic drills and explosives to get through that."

"Not keen on using explosives this close to the town. I am pretty sure it would get us way too much attention. We already seem to have a fan club." Jim pointed down the hill, but when he looked the man had vanished.

"Well, in that case we need a builder with all the right gear to drill through and then smash it." Ivan turned to Carmen. "I don't suppose your father has friends in the building trade, does he?"

Carmen thought about it for a moment, then smiled. "There are many Spanish builders, but for the security I think I know who you need. Is an Englishman who runs a company near here called ROC. If we call him from the house he can come and look at the problem."

"Why not call him from here, bonny lass?" Geordie said, drawing the mobile phone from his pocket.

"Is a nature park here. There are no towers for the signal. A satellite phone would work, but not a normal cell phone."

Jim shrugged. "And I left the satellite phone back at the hotel."

"Shall I drive you back to the house so you can phone him?"

Jim looked again at the map he held in his hand. "Not yet maybe. Do you know where the other end of the cave is? Can we go and have a look at it?"

"Is a nice place to see, but the cave cannot be seen. Never mind, we go. Get in the car."

Chapter 56

A ten minute drive down the hill, back through the neat villas and then onto the cliffs overlooking the Mediterranean brought them into a car park by a seaside restaurant. Carmen walked them along the cliff road for a short while until they reached a viewing area, with signs detailing the wildlife that could be seen around there.

She pointed up to the top of the hill that overlooked the cliffs on which stood a ruined stone tower.

"That is the *Torre del Gerro*. It was a *mirador* in the old days."

"And what's a *mirador* when it's at home?" Ivan asked.

"A watch tower. Many years ago there were big problems with pirates along this coast, so they built *miradors* to look out for them and warn the people."

Jim looked at the tower and then back to Carmen. "Why are you showing it to us?"

"The cave you want is under it. There is another marker along the cliffs and if the marker and the tower are lined up it shows where the cave is under the water."

"Can we go up and see it?"

"Of course, if you do not mind the walk. It is a little steep."

Once at the tower, Jim walked to the cliff edge and looked down at the coast beneath him, then along it at the waves pounding into the jagged rocks and sending plumes of white spray jetting into the air. He could see no sign of the cliff marker, but he could see that entering the cave from this direction would be difficult and dangerous for any swimmer.

"What are you thinking, boss?" Ivan said, walking up alongside him and gazing along the cliffs.

"Even if we could find the cave and swim into it with SCUBA gear, a sea mine is going to be way too heavy to swim out of there. I'm thinking the best way is to get this ROC construction company to make us a door in the concrete and we'll go from there."

They walked back down the hill to the lookout point to find Carmen and Geordie in deep conversation about the display on the boards.

"Ready to go? I think we need to get to your house and get your father to call this builder for us," Jim said.

"Of course. I was showing Geordie these display boards about the wildlife here. Did you know four types of whales swim through these waters when they are migrating?"

"No, but I would love to see them when we have less urgent business," Jim said.

Geordie whispered something to Carmen and they walked back to the parking area and climbed back into the car. Jim turned round to look at Geordie in the back seat. There was a broad smile across his dark features. He turned forward again, as Carmen drove off, and thought nothing more about it.

At the house, Manuel sent Carmen to bring them more wine while he went looking for the telephone number. He came back out onto the terrace and sat down with his customary groan as he eased his leg into position.

"I have spoken to Craig. He is the one who runs ROC. He will be here in the morning. He will meet you by the ruin. Carmen has spoken to Alberto, so there will be no trouble using his big track."

Jim stood up from the table. "Thank you very much. We will get back to the hotel now and have a look around for any equipment we might need. Will we see you in the morning?"

"If you collect Carmen on the way to the ruin she can help you. I will be no use on the hillside with this leg:"

They walked off down the path to where the hire car was parked. Jim noticed Geordie turn back and wave with the same wide smile on his face. He turned back to find Jim watching him.

"OK if I borrow the car tonight, boss?"

"Going somewhere interesting?"

"That place we saw on the cliff. The restaurant called Mena. I've got a date with probably the prettiest girl in Spain."

Chapter 57

Despite the slight evening chill in the air, it was still warm enough to sit outside on the terrace of the cliff side restaurant, called Mena. Geordie and Carmen took a table right alongside the railings that kept them from plunging down the low cliff to the rugged rocks below. Geordie was fascinated by the way the gentle blue waves rolled in then burst into foaming white life as they reached the rocks and then powered into the narrow inlet alongside them.

He turned back to the table to point out the line of fishing boats just leaving Denia harbour to find Carmen watching him with a small amused smile on her face. She reached across and took his hand.

"It is beautiful, is it not?" she asked. "I have always loved walking along this cliff road and hoping to see the creatures of the sea."

Geordie looked over her right shoulder to the sea again. "Well, bonny lass, you're in luck. I ordered a pod of dolphins especially for you and they're just arriving."

Carmen's hair flung out behind her as she spun round to look where Geordie was pointing. Coming along the coastline, breaking the surface one after the other, was a family of dolphins. Her hand flew to her mouth as she gazed at the magnificent animals. She watched, spellbound, as they swam slowly past them and then vanished beneath the sea. Her eyes were shining as she turned back to Geordie. He thought he had never seen a more beautiful woman, so full of joy and excitement.

They ate their meal slowly, Carmen insisting he try the famous Denia prawns and then guided him though the wide range of fish dishes on offer. Between the courses they spent the time enjoying each other's company and sharing stories of their lives. Carmen told Geordie about her fiancé who had drowned while working on one of the local fishing boats. He told her about his wife, Samantha, the actress, and how the separations had caused their marriage to collapse. They sat in a companiable silence as they sipped the coffee at the end of the meal. Then Geordie stood and took her hand to help her up from the table.

They walked hand in hand along the dark road that led them back to her father's house, where the hire car was parked. As they reached the ironwork gate Carmen turned and placed a hand on his chest before rising up on tiptoes to give him a light kiss. His arms moved smoothly around her and pulled her to him. The kiss this time was more intense and promised much.

Chapter 58

With Craig beside him, Jim looked down at the substantial concrete floor that had been laid in the ruin. Jim watched as the builder assessed and measured the slab, then took samples from the edge with a hammer, then stood up and pursed his lips.

"So how much of this stuff do you want to shift?"

"Just enough so we can get through it to examine what's in the cave underneath."

Craig brushed his overlong hair back from his forehead. and smiled. "Oh, in that case, no problem. If you want the whole lot breaking out that would take time. Just an entryway? Elio and Umberto should be able to get that done in about three days. They're Bolivians and they work like madmen. I can start in about three weeks."

Jim shook his head. "No, that's too long. I need you to start today."

Craig looked at him then pulled out his smartphone and consulted a spread sheet. He rubbed his finger alongside his nose as he considered the options.

"OK," he said, "if I pull my two best men off a job in Javea, they can start in the morning, but that's going to cost extra. I have to compensate the other client."

"Thanks. How will you do it without explosives?"

Craig grinned and brushed his hair back again. "The appliance of science. We drill the holes, then fill them with a material that expands powerfully as it dries. We leave it overnight and in the morning the holes will have cracks between them. Then we just smash it out."

"You make it sound easy."

"For us it's no problem. Digging holes is one of our specialities."

Jim pointed down to the bottom of the straight track. "Couldn't that man of yours start today?"

Craig turned around and looked along the track. "He's not with me. There were two guys hanging around down there when I arrived. I thought they were yours."

Jim looked thoughtful. "Fine, we'll be here first thing in the morning. What will you bring up here? I'll ask Carmen to get permission for you to use the track on Alberto's land."

Craig gave him the details of the equipment his men would be using and then drove off down the slope. Jim walked across to where Carmen and Geordie were sitting on a low boulder, with the girl pointing out where the eagles nested. Jim looked up as he walked to watch the magnificent birds wheeling on the air currents in the sky with hardly a wing beat.

"Do you two feel like a walk?"

"Certainly, boss. Where to?"

"I think we are being watched. There's a couple of people down the hill and there was someone there yesterday as well."

Geordie looked down the hill. "I can see one of them. Where's the other?"

"Craig saw two when he came in this morning. If you take a walk down there you could ask what they are doing and see what the reaction is."

Geordie stood up and offered Carmen his hand to help her up. They walked off down the track and Jim noticed they were holding hands. He smiled to himself. Geordie was not wasting any time, it seemed. He watched them as they walked and kept an eye on the unknown man they were approaching. The second man appeared, trotting down the hill through the orange trees. They both jumped into a small car and accelerated away before Geordie got there.

Ivan came to stand by Jim's shoulder. "What are you thinking, boss?"

"I'm not sure, but after the attack in Norway I'm just a bit nervous, I guess. The second guy was up the hillside over there somewhere. He must have been watching what we were doing."

"How do we play this then?"

Jim looked at the calm face of the big Welshman. "Once Craig and his lads start work I think we need to have one of us up here full time. The last thing we want is some random guy getting into the cave before us. But for now we need to go and collect that stuff we ordered from the sports shop."

Chapter 59

Geordie sat quietly on the small ridge above the ruin, in the shade of an orange tree. He had met Craig's workers as they arrived that morning, though he couldn't see them now as they worked inside the ruin. He could hear them as their pneumatic drill pounded the series of holes that Craig had marked out for them. What he could see was the pair of men who were watching them.

This time they had not stayed at the bottom of the odd straight track. They had climbed the hill and were looking down towards the ruin. Geordie kept very still under his bushy orange tree and watched them as they slowly moved around to try and get a better view of what was happening inside the stone walls of the ruin. He saw them switch their attention down the hill and when he slowly turned his head he could see Ivan walking up towards him.

The Welshman called in at the ruin and tried to pass the time of day with the two workers, but since they did not speak each other's language he just handed over the two cold cans of drink he had brought for them. The big man stood outside the ruin and let his eyes pan slowly around the countryside. As Geordie came into view he did not acknowledge the hand signals from his friend, but tracked his eyes back to the direction he had indicated,

There they were. The reflection from a binocular lens gave them away. Careless boys, he thought, you'll have to do better than that. He walked slowly up the hill past Geordie's position, giving every indication he was looking for him. Once out of sight of the two unknown watchers, he took a curling walk around behind them. For a big man he had a surprising talent for moving silently and the watchers did not hear him until he crouched down between them.

"Hello, lads, see anything nice down there?"

The two men rolled outwards and looked up with their mouths hanging open. The swarthy one to the right was the first to recover and grabbed for the knife at his belt. That mistake was corrected by a massive right fist to the jaw. Ivan's years of training in the boxing ring served him well and his left fist was equally powerful as he hit the left hand man.

Rubbing his knuckles, Ivan stood up and then tapped the top of his head with the flat of his hand. The British Army signal for 'come to me'. Geordie broke cover and jogged up the hill to join him.

"You never did go on the anger management course, did you?" Geordie grinned as he looked down at the two watchers.

Ivan grinned. "Silly bugger pulled a knife on me or we would just have had a friendly chat. You take that one and check his pockets. I'll have knife boy here."

They rolled the two unconscious men over and went through their pockets. Loose change and car keys were all they found until they rolled them back and checked the wallets in their back pockets. Here they found a surprising amount of cash, but no credit cards and no driver's license for either man.

Geordie looked up at Ivan as he stood over his man. "Strange to have no forms of ID on them at all. Unless they are professionals and anticipated being asked."

"That's what it looks like to me. We never got to be formally introduced to those guys in Norway, I wonder if these sleeping beauties come from the same stable."

"Looks like the boss was right to have us taking turns to watch up here. A shame we can't have any weapons in case it turns nasty."

Ivan looked around. "Their hire car seems to be over there." He pointed. "You take that one and we'll put them down with their car."

Geordie grunted as he picked the limp man up into a fireman's lift. "Damned glad we are taking them downhill. This beggar's heavy."

"Never mind. You can go back and moon over the lovely Carmen while I take my turn on watch."

Chapter 60

It was Geordie's turn on watch again as the moon heaved itself over the ridge between him and the sea. The silver light across the hillside in front of him let him pick out the individual orange trees and the jagged tops of the ruined walls. He saw the dull reflections off the tools that had been left for the final work they hoped to do in the morning to open the passage to the cave. Nothing moved in front of him.

He heard the footsteps coming slowly up the wide track before he saw the figure approaching. He smiled. The flowing hair and the poetry of swaying hips told him who was arriving. She had promised to bring him something to eat and a bottle of wine when they were talking that afternoon. He sat and admired her graceful movement. She really was remarkably beautiful.

"Hello, Carmen."

Her hand flew to her throat. "You scared me! I didn't see you sitting in the shadows."

"Sorry about that, bonny lass. Come and sit down here. I've made a nice soft spot with the branches."

She passed him the small woven basket and sat down. He reached inside to find the promised bottle of wine and two glasses. He set them on a flat rock and then brought out the sandwiches wrapped in paper. He passed one to Carmen and sat watching her as she unwrapped it. He thought the moonlight made her even more beautiful, if that was possible.

"What are you looking at, Geordie?"
"Perfection."

She smiled and reached out to take his hand. Her fingers were warm and smooth in his as he stroked her palm. He looked into her eyes, then put down his food and pulled her gently towards him. Her hand slid around the back of his neck as she kissed him. Then he felt her other hand slide down his body and unfasten his belt.

Her eager fingers opened his clothing and clasped him, stroking him and sliding her leg across his. He lay back on the picnic blanket and let her climb above him. She sighed as he entered her and she started to move gently as he slid deeper and deeper.

On the ridge above them the night vision glasses showed the couple as brighter green shapes moving rhythmically against the darker green of the cool earth. Cold eyes watched as they moved together faster and then faster. The watcher heard her cry in the still night as she reached the moment of release and fell across the big man's chest.

He watched as she recovered herself and rolled to lie beside her man and he watched as they kissed before she left and walked slowly back down the gentle slope.

Chapter 61

The three soldiers and Carmen stood by the ruin just after sunrise as Craig and his two men arrived in their open backed truck. They jumped down and walked across to see what progress the expanding material had made in the concrete slab. Two days of heavy drilling had put a line of drill holes around the point they wanted to enter and now the holes were linked by significant cracks.

Craig spoke to his men in fast Spanish and they set to work with heavy hammers and crowbars to increase the cracking. After half an hour of heavy work the two South Americans were sweating profusely, but the slab was slumping into the hole they had made. A wire rope looped around one corner was led out through the doorway in the ruined wall and then fastened to the tow hook of the truck. Umberto climbed into the cab and drove slowly forward. The slab reared up and then crashed to one side in a small cloud of dust.

Jim and the others came forward and found themselves looking down into a ragged hole in the concrete. Below it they could see the tumbled ground dropped away into a low cave that was seeing the light of day for the first time in many years.

Jim and Ivan shook hands with Craig and waved to his two men as they drove away down the gently sloping hillside. Geordie walked back from where they had dropped their equipment carrying four caving helmets with headlamps and four large flashlights. The canvas bag over his shoulder also held heavy duty gloves to protect their hands from the rough stone they anticipated.

Jim turned around and looked at Carmen. "Are you sure you want to climb into this cave? We can handle it from here."

"Thank you for the consideration, but this is my family's land and I would like to see what has been here all these years."

"What colour helmet would you like, Carmen?"

"Thank you, Geordie. I will take the green one."

"OK, boss, that's blue for you then and Ivan gets the red. I always think yellow suits a dark complexion, don't you? Just like my medallion."

Ivan took the helmet he was handed. "I don't think there is any need for a fashion discussion about a plastic helmet." He turned on the headlamp. "Guess I'll go first? If I can get through, any of you three can."

The Welshman climbed down into the hole, taking care not to gash himself on the ragged concrete edge. He slithered down the first part of the slope on the loose rock and debris to find himself standing in a cave that vanished into the darkness. It was about two meters high and maybe the same in width. The floor bore the marks of the tools that had been used to smooth it out, ready for the nuclear devices to be brought in. Ivan turned on the powerful flashlight in his hand. In the beam the cave stretched away from him with a very slight downward slope. He could see no sign of the end.

Ivan heard Jim's voice from behind him. "OK to come down yet?"

"Yes, come on down, boss. It's all clear so far."

He moved forward to make room and watched as Jim slithered down the slope and into the cave. He was quickly followed by the other two members of the party. He noticed Geordie was very careful to help Carmen down the slope, maybe just a little too solicitous. He could see that Jim, as usual, was struggling to bring his claustrophobia under control, the way he did whenever they were in a tight space. He shrugged and turned into the darkness again.

Ivan walked carefully forward with the other three following him. Nobody spoke; none of them knew quite what to expect. The walls of the cave stretched away from them, but there was no sign of the roof getting any lower. The smoothed floor made walking a lot easier. As they came around a slight bend Ivan could see that the way ahead had been at least partially blocked by a rock fall. It was not a cave-in, just a slab of rock that had slid down the cave wall and blocked the path.

Ivan moved forward to examine it. "Geordie, can you come up here? I need your mining expertise."

Geordie patted Carmen on the arm and then walked past Jim to get to where Ivan stood running his flashlight beam over the rock. He turned around to the ex-miner and then pointed to the blockage with his thumb.

"You reckon you and me could roll that over to one side and out of the way without causing problems?"

Geordie examined the stone walls around the fallen rock. He could see no sign of any other loose pieces ready to fall. He took a firm hold on the rock and heaved backwards.

"Feels like the two of us should be able to shift it and I can't see any nasty surprises waiting for us." He looked past Ivan at Jim. "Probably best if you and Carmen take a few paces back just in case, though, boss."

"You don't need my help?" Jim asked.

"Thanks for the offer, but there really is only room for the two of us to get in here."

Jim took Carmen by the elbow and shepherded her away from where the two big men were getting into position. Once clear, they turned and watched as they got ready to heave. Ivan nodded and the two men grunted as they strained at the rock. They heaved it upright and then twisted it around, then jumped clear as the stone fell with a resounding crash to the floor of the cave, raising a cloud of choking granite dust and clearing the way to let them progress.

Carmen giggled as the two men appeared through the dust cloud, both of them plastered with the fine grey granules. "You are both the same colour now. You look like brothers."

Geordie's brilliant smile broke through the mask of dust while Ivan just grunted. As the dust in the tunnel settled, Jim walked forward shining his big flashlight. He was the first to see the hole to the right in the cave wall. Only a meter and a half high and maybe another meter wide, it seemed to go back a decent way. He crouched down and shone his light into it. His mouth dropped open and then he crawled into the hole on his hands and knees.

He was back a minute later. He stood up in the cave and looked at his three companions. They could see from his expression that something significant had happened.

"You are just not going to believe what I have just found in there. Not in a million years. Come on, follow me, but be careful what you touch."

Chapter 62

Ivan crawled through the hole after Jim and stood up when he reached him. He looked around, but saw nothing in the darkness until Jim turned on his large flashlight.

"What the hell is ...? That's an aircraft tail section!"

Jim swung the light to the right and the rest of the aircraft appeared. By now Geordie and Carmen had entered the new cavern and stood staring at the machine before them.

Carmen drew in a shocked breath. *"Dios mio. Es verdad!"*

"Say what?" Geordie asked.

She looked at him and back to the aircraft. "It's true. There were stories, when I was little, that Franco had ordered bases hidden in the hills in case of a counter revolution, but we all thought it was just government lies."

Ivan ran his hand along the riveted metal skin of the fuselage. He looked at the red and gold roundels that marked it as belonging to the Spanish Air Force. Then he looked at the strangely bent wings. They dropped down from the main body and then rose up again. He looked at the long cockpit and when he peered inside he could see two seats through the dusty glass. The machine gun still rested in its mount at the rear of the cockpit, ready to be used by a long dead gunner.

"I don't get this," Ivan rumbled. "Unless there is something like it that I don't know about, this is a World War Two German Stuka dive bomber, but the markings are Spanish. How does that work?"

Jim came around the end of the wing from where he had been examining the propeller and engine, "Must be left over from the Condor Legion. During the Spanish Civil War, General Franco got help from the Germans and Italians. The Germans even sent squadrons of aircraft with pilots and support crews. This must be one of them."

Geordie's voice echoed through the darkness. They hadn't noticed he had wandered off. They looked to where the sound had come from and saw him standing, shining his flashlight on another Stuka, which was parked with its tail into the corner of the cavern. They walked around the first aircraft to go to look at the second and Ivan's flashlight beam passed across another shape covered in a large, dusty, green cloth sheet.

"That looks interesting." Jim swung his flashlight around to expose another aircraft, standing at the front of the cavern and covered in dust sheets.

They walked around it pulling the covers off and raising clouds of dust. This was a much larger aircraft with two engines and a large multi panel glass cockpit that looked like some kind of a greenhouse. This one also had the Spanish roundel on the fuselage and wings and the cross of Saint Andrew on the tail fin.

"I recognise this one. I had a plastic model of it hanging from the ceiling of my bedroom when I was a boy," Geordie said. "It's a Heinkel III; that's the bomber they used to pound London during the Blitz. I don't remember my model having so many guns though."

Jim shone his flashlight along the length of the plane. There was a machine gun right in the nose, another on the upper spine, one each side behind the cockpit and mounted below the fuselage was a shape that looked like a canoe, with a machine gun poking through at each end. Just behind the glass of the cockpit someone had painted the aircraft's name – *Pedro*.

"Well, that answers the question about that long straight track. It must be the runway for these beasts to take off from." Ivan said as he shone his light up at the front wall of the cavern. "And this looks like the way out."

The massive doors stretched across the cavern, supported by powerful hinges to allow them to swing inwards. At the point where the two doors met there were support wheels to help them to swing open without overloading the hinge mechanisms. Gouges in the concrete floor showed where they had been operated so long ago.

Carmen stood silently in the middle of the cavern, overcome by what she was seeing in a place she thought she knew. The three aircraft stood on deflated tires with equipment scattered around them. In a side cavern they found bombs sitting on trolleys ready to be pulled out and loaded. Boxes of double drum magazines for the machine guns were lined up along benches. Flags and banners hung from the walls and slogans were painted on the stone. She shook her head sadly and walked back to join the three men.

"Finished looking around, everyone?" Jim asked. "This is a fascinating find, but we have more important equipment to deal with first. Let's move on."

Chapter 63

They crawled back out of the small hole and back into the original cave. Turning right, they walked down the gentle incline with Jim in the lead this time. They walked for an appreciable distance before he paused and held up his hand.

"Can you hear that?"

They listened intently. "Water?" Ivan said.

"I think so. We must be getting closer to the sea cave Manuel told us about."

They walked on and, as they rounded a gentle bend, they saw the cave with the sea gently rocking in it. The light coming through from the outside caused dappling all around the roof of the cavern and let them switch off their headlights to conserve the batteries. They walked into the cave and stood on the dock that had been hacked out of the rock. At each end pillars of stone had been left standing to act as mooring posts and wooden beams had been secured along the dock edge, to prevent damage to any boat tied up there.

Geordie looked around. "All very nice boss, but no nukes in here,"

"I didn't expect them to be sat on the dockside. The corrosion from the salt water would have been a major problem, even if they were designed to be put in the sea. My guess is there must be some kind of storeroom nearby."

The four of them split up, with two going in each direction from the dock. Geordie and Carmen rounded the rock wall at the left end of the dock and found themselves facing a dull steel door, with four hatch handles dogging it closed. Carmen walked back to the edge of the dock and called Jim and Ivan back from where they were searching. Geordie had heaved two of the hatch handles open by the time they arrived and was struggling with the third. Ivan stepped forward and, with a heave of his broad shoulders and massive arms, he swung the handle to the open position.

The fourth handle proved to be a challenge even for Ivan and it took both of the two big men together to heave it open. They stepped back sweating as Jim took hold of the door and pulled it towards him. The weatherproof seal around the door edge resisted, but then gave up the struggle and allowed the door to swing. Jim shone his flashlight into the room that was revealed and found himself looking at four large sea mines, each mounted on a metal handling trolley and ready to be pulled out into the cavern.

Ivan stepped through the doorway and took hold of the handle of the first trolley. He pulled it towards him and with an effort the contraption began to move. He pulled it clear and took it out onto the dockside.

"That's going to be a damned long pull to the entrance way, boss."

Jim walked around the mine, touching it with his fingers. "More importantly," he said looking at Ivan, "it's never going to fit through the doorway we made in the concrete slab unless we get Craig back and open it up to the original size."

"Getting four of these bloody things out and then down the hill and away is going to be one hell of a job, boss," Geordie said. "Even then, how do we move them and where do we take them?"

Jim looked at the mine and the cave they had just come down to get here. Moving something up even that gentle slope would be heavy going. He looked back down at the water and at the entrance cave that led out to the sea.

"Seems to me, the only sensible way is to get the Royal Navy to bring one of their inshore subs around and get them to collect these in the way that was intended. Unless you two really want to tow these great lumps through that cave?"

Chapter 64

Jim left his three companions exploring the aircraft cavern as he walked on to get back to the entrance, where his satellite phone would be able to pick up a signal. He climbed out through the hole and stood in the doorway of the ruin waiting for the phone to find the satellites. He looked around the hillside as he waited, but could see nobody nearby.

The screen on his phone indicated that he now had a connection and so he dialled the number he needed in the Ministry of Defense. He lifted the phone to his ear and listened to the ringing tone from the other end. As he heard the voice from London answer the phone was snatched from his hand in a blast of noise. For a second he stared in amazement at the smashed phone on the floor by the rock wall behind him. As the second bullet struck the rock and sent splinters into his cheek and forehead he realised what was happening and dived back into the cave.

He paused for a moment or two to clear his head and then risked a peek out of the hole to try and identify where the gunman might be. A third round struck the concrete slab and ricocheted up into the stone wall at the back of the ruin. He rapidly withdrew into the cave and set off back to the aircraft cavern at a dead run. Skidding to a halt, he dropped to his knees and crawled in.

"Ivan! Geordie! To me quickly!"

The two men appeared rapidly out of the darkness. "What the hell did you do that on?" Ivan said as he looked at Jim's damaged face.

"I've just had the satellite phone shot out of my hand. This lot was done by stone splinters from a bloody near miss," Jim said, indicating the blood trickling down the right side of his face.

"So it looks like the guys in Norway were not the only ones," Geordie said. "But at least we've got some cover down here."

"Only for the time being. Without weapons we are trapped and eventually they are going to realise that and come in after us."

Ivan and Geordie grinned at each other and then looked at Jim. "Oh, I wouldn't think it's all that bad," Ivan said as he turned away. "You take the far one, Geordie."

Puzzled, Jim stood and watched his two men walk quickly away. Ivan climbed up onto the wing of the nearest Stuka and slid back the glass canopy then climbed inside. A minute later he emerged and climbed back onto the wing and back down to the ground. He walked across to Jim with a cheery smile on his face and a machine gun over his shoulder.

"We haven't been idle while you were making new friends, boss. We had a look round and found that these guns can be taken out of the aircraft by just pulling out two mounting pins. These two drum magazines are loaded and there are plenty more stored across the other side here."

Geordie walked around the tail of the Stuka carrying the gun from the second machine. Jim shook his head in disbelief. He might have known these two resourceful men would find a solution.

"First order of business," Ivan said. "Send them a message that coming down here is not a good plan. Do you know where they've set up their position?"

Jim shook his head. "Didn't see. I was too busy trying not to get shot. But the rounds came through the doorway of the ruin, so they must be somewhere down that side of the hill."

"That's fine. One long tracking burst of fire through the doorway and they should get the message." He turned to Geordie and fished a coin out of his pocket. "Heads or tails, mate?" he said, flipping it into the air.

"Tails," Geordie said.

Ivan caught the coin and looked at it. "Tails it is. Your choice: do you want to pop up and fire or would you rather be the backup in the cave?"

"Miss the chance of firing a machine gun at the bad guys? Never happen. I'll do the firing this time."

Ivan grinned. "How did I know that? OK, you lead the way and listen out as you go in case they've decided to come in here already."

Jim stopped the two men as they headed for the small entrance to the aircraft cavern. "Don't get cocky. I was lucky. Just get your burst off and then get into cover PDQ."

Geordie's grin dropped from his face. "Will do, boss. Look after Carmen for me, eh?"

"Of course. Where is she, by the way?"

"We gave her the job of finding out how the doors work to see if we could get the nukes out that way. She should still be over that side of the cavern."

Chapter 65

Geordie walked quietly through the narrow cave carrying the machine gun across his chest. Unusually for him he was silent; listening intently for any sound that might indicate the enemy was coming into the cave. He reached the bottom of the rubble slope and paused looking for any movement or any shadow that would tell him there was someone waiting above. He saw and heard nothing.

He turned and nodded to Ivan, then removed his yellow plastic caver's helmet and put it carefully down at the side of the pathway. He cocked the weapon, drew a deep breath and then lunged up the slope. He did not bother to aim, but just swung the weapon into position and fired while sweeping slowly from left to right. He was rewarded by a scream of pain from the orange grove in front of him, just before he dropped back into the hole.

Geordie sat down on the cave floor and removed the now empty double drum magazine. He fitted the full one that Ivan tossed to him and then grinned at the Welshman.

"Score one for the good guys. That should make them think twice about coming in here."

Ivan looked past his friend at the sunlight pouring through the entrance hole. "It should, but that still leaves us stuck down here and them up there. Plus, if they start throwing grenades in, we could be in trouble. Best we get back a way and set up a defense point beyond shrapnel range."

Geordie agreed and, picking up his helmet, he followed the big Sergeant Major back though the cave, towards the aircraft cavern entrance. Ivan stopped and looked back.

"This should do. We'll set up here where we can just see the entrance. You take first watch and I'll go and get some more ammunition. If you're bored, you could start making a sanger out of these loose rocks."

Geordie put down his weapon and started to pick up the rocks that lay around. He piled them in a semi-circle across the narrow cave to make an improvised gun position, similar to those that are often seen in the mountains of Afghanistan.

Ivan ducked back through the smaller hole and emerged in the aircraft cavern. He could see the two flashlights held by Jim and Carmen moving across the large Heinkel. He walked over to them to report progress. By the time he got there Jim had opened the crew hatch and was climbing inside.

"Looking for souvenirs, boss?"

Jim's head reappeared through the hatchway and he looked down at Ivan grinning up at him.

"Not really, Ivan. I've had a crazy idea and I want to see if I can make it work."

"Care to share?" Ivan asked.

Jim jumped down from the aircraft and looked at Ivan. "So how did it go?"

"Geordie hit one of them, but we don't know how badly and we don't know how many that leaves."

"So we're stuck in here. I thought that might be the case. So my crazy plan might be the way forward, but it's one hell of a long shot."

Ivan looked at Jim and then at the old aircraft standing silently behind him and shook his head. "You want to fly out of here, don't you? To quote the great John McEnroe, 'you cannot be serious'."

Jim glanced up at the large dark green aircraft they stood beside. "I'm open to any better suggestions, but until I hear one I'm staying with crazy."

Chapter 66

Ivan went back out into the cave carrying the extra magazines he had promised Geordie. He set them down behind the wall of the makeshift sanger and looked along the pathway to the entry hole. Anybody risking that way in had no chance as long as they had a person sitting here with the machine gun at the ready.

"Has the boss come up with one of his cunning plans yet?" Geordie asked.

Ivan sat down next to him and looked along the path. "Oh yes, and this one's a little belter. He wants to fly us out of here."

Geordie chuckled. "Nice one, but what's he really going to do?"

"Sorry, mate, but I'm not kidding. He's inspecting that bomber in there now, to see if he can get it going."

Geordie sat up straight. "You're serious? But that damned thing must be seventy years old. Lord only knows what happens to planes that sit around for that long. I mean, I know we got those submarines going which were that old, but an aircraft is something different. You can't swim away if that goes down."

"All true, but as he said to me, until someone comes up with a better plan he is going with crazy and you know him. If anybody can pull off crazy, it's him."

Geordie lay down again behind his wall of stones, then turned and looked at Ivan. "Mad as a box of frogs. I think one of us better go and help him if we are going flying. Just make sure he books us a nice stewardess with lots of cold beer for the inflight catering."

Ivan heaved himself to his feet. "I'll come and relieve you shortly."

Geordie grinned. "Thanks, but don't call me shorty."

Ivan kicked Geordie's boot as he went by. As long as his friend was still making his ridiculous jokes everything seemed normal. He walked back down the passage to have another look at the dock in the sea cave. He searched the whole cavern, but there was no other way out than the underwater cave and none of them was going to swim that far carrying a nuclear bomb. He walked back up to the aircraft cavern, checking the pathway as he did so. It would be tough, but he thought it would be possible to pull the mines up here on their trolleys.

He sighed and ducked down into the small entrance to the aircraft cavern. As he emerged he found Carmen walking past carrying something heavy. He reached forward and took it from her, she smiled with relief. When he shone his headlamp down at the object he held he found it was a large foot pump with twin cylinders to produce high pressures.

"What does he want this for, Carmen?"

"Is for pumping up the tires on the big airplane."

Ivan walked across the cavern to the Heinkel to find Jim standing on the wing with the engine cowlings open. He had tools laid out around him and was removing a component.

"It won't fly if you take it to pieces, boss."

Jim turned round and looked down at Ivan. "Ah, Carmen found the pump, good. Can you put some air in the tires so we can see just what state they are in?"

Ivan put the heavy pump down and looked up at Jim. "So what's the story on the engines?"

Jim sat down on the wing and wiped his hands on a rag. "They've got oil in them and they will turn over when I walk the propeller around, so we know they haven't seized up. The batteries are obviously completely dead after all this time, but aircraft of this era often had hand cranks to start them as a backup. This one is no exception. If you take off this electric starter motor here the hand crank can be fitted and the engine started."

"Are you seriously saying we can hand crank an engine of this size?"

Jim grinned. "Why else would I bring two strong soldiers with me?" He hesitated. "Look, I know you think this is insane, but I've considered all the options and this is all I can come up with. Now the sat phone is smashed, we are on our own in here with no food or water. Our time is severely limited and those clowns outside are taking this seriously."

Ivan stood and contemplated Jim for a long moment before he sighed. "All right then, I can't think of anything else either, so what do you want me to do?"

"Start by testing the tires and then make sure all the defensive machine guns on this beast are functional and loaded."

Chapter 67

Geordie heard the metallic thump from the entrance hole and saw the two hand grenades roll in to the cave. He was far enough back to be safe from shrapnel at that distance, but lowered his head behind the rocks anyway. The two explosions close together echoed off the stone walls and made his ears ring. As the dark smoke of the blasts cleared he could see a shadow moving around the entrance. He lifted the gun into place and rested it on the rock pile in front of him, then waited.

A head appeared as someone looked into the cave and quickly withdrew. Geordie waited quietly. The head appeared again and he heard voices, with one obviously giving orders. He watched as a man dropped through the hole with a sub-machine gun at the ready. Hidden way back in the darkness of the long thin cave, Geordie was out of sight as the man peered towards him.

The man cocked the weapon and raised it, then fired a long burst down the cave. Geordie had lowered his head as soon as he saw what was happening and the rounds passed safely over him. Having had a clear declaration of intent, Geordie rose up silently and fired his own weapon. The 7.92mm rounds were horribly effective and the intruder was thrown back with a scream onto the rock slope behind him.

Geordie watched as the man struggled out of the hole, whimpering and dragging his bloodied legs behind him. The MP5 sub-machine gun lay where it had been dropped, but Geordie felt no need to go and collect it. As he watched an arm swung into the hole from above and a grenade bounced and rolled along the tunnel towards him. It was a good throw and the bomb came a lot closer than the first two.

It exploded and the shrapnel flew in all directions. Down behind his improvised wall Geordie was safe, but he did hear hot metal fly over him and when he looked around there were small pieces of smoking shrapnel scattered nearby. He saw the shadow pass across the entrance hole again and fired a short burst towards it just to announce his continued presence.

There was a pause and Geordie could just hear the whispers from outside the cave as the attackers considered their next move. As he waited to see what surprises they had for him he felt movement behind him and smelled Carmen's perfume as she walked up next to him.

"Lie down here next to me, bonny lass, and turn off your head lamp."

"I do not think it is time for that, *cariño*."

Geordie grinned; he did like his women with spirit. "No, love, but you do need to take cover in case they throw something nasty in here again."

She snuggled in next to him and peeped over the rock pile. "What will happen now?"

"I wish I knew. No doubt we are going to find out. Hello, look at that!"

Ahead of them a stick had been pushed through the hole and was waving slowly side to side with a white rag tied to it. He heard a voice echo down the cave.

"English, we need to talk. You come near the hole and we speak, no?"

"No!" Geordie yelled back. "I know a trick worth two of that one. How about you come into the cave unarmed and talk from there?"

"You no shoot?"

"I won't shoot." Geordie turned to Carmen and spoke quietly. "Stay low. I don't want them to see you."

She put her head down on her arm with her lovely face turned towards him. He gazed at her for just a moment before he pulled himself together and aimed the gun down the cave. There was a short hesitation before a man dropped down through the hole waving his white flag nervously.

"You no shoot?"

"What do you want, mate?"

"I think is time you come out. All we want are big bombs. We take them, you go free, everybody happy, no?"

"I don't think so, but thank you for the offer."

"You not understand. We know there is not a way out except here." The man pointed to the entrance hole above him. "I have seven men sit here with guns. You cannot get out, is foolish you not make a deal with me."

"We're quite happy in here, thank you."

"This is foolish. We watch you come in here. You have no food, no water. You cannot get out. I give you last chance to live."

Geordie paused. The man was right, but he was pretty sure there would be no chance of living once they stepped out of the cave. He looked down at Carmen and contemplated what her fate might be. Not acceptable in any way.

"You've made your offer, friend, now bugger off before I get bored."

The man shrugged and turned away. As he left he grabbed the MP5 from the ground and exited the cave. Geordie heard movement from behind him again and turned to see Jim emerging from the hole in the cave wall.

"You heard all that, boss?"

"I did. Nicely done, by the way. The unfortunate thing is that he is right. We do have no way out unless my attack of insanity works."

Geordie grinned. "So how are we coming on with 'Wilson International Airways'?"

Jim sat down and leaned his back against the cave wall. "Strangely enough, not too bad. There are things wrong with the aircraft, for sure, but so far no show-stoppers. This might actually work if we can take that lot by surprise."

"Why surprise?"

"When we swing those doors open they will see the aircraft and we will be a damned big target for seven guns outside. Anyway, what did you think of that guy's accent? Where do you think he's from?"

"No idea, boss. I'm rubbish at accents. They're all Greek to me."

Jim chuckled at the old joke, but Carmen sat up with a frown across her face. "Why do you laugh? My Geordie is right: he is a Greek."

Jim looked at Geordie, who nodded slowly. "Well, that explains a lot, eh, boss?"

"Christophides. It seems he wants some more nuclear weapons to sell to other crooks. He must have been following us since we left his place in Cyprus. Keep watch, Geordie. He won't have given up yet."

Chapter 68

Jim went back to the Heinkel to find Ivan climbing out of the crew hatch. The big man was wiping his hands on his sleeves to remove the oil from his hands. He looked at Jim who could see that he was looking a little happier.

"The machine guns are fine, boss. I've also had a look round inside the plane and I don't know who these guys were, but they've left it in pretty good state. They obviously intended to come back one day."

"So you think it might work?"

"I wouldn't go that far yet, but it looks a little less crazy than it did an hour ago."

"Did you try pumping the tires up?"

"I did, and against the odds they are holding air, but the rubber is pretty perished so you better land this thing pretty gently."

"Land a seventy year old aircraft that I've never flown before gently? OK, got that. Now then, we have to decide what to do about the sea mines. Do we dump them off the dock and get the navy to come and get them later or do we jam the storehouse door somehow?"

Ivan grinned. "I think crazy must be infectious. I have an idea for that. This is a bomber, right? Well, I had a look in the bomb bay and there are hand-cranked winches in there for lifting the bombs into place. The fittings won't work with the mines, but we should be able to lash something up that will work for one flight."

"So now you want us to fly out of here, carrying four nuclear devices, in an aircraft we never used before and you call me crazy?"

Ivan smiled happily and nodded. "Mental, isn't it? But, as you say, we have no other options. If we leave without the nukes they could end up in the wrong hands and then all hell gets let loose on the world."

Jim slapped his Sergeant Major on the shoulder. "Now you're getting it. I'll do you a deal. I'll work on getting the aircraft fit to fly and you get the nukes loaded into the bomb bay."

"I'm going to need Geordie's help. It's not a one man job, dragging them up that slope and then loading them."

"Then Geordie is going to have to give his lady friend a crash course in gunnery."

"Ah, you've noticed that, have you?"

"What? The cow eyes and touching each other every chance they get? Yes, even I noticed the clues. He deserves a break after Sam left him like that and they make a handsome couple."

"I'll get on it. With a bit of luck the clowns outside will decide to starve us out."

Chapter 69

With Carmen sitting in the darkness behind the rock wall and watching the entrance, Geordie and Ivan walked down to the dock in the sea cave to start moving the sea mines. Together they pulled the first one to the foot of the slope up toward the cavern where the aircraft waited. They hauled it up the narrow pathway, struggling to find room to get a full strength pull on the heavy trolley with its deadly cargo. After struggling for around two hundred meters they stopped for a break. Geordie chocked the wheels as Ivan held the load in place.

"This isn't working too well, mate." Geordie panted. "Unless we can find a better way to pull this, we are going to be creamed before we've finished."

Ivan nodded as he tried to control his breathing. "You're damned right. I'll stay here with this to make sure it doesn't escape and you see what you can find in the aircraft stores."

Geordie heaved himself away from the wall he had been leaning on and walked up the long slope. He checked that Carmen was all right before he ducked through the low opening into the side cavern.

He searched around until he found what he was looking for, then set off back down the path to Ivan. Once there, he handed the Welshman a wide webbing safety belt that had been removed from one of the Stukas and put the other one on himself. Once they were lashed into the harness, Geordie tied a length of stout rope to his harness and the other end to the trolley. Ivan did the same, using a different length of rope, so that they could pull in tandem and not trip over each other's feet.

Both men leaned back and took the strain with their boots gripping the floor of the cave. "Ready?" Ivan asked. "Then three, two, one, pull!"

With both now able to exert their full strength, the trolley started to move more freely up the slope. Once they had it moving they didn't want to stop, so carried on pulling like a pair of pit ponies until the heavy load was level with the hole in the cave wall. Once there, Geordie leaned into his harness while Ivan chocked the wheels with stones again.

Once they were sure the trolley was not going to run back down the slope the two sweating men relaxed and drew breath. Ivan stood and appraised the size of their load and the height of the hole they had to get it through.

"Well, thank the Lord for that. It looks like it's going to just fit through there without having to smash more rock out of the way."

Geordie came across and looked at the hole. "We were due a bit of luck after that pull. Once we've got this bloody thing in there, I'm going to have another look round. Heaving another three of these up that path is going to ruin us."

Ivan nodded and wiped the sweat from his brow with the back of his hand. "I'll buy that. I'm getting too old for this stuff. Next time the boss goes on one of these jaunts I think I'll be busy elsewhere."

Geordie grinned and then went to pick up his harness again. Once Ivan was ready as well, they started heaving the trolley round and through the hole. Ivan had been right, it just slid under the overhanging rock and into the cavern beyond. Once inside on the level surface, it was a relatively easy pull to the side of the large two-tone green aircraft and underneath it to where the bomb bay doors were now hanging open.

Leaving the mine where it was, they went in search of anything that could help them move the next three heavy loads. Ivan found a large coil of rope at the back of a storage area and Geordie found a set of iron pulley wheels. It was the work of less than an hour to rig the pulley wheel with the rope and to run the loose end down to the dockside. They heaved the next mine out of the storeroom and pulled it to the start of the upward path. Once it was tied securely to the rope, they walked back up to the other end and started to heave on the rope end that came out of the pulley system they had created.

The rope slid through the cast iron wheels easily until the weight from the bottom started to be felt. Then it became a little harder, but once they had dropped into a steady rhythm the rope continued whizzing through the wheels and the load crept up the incline towards them. It was still hard, taxing labour, but far more effective than the direct pull had been, and within a fairly short time they had the second device standing next to the first.

"You know, Ivan, about now a really cold beer would go down extremely well."

"Never mind, I'll buy you one when we get to Gibraltar."

"How do you know we're going there? Has the boss said?"

"I haven't asked him, but where else could we go? We can't land on a Spanish airfield and that plane doesn't have the range to fly to the UK from here. The only British territory within range is Gibraltar and there's a military presence there as well, so we can hand these things over."

"Makes sense. Right then, cold beer in Gibraltar it is, but first we have to work up more of a thirst."

Chapter 70

Jim walked the propellers round to get the lubricating oil pumped to all parts of the engine before he attempted to start them. Having been left for so long, all the oil had naturally dropped into the engine sump. He had checked that the flight controls moved freely and were still properly connected to the flight control surfaces. He could do nothing about the instruments or the radio, with no battery power available. He would just have to trust that they would function once the engine driven generators kicked in.

The tires seemed to be holding pressure, but he was worried about the deterioration in the rubber of the sidewalls. It might last for a take-off run, but the impact of a landing could rupture them and cause a serious problem. There were no spares available and even if there had been, they would be the same age and subject to the same problems.

He found some clean cloth in a side bin against the wall of the hangar and wiped as much dust off the cockpit glass panels as he could. Water would have been much more effective, but there was none available, without a trek down to the sea cave. He checked the fuel tanks of the aircraft and found that they had been left full. He operated the water drains of the fuel tanks and was delighted to find that there was very little evidence of condensation.

Having checked everything he could think of, he walked around the aircraft looking for anything else that might have gone wrong over the years it had been sitting here. Then he climbed into the cockpit and started to familiarise himself with the controls. As he sat in the pilot's seat he realised just how much glass he had in front of him and how vulnerable that was going to be to enemy fire as he exited the hangar. There was nothing he could do about that.

Having done as much as he could, Jim climbed through the aircraft fuselage and out of the crew hatch to find Ivan and Geordie pulling the last of the nuclear sea mines alongside the bomb bay. They stopped and leaned on the heavy load they had just heaved up the slope, both men were drenched in sweat and panting from the exertion.

"Nice work, guys. I wish I had something cold for you before we try and load these things into the aircraft."

"Never mind, boss. Ivan has promised me a cold beer when we get to Gibraltar."

Jim looked at Ivan. "That was a good guess."

"Not much of a guess. Just like trying to fly this thing out of here, there aren't many alternatives, are there?"

Jim agreed. "Not many. I've checked the plane as far as I can. But everything hinges on being able to start the engines and get away before we get shot to pieces. If they don't start, we are royally screwed and out of ideas."

"What's that expression about eggs and baskets?" Geordie grinned. "At least if we make it, we are going to have one hell of a tale to tell, one of these days."

Jim patted his man on the shoulder. "When we make it. We need all the positive thinking we can muster. Are you two ready to start getting these things up into the bomb bay?"

Ivan sighed and pushed himself upright from where he had been leaning on the mine. "As ready as we're going to be. We might as well start now."

Jim climbed up inside the bay and freed the first of the bomb winches, letting the wire cable drop down until it just touched the heavy metal loop on the top of the first mine. Ivan released the clamps that had held the device to the transport trolley and Jim started to wind the handle. The gearing in the winch made it fairly easy to turn the handle, but also meant that a lot of turns were going to be needed for each load.

As the first mine reached the top of its travel, Geordie ducked into the bay and started to weave the heavy rope around the mine to secure it in place. It took some time, but once he was done Jim was surprised at how firmly the mine was located in the top of the bomb bay.

They hooked up the second mine and were about to begin the lift when there was an echoing explosion from the cave tunnel, followed by a burst of automatic fire. Geordie ran to the hole in the cavern wall, snatching up the spare MG15 machine gun as he passed the bench it was lying on. He skidded into the hole and crawled through, his heart in his mouth.

He need not have worried. Carmen had handled the attack exactly as he had trained her. She smiled over her shoulder at him as she calmly changed the drum magazine on her weapon. He dropped down beside her, hugely relieved.

"Are you all right, bonny lass?"

"*No problema, mi amor.* The gun is easy for me to use and the people outside, they stay there now, I think."

"What happened? Did you hit anyone?"

"They threw in one of their little bombs and after it went bang somebody tried to come in. I shoot and he goes back out as quick as he can. He was not hurt, but I think he was very scared."

Geordie leaned over and kissed her gently on the forehead. "You're wonderful and I wish I could stay with you, but we are in the middle of something right now. I'll be back as soon as I can."

With that, he climbed to his feet and walked back to the entry hole and through into the cavern. He put the machine gun down where he could reach it quickly again if needed, then walked back to where the loading was happening.

"All OK, Geordie?" Jim asked as he started to wind the winch handle.

"Fine, boss, just fine. The baddies decided to have another go and Carmen chased them off in fine style. I think they will think twice before they come in that way again."

Jim stopped winding and looked down at Ivan. "The problem is going to be when we fling those doors open and they see what we are trying to do. They'll have people down that tunnel like rats up a drainpipe and we'll be getting fire from two sides."

"Keep winding, boss. I'll solve that one for you," Ivan said.

Chapter 71

Before the escape plan was attempted Jim decided to have a council of war. The three men went out into the long cave tunnel and sat down with Carmen behind the rock sanger. Jim explained what he was trying to do.

"You know I want us to fly the mines out of here, but I think I ought to spell this out for you before we finally commit. We have a few advantages. First, the people outside do not know we have an aircraft in here, so when they hear the engines start they will be confused as to what is going on. Next, they do not know that the cliff face they see at the top of that wide straight track is actually made up of two camouflaged doors. They will probably not be watching them, so will be out of position. Thirdly, even when they do see the aircraft emerging they will not be expecting us to have teeth. Those machine guns should let us keep their heads down to some extent. That's the upside."

Geordie looked at Carmen and then at Jim. "I think we know the downside, boss, but you'd better spell that out for Carmen, too."

Jim looked at the girl waiting expectantly and nodded. "I was going to. Carmen, you need to understand this is one hell of a risk. We will emerge from the cavern slowly and while we are gathering speed they will be shooting at us. Bullets go straight through an aircraft skin; there is no armour. Plus there is no guarantee this thing will fly. We could end up running out of runway and crashing into the orange groves. We have no maps, so I will have to fly us along the coast until we see Gibraltar. I don't know if we have the fuel for that. Last of all, this is a very old aircraft, it could just fail and fall out of the sky."

Carmen sat up and looked at Jim very seriously. She took Geordie's hand and squeezed it gently before she spoke.

"I heard you say we have no other choices. So we have to go."

"Not quite true. We could go and you could stay in here and leave later."

She shook her head and gave Jim a small smile. "I think no. When those men come in here and find me, I think it will not be good for me. I will go with my Geordie."

Jim sighed. "I was hoping you'd say that. We need you to make my plan work. I could do with an extra couple of people, but we have to work with what we've got. I'm going to lay out a plan and if we all do our part we have a chance. Not a good one, but a chance. Now Carmen wants to go, but what about you two? Any objections?"

Ivan cleared his throat. "I've been thinking since you came up with this madness and I can't think of anything better. You're right, it's a long shot, but the alternative is being starved out of here and almost certainly getting shot as we emerge. I'm in."

Jim turned to the last in their party. "Geordie?"

"Boss, there might be a practical problem to solve, so you need me and anyway there's no way

I'm going to miss out on Ivan buying me a beer in Gibraltar, when we get there."

Jim stood and dusted himself down. "Right then, let's get ready. I'll walk through my choreography and then brief you, but in the interim, Ivan, you were going to solve the problem of people coming at us through that hole in the cavern wall."

Chapter 72

Ivan busied himself sorting out the way to block the entrance from the long cave while Geordie checked once again that the doors were going to open when needed. Were the doors to stick halfway they would be in a very vulnerable position. Jim went back to the Heinkel and carried out the pre-flight checks he had been taught when trying to qualify as an army pilot. Carmen stayed behind her mound of stones in the passageway to protect the men while they worked.

Eventually Jim could think of nothing else to check and called his men over. "Right, guys, the engine crank handle is in place up there on the starboard engine. Once I am in the pilot's seat I will work the controls to put them into the starting position. When I shout I need you to crank the engine round as fast as you can manage. It might take a while."

Ivan looked up at the crank handle protruding from the rear of the engine. "We can do that, right enough, but what about the other engine?"

Jim gave him a weak smile. "That's the first big risk. Once the first engine starts, the generator mounted on it should start to produce electrical current almost immediately. I'm counting on that to start the port engine."

Ivan looked at Geordie and then back to Jim. "So if we assume you are lucky and it starts, what will we be doing?"

"As soon as we have started the engines, I need Carmen to get in here pretty damn quick. I need her in the nose gunner position so she can give us some suppressing fire once the cavern doors are open. As soon as she is in the cavern, you put your blockage in place and then you two swing the front door open as fast as you can. You then run like hell round to the crew hatch and get in. One of you take the gunner's position in that thing that looks like a canoe under the fuselage and the other take the gun on the starboard side, since that is where the ruin is and I'm hoping they are concentrated over there."

"That all sounds very exciting, boss. Then what?"

"Then I push the throttles forward and we find out just how good German aircraft engineering was, back in the day. Any questions?"

"Just one, boss." Ivan grinned. "You are aware that we are all certifiable for even attempting this, right?"

"As I think you said before, 'mad as a box of frogs', but I've still not heard any alternatives. Geordie, can you go and tell Carmen what we need her to do, and make sure she knows she has to move like greased lightning once this all kicks off."

Chapter 73

Jim strapped himself into the pilot's seat and then nervously heaved the old webbing straps even tighter. If anything went wrong with the aircraft or their escape he had to stay in the seat to try and save the lives of his friends. He controlled the empty feeling in the pit of his stomach in the same way he had before going into combat. He looked out of the starboard window of the cockpit and saw that Ivan was waiting with the engine starting crank in his hand. Geordie stood on the wing behind him ready to take over when the Welshman tired.

He checked again that the switches and control levers were in the right position as far as he could tell and then gave Ivan the signal to start. The big man bent to his task and heaved on the crank handle, which started to turn, painfully slowly. Ivan kept up the pressure and the turning became faster bit by bit. Jim was waiting until he guessed that the engine was at a suitable speed before he made the attempt. He saw Ivan look up at him as he spun the crank and he could see the sweat already starting to run down the big man's face.

Judging the time was right, Jim flipped the switches in front of him and watched the engine dials intently. The engine shuddered and the airframe shook slightly. But there was no sound of the ignition system kicking in. Jim swung his head to the right in time to see Geordie grab the crank and start to turn before the momentum was lost.

Jim flipped the switches back to their original positions and waited for the speed to build up again before trying again.

This time he waited until the engine was turning faster. He could see the needle in the dial in front of him that measured engine revolutions was now starting to flicker. He threw the switches again and the immediate resistance told him there was pressure in the cylinders, but still the engines showed no sign of starting as Ivan stepped forward to resume his place at the crank. Even from inside the aircraft Jim could hear the grunt of effort as the crank was wound again and the engine revolutions increased.

Jim knew this could not go on. His two men were strong and fit, but continuous effort at this level would wear them out rapidly. The rev counter now showed a recognisable reading as he threw the ignition switches once again. The engine coughed once and Jim saw Ivan redouble his efforts. It coughed again and then again. Ivan was now red in the face and pouring sweat as he slammed the crank handle around and around. Jim could see his mouth moving and smiled as he remembered the Welshman's theory that judicious use of the proper swear words will always increase efforts.

The engine coughed, then again and again, and then with a roar it started. It was running rough for certain and pushing out a vast cloud of thick white smoke as the preservative oil was burnt out of the cylinders, but it was running. As the revolutions built up the roughness faded as all the cylinders began to fire. The smoke filled the cavern, stirred about by the spinning propeller. Jim could just see Ivan pulling the crank handle clear of the engine and fastening the engine covers back in place. He looked down at the instrument panel. Dials were flickering into life across the board, showing him that the electrical power he needed was flowing through the old aircraft.

Whispering a prayer to whatever saints protected madmen and fools, he pressed the button to start the port engine. The electrical starter motor whined loudly and the engine began to turn. He watched the propeller spin up and then threw the ignition switches. The propeller slowed, but the starter motor kept turning and after two or three more seconds the first cylinder coughed as it fired. Then another and another. The engine roared into life and gushed even more oil smoke into the cavern.

Out of sight in the artificial fog, Ivan ran to the cavern entrance hole and called Carmen to him. She fired a burst at the end of the cave and then abandoned the machine gun she had been holding and ran, as she had been instructed. She ducked through the hole and ran to the throbbing aircraft, coughing in the thick smoke. Ivan untied the rope that had been holding the four heavy mine support trolleys and let them fall across the entrance. The first one blocked it and then each subsequent one fell forward to hold it in place.

Jim leaned to one side in his seat as Carmen climbed past him into the glass nose of the Heinkel. She took her position, flat on her stomach, behind the machine gun and cocked the weapon. In front of the aircraft Jim could no longer see the doors through the cloud of swirling smoke. Then the smoke became lighter as the sunlight flooded in from outside when the doors were swung back. He felt the aircraft rock as his two men clambered inside and then Ivan was at his shoulder.

"Go, boss! We're in!"

Ivan retreated back into the fuselage to take up his position at the starboard waist gun. He saw Geordie snuggling down onto his belly in the gunner's position slung beneath the aircraft, in the canoe shaped turret. In the cockpit Jim pushed the throttles forward slowly, careful not to stall the old engines. With the cavern doors open, the smoke was thinning rapidly as the propellers swirled it around and out into the open air. Jim could now see the artificial stone mounted on the outer side of the doors. Even knowing it was false, it still looked convincing.

With the throttles now on their forward stops Jim released the brakes and the aircraft jerked and started to move. It accelerated rapidly and the bright sunlight flooded the cockpit as they cleared the front of the cavern. In front and to the right of them, Jim could see startled men jumping up out of cover and staring at this apparition from the past emerging from a mountain. He saw them recover their wits and the weapons all around them came up into the aim.

The machine gun in the nose began its harsh chatter as Carmen fired a burst over the men's heads. A second later Jim heard the gun beneath him join in and a stream of tracer rounds flew across the hillside from Geordie's weapon. As they moved forward, still accelerating, Ivan opened fire from the right hand side as well. The men outside dived for whatever cover they could find, but they had not panicked as much as Jim had hoped and they started to return fire.

The glass panel to Jim's right crazed and shattered as it was hit. He could hear and feel the rounds hitting the fuselage and punching through the thin metal. There was nothing he could do but hold the throttles forward and try to get out of range. More rounds punched through into the cockpit, but he did not allow them to distract him.

Below him, Geordie had spun round and was now using the machine gun at the rear of the canoe shaped turret. With the dust being kicked up behind them from the aircraft's progress down the track, he couldn't see their assailants, so just fired in the general direction of their positions.

Jim kept the aircraft in the centre of the track and waited as long as he dared for the forward speed to build up. With the end of the track now approaching rapidly, he eased back on the control column. The ancient aircraft bounced once and then lifted into the air. She climbed slowly and Jim eased her around to the left to fly along the valley in front of them while still climbing. He operated the control and heard the undercarriage slam into the bays beneath the wings. With the wind resistance now reduced, despite the remarkable heaviness of the controls, he could feel the aircraft becoming more responsive, more alive under his hand. They were clear. It had worked.

Chapter 74

Jim looked quickly around him. The massive orange cliffs of the Montgo were to his left and a perfect saddle shaped mountain to his right as he headed the aircraft to the south. As he cleared the Montgo he could see the town of Javea opening up below him and he took his aircraft across the town and across the wide bay to pick up the coast. Once across the bay, he took the aircraft round to the right in a gentle turn and settled it down to follow the cliffs and beaches all the way to Gibraltar at the southern end of Spain.

Ivan reappeared at his shoulder and looked around the cockpit. The broken and missing panes of glass were letting the wind scream in and he had to shout to be heard.

"Bloody marvellous! You did it! I thought we were going to end up in a blazing wreck for sure."

Jim nodded and yelled back. "We're not home yet. These controls are way too heavy. There's something wrong. I'm not sure I can hold her in the air all the way to Gibraltar."

Ivan looked at Jim. The effort was obvious in his face and he was beginning to sweat as he hauled backwards to keep the aircraft from diving towards the hungry sea below.

"How can I help?"

"First get Geordie on that radio. See if he can raise the airfield at Gibraltar and tell them we are coming. Then you get in front of me and put some back pressure on the control column while I work out what the hell is wrong."

Ivan nodded and went back into the fuselage to speak to Geordie. He was back in moments and climbed past Jim to sit with his back to the nose of the aircraft, and with his foot pushing back on the control column. With the pressure on his arms eased, Jim started looking around to see what he had missed in his pre-flight checks.

Geordie sat himself down on the small stool that swung out from below the radio operator's plotting table. He stared at the ancient contraption as he trawled in the dusty corners of his mind for the German words he had learned when serving in that country, years before. His fingers wandered across the switches and dials as he mouthed the words engraved into the front panel of the radio. He found a switch that looked promising and flicked it up. There was a pause until the dull orange lights behind the dials started to glow.

He picked up the dusty headset and put it on. As soon as the radio was warmed up he was deafened by the high pitched electronic screech in his ears. He ripped the headset off and threw it to the table in disgust. Standing up, he made his way forward to report to Jim.

"Sorry, boss. All I'm getting is the same screeching I got from that damned radio in Norway. It's not useable."

"What the hell is it with you and radios?" Jim said. "Look, get forward and take over from Ivan. Maybe he'll have more luck."

The two soldiers changed places and Ivan climbed past Jim and back into the crew area. He picked up the headset and put it on. There was no screeching, just the hiss and crackle of static. He turned the tuning dial slowly, listening intently for any intelligible sounds. As he did so he looked idly out of the small window to his left that seemed to be there just to give light to the operator's table.

A shadow on a cloud caught his eye and he looked up, craning his neck to see further upwards. Heading right for them was a civilian airliner. A second or two of staring at it open mouthed was enough to confirm it was on an intercept course and that the crew had not seen the bomber below them. Ivan leapt out of his seat, smashed his head against the low ceiling of the fuselage and blundered forward to Jim. He slapped him on the shoulder and pointed up and left.

"Take her down! Take her down now!"

Jim looked up to where Ivan was pointing and saw with horrible clarity that a mid-air collision was imminent. He forced the control column forward and sent the aircraft into a dive. As the airspeed increased the engine note changed to a higher and higher pitch. The sea rushed towards them as Jim fought to bring the old machine back out of its death dive. After what seemed an age the nose lifted and Jim was able to relax just a little as he brought the plane back to a gentle climb away from the sea.

He looked to his right to see the airliner continuing its landing approach to an airport set just back from the coast. That must be Alicante, where they had flown into just a few days before. That had been way too close for comfort.

Jim looked up at Ivan. "Thanks! Keep looking out as much as you can. Geordie! I need you to keep a lookout as well and go forward and tell Carmen to do the same. We can't risk that again."

Once Geordie was sure Jim had a firm grip on the controls, he moved his foot and turned over to crawl forward. He crawled alongside Carmen in the cramped nose cone and patted her on the shoulder to get her attention. She did not respond. He put a hand on her shoulder and shook it, thinking she must be asleep. There was no response. He took hold of her arm and shoulder and rolled her to the right. Her head lolled down. Her eyes were open, but the light had gone out of them. Her beautiful face was pale and stiff. With his heart in his mouth Geordie looked along her body to the patch of blood covering her chest. There were two jagged entry wounds, where bullets that had smashed through the airframe had distorted and tumbled as they flew, before smashing into her and ripping her heart apart.

Geordie's world started to tear and crumble around him. "Oh sweet Jesus, no. Not you. Oh dear Lord, no."

He looked up at Jim with stricken eyes and the tears rolled down the dark skin of his cheeks. He saw Jim's face crumple as he, too, realised what had happened. Geordie gently closed those lovely eyes and rolled her back into her position behind the gun. There was nothing more he could do for her now; that would have to wait until they landed.

Ivan came back into the cockpit to report some success with the radio. As he ducked in he took in the frozen tableau in front of him. It took a second before he realised what it all meant. He lowered his head and said a short prayer for the young woman who had risked so much with them. Then he turned to shout to Jim.

"The radio is working! I haven't got Gibraltar yet, but the Air Traffic Control at Alicante is yelling blue murder. They demand that we identify ourselves and they say we must land at Murcia or we will be shot down."

Chapter 75

Jim looked down at the instruments in front of him. The air speed indicator was working, but the altimeter had failed completely. The engine dials showed the oil pressure and the RPM were in the green, while the compass slowly revolved with no apparent intention of showing any particular direction. As long as the weather stayed clear they could follow the coast and eventually find the Rock of Gibraltar. He had no idea where Murcia was and no way to find the airport, even if he was minded to land there.

He turned to Ivan and yelled, "Ignore them! We can't do what they want anyway! Keep trying to pick up Gibraltar airfield!"

Ivan nodded and pulled back out of the cockpit. Jim returned to trying to work out what was causing the aircraft to try and fly down into the sea. He looked at Geordie who still knelt by Carmen up in the nose of the aircraft.

"Geordie! I need you. Get back here and help with this control column."

Geordie nodded sadly. He looked down at the lifeless form that had once been Carmen. With a tear still on his cheek, he climbed back into the position where he could exert backward pressure on the control column to relieve the strain on Jim. While Jim wanted to try and comfort his friend, yelling over the sound of the wind through the broken windows was not the way to do it.

He searched his memory for the things he had been taught during his flying course before he had been failed and sent back to his normal unit. The training aircraft had been much simpler and a lot more modern. He looked down to his side at the ancillary controls he had been ignoring up to now. As he looked he realised he was staring down at the trim wheels that adjusted the flight control surfaces. He started to spin the first one back. At first there was no effect, but then he could feel that the forward pressure on the controls was easing. He kept on turning until he felt able to let Geordie stop pushing back.

Jim waved Geordie to move back alongside him. "Geordie, get Ivan to help you and move Carmen back into the crew compartment back there. The landing could be rough, so find a way to keep her from being thrown around."

Geordie nodded dumbly and went rearwards to find Ivan. As he reached the radio operator's position the old radio screeched through the headset again and Ivan snatched it from his head. He and Geordie went forward and, as gently as they could, lifted Carmen out of the gunner's position and into the rear area of the aircraft. They wrapped her in Geordie's jacket and strapped her into one of the crew seats. Then Geordie returned to the cockpit and looked enquiringly at Jim.

Jim pointed forward. "Take the gunner's position and keep a lookout for other aircraft. The last thing we need is a run-in with another airliner full of tourists."

Geordie nodded, but said nothing as he climbed forward to where Carmen had died. He paused as he touched the bloodstain where she had been, then lay down and started to watch all around. Jim watched his man from the pilot's seat; there was nothing he could do to comfort him.

The flight continued, with Jim watching the instruments nervously while trying to scan the sky ahead and follow the coast. He estimated he was somewhere around three thousand feet up and maybe half a mile out to sea. His main worry was that he had no idea how far it was to Gibraltar and how far this old aircraft could fly on the fuel he had on board. Once he got there, he knew he would have other problems, but for now he was trying to decide where to put the aircraft down if he ran out of fuel. None of the options were appealing.

Geordie looked around him as he lay on his stomach in the forward position. Below him he could see the azure blue of the Mediterranean stretching away to his left. To his right the coast look brown and dusty with patches of white walled houses tumbling down the hillsides like spilled sugar cubes. He looked up and around, but saw no other aircraft near them, so turned his attention back to the occasional ship that plowed up the coast, leaving a pure white wake behind it.

Away to his right a city came slowly into view, set back a little way from the seashore. He could just make out the spires of a large church or cathedral when the glint of sunlight above the city caught his attention. He strained his eyes to see what had caused it, but saw nothing initially. Then there was another flash and he saw the two specks climbing into the sky. As he watched, the specks became two aircraft heading towards them on an intercept course.

He rolled over and yelled to Jim, pointing in the direction of the newcomers. Jim looked that way until he, too, saw them and nodded to Geordie before yelling back to Ivan that they had company.

Chapter 76

The two small, two seat jet aircraft took up position off the port wing of the Heinkel. Jim looked across at the dull silver airframes with the bright orange flashes that marked them out as training aircraft. He saw the person in the back seat of the nearest aircraft taking photographs, while the pilot pointed in the direction he wanted the old bomber to turn. The first of the jets moved in front of them and started a gentle turn to the right to lead them to the airfield at Murcia. Jim ignored it and stayed on the course he had set.

He looked left to see that the second trainer had closed in on his wing tip and was pointing at the lead aircraft to indicate Jim should turn and follow him. Jim gave him a jolly wave and then turned his head forward and stayed on course. The first aircraft returned and took up position off the starboard wingtip. Jim looked from side to side watching their activities and saw that the port aircraft was easing closer, while the starboard one moved gently away. He decided to ignore the shepherding they were attempting and maintained his course along the coast.

The lack of a radio on the correct frequency made life more difficult for the Spanish Air Force pilots, though it relieved Jim of the need to tell them he was not going to follow them. They tried to encourage him to turn a few more times and then they both climbed up above him and turned away. Ivan came forward and looked around

"Looks like they have given up!" he yelled.

Jim shrugged noncommittally. It seemed unlikely they were going to be allowed to carry on through Spanish airspace without further interference. He was right. The first aircraft appeared over Jim's head from behind in a shallow dive. Once in front of the Heinkel it pulled up and turned right yet again. The buffeting from the jet blast shook the old airframe, but caused no other problems. Seconds later the second aircraft executed the same risky manoeuvre and again the airframe shuddered. Both aircraft climbed and disappeared, then they did it all over again.

This time they reappeared off Jim's port wingtip as they had the first time. The pilot of the lead aircraft was clearly exasperated by Jim ignoring him and his hand gestures were much more aggressive and forceful. Jim waved to him gaily and gave him his best beaming smile before carrying on down his chosen course. The two jets tried a number of times to force the Heinkel to turn, but Jim was having none of it and let them fly around him without taking any action.

Eventually the two jets turned away and headed back towards the coast, in the direction they had approached from. Geordie scanned the sky and turned over to look back at Jim and Ivan. He shrugged his shoulders and raised his hands palm upwards. Geordie might not know what was happening, but Jim was pretty sure they had not seen the last of the Spanish Air Force.

It was another half an hour before Geordie spotted the two dark specks against the cloud behind them. These two were approaching fast, really fast. They came alongside the wing as the first two had done and Jim could see that he was now being looked at from the cockpits of two Eurofighter aircraft rather than unarmed trainers. The big fighters were having trouble slowing down to keep pace with the old lumbering bomber. Jim could see the pilots struggling to keep the fighters from stalling.

The pilot of the closest aircraft gave the now familiar signal that Jim was to turn towards the coast and once again Jim gave him a jolly wave and a big smile. Jim could see the big helmet moving side to side as the pilot shook his head. He accelerated away in front of the Heinkel followed by his wingman. The three men in the bomber watched them fly way out in front of them and then turn back to approach them nose to nose. The two large fighters got bigger and bigger as they approached. Just before impact the pair split and one went each side. The buffeting from their combined jet blast jarred the old aircraft and Jim scanned the instruments quickly in case they had done damage.

"What do you reckon the next stage is, boss?" Ivan yelled.

Jim looked round at Ivan standing alongside him. "Depends if they want to use missiles or their cannon."

Ivan looked at him quickly. "Would they really do that? That wasn't in the escape plan at all."

Chapter 77

Geordie lay on his back and watched the two Eurofighters circling above them. He guessed they were getting instructions from base as to what they were allowed to do next. He looked back at Jim and was amazed at how calm he looked as he flew the old aircraft along at its leisurely pace. He got Jim's attention and then patted the machine gun and raised an eyebrow at his team leader. Jim shook his head and mouthed the word "NO."

The sun glinted off one of the aircraft canopies above them as the lead fighter rolled into a shallow dive towards them. The second aircraft seemed to pause for a short while and then he too rolled into the same shallow dive. Geordie sensed their intention and yelled to Jim.

"They're attacking!"

Jim nodded and yelled back. "Keep pointing at them and tell me when they fire!"

Ivan came back into the cockpit. "I can hear Gibraltar airfield on the radio."

Jim nodded and jerked his thumb over his shoulder. Ivan spun round and looked up to where he had seen Geordie pointing. The fighter diving towards them looked as though he meant business. The Welshman stared in fascination as the aircraft got rapidly bigger. Behind him in the nose of the aircraft Geordie kept his finger pointing at the attacker and, as soon as he saw the first flicker from the barrel of the cannon, he yelled hard at Jim.

Jim stamped on the control pedal and the aircraft skidded across the sky. He watched as the burst of tracer cannon shells flew past him and down into the sea. The fighter itself followed, causing more violent turbulence. Geordie was now intent on watching the second aircraft as it made its run. He yelled his warning again and this time Jim spun the control wheel to the right and rammed the column forward, into a turning dive.

The turn this time had not been as successful and two of the rounds from the burst smashed into the rear fuselage, causing it to shudder. Ivan moved quickly rearwards to check on the damage while Jim levelled the aircraft out again and returned to his original course. The first fighter appeared at his left wing again and again the pilot indicated the bomber should turn inland. Jim did not wave this time. He stared ahead considering his options.

Then he smiled at Geordie and pointed ahead. Geordie rolled over and looked forward. There, emerging from the sea haze, was the massive bulk of the Rock of Gibraltar. Jim looked at the fighter pilot to his left and raised a thumb in his direction to indicate compliance. He remembered that the old sign for an aerial surrender had been to lower the undercarriage so he operated the appropriate switches. He heard the wheel bay doors open below him and the landing gear legs start to move. Then he felt the judder and everything stopped.

Geordie rolled across and peered under the wing to the right and then to the left. He moved back to Jim and yelled over the wind noise. "Two small problems. The undercarriage has stopped about half way down and, at least on the starboard side, the tire has been shredded."

Jim turned to face the pilot in the aircraft off his port wing and shrugged. He gave a fine impersonation of helplessness while attempting to lower the wheels. The increased drag had slowed the bomber and the fighter could no longer stay alongside him, so flew off to one side and started to circle back. He had apparently not noticed that Jim had not changed course.

Chapter 78

Jim leaned around in his seat and shouted for Ivan who appeared from the rear crew compartment. "Have you got through to the airfield at Gibraltar?"

"No, not a chance. I can hear them, but I've been trying to transmit for the last few minutes and they aren't hearing me."

Jim pointed ahead. "Well, the airfield is somewhere next to that bloody great lump of rock. I can't see any aircraft in the circuit, but can you listen and see if they are talking anybody down. I don't want to ruin this at the last minute."

Ivan nodded without speaking and moved back to the radio position. Jim turned and checked where the Spanish fighters were and saw one coming into a slow gentle turn to take a pass by his wing. He considered his limited options again, then shouted to Geordie.

"Geordie! Get back here." He paused while the big man climbed back to him. "I need you to find the manual winch mechanism for getting those wheels back up. I'm probably going to be flinging the aircraft about a bit so hang on."

Geordie nodded grimly and went to move back in search of the wheel raising device when Jim stopped him. "And keep an eye on where we are. When we get close to the airfield you and Ivan need to make sure you are strapped in to one of the crew seats. It's going to be rough."

With Geordie gone into the rear with Ivan, Jim was alone in the cockpit. He turned and checked where the two fighters were now. The reduced speed was causing them some difficulty in staying with him, which suited his plans beautifully. He waited until both aircraft were facing away from him in one of their wide circles and pushed the control column forward to take the Heinkel into a dive. His unexpected manoeuvre had the desired effect and the two fighters had some difficulty reacquiring him as they came around to where they anticipated him to be. By the time they spotted him he was low down and skimming across the surface of the Mediterranean at no more than a hundred feet.

It took them a little while to line up to overtake him from the rear without the jet blast forcing the old aircraft into the sea. Jim meanwhile was using the rudder pedals to cause his aircraft to skid sideways backwards and forwards across his chosen path. The strange manoeuvre caused the problem to be more difficult for the two advanced fighters and they circled to consider and debate the best way to address the issue.

By the time they had decided on their joint course of action Jim could see the main runway in the British Overseas Territory of Gibraltar. Thankfully there were no aircraft on approach or taxiing on the ground. He would ideally like to have made a pass over the airfield and then swung around to make his landing. That would have warned Air Traffic Control and the Emergency Services that he was coming. With two Spanish fighter aircraft coming for him, that was not going to be possible.

A sweating Geordie appeared back in the cockpit. "OK, boss, they are up as far as they are going, but the wheel bay doors are still open." He looked up and saw the runway approaching rapidly. "Bloody hell!" he said as he dived back to get himself into the relative safety of a crew seat.

The Heinkel crossed the runway threshold at about fifty feet up. Jim throttled back as far as he dared and continued to let the aircraft sink down towards the tarmac that was flashing by. Judging his time to perfection, he wrenched the throttle way back and switched off the fuel pumps just as the two propellers gouged into the concrete and distorted violently. The metal screamed as it churned the solid ground and the wheel bay doors were wrenched off and spun to either side.

The main fuselage touched down and Jim removed his hands from the control column. There was nothing he could do from now on. For long seconds, the tortured aircraft screamed along the runway until a wing dropped and smashed into the ground at the side of the concrete strip. The whole aircraft was flung into a rapid and violent spin until the wing was ripped off by the force of the impact. The fuselage continued to slide sideways and then came to a shuddering stop, tilted over at about thirty degrees.

Jim let out the breath he had been holding in a long heartfelt sigh and then started to unlock his harness. He could hear Ivan calling to Geordie behind him and was mightily relieved when he heard the second voice answer. As he started to lever himself painfully out of his seat he could see the bright red fire engines roaring across the field towards him, followed closely by RAF Police vehicles. This was going to take some explaining.

Chapter 79

Ivan sprung the crew hatch open and one by one they emerged onto the concrete runway. The first fire truck had gone by them and was dealing with the detached wing that had caught fire as the integral fuel tank ruptured and sprayed aviation gasoline across the hot engine. The second truck pulled up alongside them and Jim could see the fire officer standing through the cupola and aiming a large silver foam cannon at them.

A Royal Air Force blue Land Rover with the distinctive yellow stripe of the RAF Police skidded to a halt and a very irate young officer flung open the door and stomped towards them. "Who's the pilot of this aircraft? And what the hell is it anyway?"

Jim turned wearily to face the red faced young man. It had been a long day. "I'm the pilot and it's a Heinkel He111. Now I need you to .."

"Frankly I don't care what you need. What do you mean by crashing that thing here and why were those Spanish Air Force aircraft chasing you?"

Jim sighed. "All in good time, but first ..."

"Answer my questions!"

Jim paused and looked the young officer in the eye. "First, you say 'sir' when you speak to a superior officer and you don't interrupt him. Next, I need you to secure this aircraft and get some armourers over here now to unload four nuclear weapons that you will find in the bomb bay."

The flustered young man was not quite ready to give up yet. "How do I know you are an officer and what do you mean, nuclear weapons?"

Jim reached into his pocket and retrieved his military ID card, then handed it to the officer. "Major James Wilson, Royal Engineers on a classified task for the Prime Minister which involves nuclear weapons. Now stop being a pain in the backside and do as I say. Plus, I need an ambulance here as well. We have a casualty."

The young man looked up from the ID card in his hand and swallowed. He drew himself up and saluted, then turned away and started issuing instructions to the three RAF policemen who stood behind him. Once they had scurried away to start making the required arrangements, he turned back to Jim.

"And the casualty, sir. What are the nature of his injuries?"

"Unfortunately, she is dead. She has two bullet wounds that appear to have pierced the heart. The complication is that she is a Spanish civilian, so she needs to be handled very carefully."

As he spoke the ambulance arrived and two orderlies jumped down from the cab. "I hear you have a casualty for us, sir?" the blonde driver asked.

Jim pointed to the open crew hatch in the fuselage side. "Yes, in there. She's dead, I'm afraid, but treat her gently."

Jim and his two men stood back while the two medics, assisted by some of the fire crew, went into the aircraft and brought Carmen's body out. They placed her on a stretcher and carried her around to the back of the ambulance. Once the doors were closed the medic came back to Jim and the others.

"So what do you want to do with the stiff then, gents?"

Geordie's arm came back and was just about to smash a fist into the medic's face when Ivan grabbed it and pulled him away. "No, no, that's not the way to do it. Let me show you the correct procedure."

With that Ivan walked to the startled medic and took him by the shoulder. He then sank a fist into the man's stomach, causing him to double over in pain and then vomit onto the runaway. Ivan grabbed him by the shoulder again and wrenched him vertical before pushing him hard against the side of the ambulance.

"That lady you have in your care is Carmen Sanchez Domingo and she has just died serving our country. You will treat her with the utmost respect and you will remember her name until your dying day. So now, tell me her name."

The man drew a shuddering breath. "Carmen Sanchez Domingo."

"That's Carmen Sanchez Domingo, Sergeant Major, to you. Now say it again."

"Carmen Sanchez Domingo, Sergeant Major."

"Good. Now get in your vehicle and get her away from here. And a word of advice for you.

You see that black guy standing there? If you see him coming towards you, run."

The RAF officer turned to Jim with his mouth hanging open. "I can't believe your man assaulted a medic right in front of me. I'm going to have to arrest him."

"You will do no such thing, Flight Lieutenant. That never happened, do you understand? Never happened. And if your medic whines, just tell him he's lucky. Geordie would probably have done him quite a lot of damage."

The young Flight Lieutenant looked at the determined Major standing before him and realised it was time to keep quiet and do what he was told. He raised the hand held radio and spoke into it, demanding that the armourers get out to the crash site urgently. As he was speaking Geordie walked over to speak to Jim and the radio in the young officer's hand gave out the now familiar electronic screech.

Jim looked thoughtfully at Geordie. "Walk away for a few yards, will you?" As Geordie did so Jim took the radio from the RAF officer's hand and pressed the transmit button. "Now walk back to me." As Geordie obeyed, the screeching started again. "It's you. Are you carrying something electronic?"

"Not me, boss. Just money in a wallet and a pocket knife."

Jim looked at the tall Staff Sergeant and noticed the gleam of gold at his neck. He reached forward and pulled the heavy gold pendant he had been given for luck in Cyprus out of his shirt.

"Take that off for a minute and give it to the Flight Lieutenant here." Geordie handed the pendant over. "Now you walk away while I run this radio over Geordie."

The RAF police officer walked away holding the pendant and Jim held the radio near Geordie and pressed the transmit button again. There was no sound but the gentle hiss of static. He turned and waved the young officer back towards him. As he approached the screeching began again.

"Well, what the hell is causing that?" Geordie asked.

Jim took the pendant and looked at it carefully. "I have a theory about that." He turned to the Flight Lieutenant. "I need your driver to take me to your base electronics workshop. These two will stay here and help with unloading the nuclear devices when your armourers finally arrive."

The weapons had been removed from the crashed aircraft by the time Jim returned and a mobile crane was just moving into place to lift the wreckage off the runway and onto the back of a large gray flatbed recovery truck. Jim waited until the weapons were loaded and on their way to safe storage before he called his men to one side.

"You remember how we couldn't work out how they kept coming straight to us in Norway without needing to follow our tracks? Well, here's the answer," he said, holding up the glittering pendant. "This little gem that Christophides' daughter gave you is a transmitter. It has a GPS device inside it and the neck chain is the antenna. Clever, eh?"

Geordie growled slightly under his breath. "So I've been bringing the thugs that Christophides sent straight to us all this time? Let me have it back please, boss, I'll smash it right here."

"Not so fast," Jim said, swinging the pendant away from Geordie. "Keep wearing it for a while. We may be able to use it to our advantage at some point."

Chapter 80

Ivan stood quietly behind Geordie watching him move carefully forward and take a position behind a small bush from where he could see the large white villa. He smiled slightly as he walked silently forward and dropped to the ground next to him.

Geordie rolled left and stared at the apparition that had appeared next to him. "How the hell did you get here? How did you know where I would be?"

Ivan grinned. "And good morning to you, too. How's the plan working out?"

"What plan? And, come on, how did you find me?"

Ivan raised his head slightly and looked at the villa then turned to Geordie. "Not too difficult really. I saw your face when we found out about the pendant. I could see you were planning something. Then you spent so much time on the computer in Gibraltar I knew you were up to no good. So I went and checked your browsing history when you went off to get a shower."

"Does the boss know you are here?"

"No, mate. He thinks I'm on my way to a parish in Wiltshire to check in and he thinks you are staying in Denia for Carmen's funeral. How did Manuel take it when you took Carmen home to him?"

Geordie sighed. "Not well. That girl was his pride and joy. He just sort of crumpled when he saw her. The rest of the family came round and they were pretty devastated, too. They bought the story about the car accident, though. I told Manuel the truth and somehow that helped him a bit, that she died for a reason. I told him that I loved her and he told me that she had confessed to him that she had feelings for me."

"Pretty rough, then?"

"Yeah, pretty rough, but now I pay the bastard back."

Ivan looked down at the distinctive wooden stocked Dragunov sniper rifle that lay in front of his friend. "I take it that Mike Donald got that for you?"

"Yeah, he's a good guy. Even took me out to the ranges at Dhekelia to zero it in. It's ready now and so am I."

Ivan picked up the powerful binoculars and scanned the house. He could see the wide open terrace where they had eaten lunch. He tracked to the right and spotted the uniformed security guards climbing the hillside outside the walls of the extensive garden. He looked back at the villa and could see no other security people.

"So how have you managed to convince the security force to chase up the hillside?"

Geordie gave a tight little smile. "If you look up near the top of the hill you might see some goats wandering about."

Ivan lifted the binoculars again and scanned up the slope. He saw nothing for a moment and then a scraggy goat wandered from behind one of the shady pine trees. Then another until he could see seven or eight of them eating the scrubby grass.

"I've got them. So what?"

Geordie lifted the rifle and focused the telescopic sight before he answered. "If you see a black one with really curly horns, that's our decoy. He's got a very nice pendant of Saint Anthony round his neck. I relied on them keeping a check on where I was."

Ivan chuckled. "They are going to be so irritated once they catch up to it."

Geordie nodded. "I picked a skittish one. I guess he is going to keep moving away as they get closer to him. He should lead them a merry dance while I do what needs doing."

Ivan laid the binoculars down and looked at his friend who was still looking intently through the scope. "Are you sure about this?"

"Never been more sure about anything in my life."

He stiffened as he saw Christophides walk out onto his terrace. He saw the Greek arms dealer raise a pair of powerful binoculars to watch his security people scrambling up the hillside beside the villa. Geordie saw him lower the binoculars half way and turn his head towards the French doors just as Calanthe, his lovely daughter, came through wearing a simple white dress and carrying two glasses of something cold. Through the powerful sight optics he could see the condensation running down the glasses.

He adjusted his position to make the rifle steadier and controlled his breathing. The range was around six hundred meters. Well within the capabilities of the weapon.

Christophides turned and reached out for his glass just as Geordie fired. The powerful 7.62mm round punched through the arms dealer's back, directly between the shoulder blades. He dropped like a felled tree as his blood spattered across the white dress in front of him. Geordie could hear the girl's shocked scream from where he lay.

Geordie lowered the rifle and his shoulders sagged. Ivan waited a moment or two and then patted his friend on the shoulder.

"OK, he's had his payback. Now it's time we weren't here."

The two men slithered backwards into the cover of the trees behind them, then hiked through the wood for two kilometers to where Geordie had left his car. As they got closer Ivan could see that his own hire car was still there, parked neatly behind Geordie's.

The Welshman turned to Geordie. "We better get that rifle back to Donald so he can put it away before the police get called. When are you booked to leave?"

"I'm on the morning flight out of here tomorrow."

"That's handy, so am I, and it's your turn to buy the beer."

They sat in Donald's living room later that evening watching the football on the TV and not speaking, when Ivan's friend came into the room.

"Good thing you two are leaving so soon."

"Why's that?" Ivan asked.

"Just had a call from a friend of mine, asking if I want to make some money. It seems the lovely Calanthe has taken over her Dad's business right away. She's using you to put out a message to her own people and her rivals. She's put a contract out and you two, plus your friend the Major, have got a price on your heads and it's a big one. To make it absolutely clear to everyone that she's a bad bitch to mess with, the contract includes your families."

Chapter 81

Jim and his two men had been summoned to see the Prime Minister and had dutifully turned up at the main gate of the Foreign Office, as instructed. They were ushered through the central courtyard of the old building and then out through the tall wrought iron gate that leads into Downing Street. A civil servant was waiting to shepherd them across the short street and into the front door of Number 10. They were shown into the waiting room and left to their own devices.

They sat quietly until Ivan turned to Jim. "Boss, we have some bad news for you."

"Go on."

"It seems Christophides' daughter has taken against us in a big way and has issued a contract on us."

Jim sat up, and paid attention. "Why the hell would she do that and why her?"

Ivan cleared his throat. "It seems she took over his organisation when the old man died."

"I'm sorry," Jim said. "I get the feeling I'm missing something here. What else?"

Geordie shifted uncomfortably in his chair. "It's my fault. I didn't think he should get away with causing Carmen's death, so I went to Cyprus and sorted him out."

"And 'sorted him out' means what, exactly?"

Geordie looked down at his boots and then up at Jim. "I shot him. Nice clean shot between the shoulder blades. I used the tracking device they planted on me as a distraction so they know it was me. But I guess she decided we were all involved."

Jim sat back in his chair and looked at the ceiling. "Charming. That's all I need."

Ivan turned to him. "There's more. She's included all our families in the contract. It seems she is using this as a way to exert control over the organisation and show she is a hard case to any rivals."

Jim was about to answer when the door opened and the civil servant returned to show them in to see the Prime Minister. They walked across the hall and into the Cabinet Room with its famous oval table. Phillip Morton rose from his seat as they came in.

"Welcome, gentlemen. Please sit down." He said, indicating the chairs on the opposite side of the table.

The three men sat down and waited. Morton resumed his seat and rested his elbows on the highly polished wood. He steepled his fingers in front of his face and contemplated them before he spoke.

"Gentlemen, your country owes you a debt for what you have done in recovering what could have been some very embarrassing devices. You seem to have had some interesting adventures. I have a formal protest from the Government of Spain to deal with and some interesting questions from the government of Belize. Plus, the Norwegians want to know if we can shed any light on a missing fishing boat."

Jim leaned forward. "I can provide a detailed report if you wish, sir."

Morton shook his head and gave Jim a tight smile. "To be honest, Major, I don't want any record of this action on file anywhere. Written reports have a nasty habit of resurfacing. My senior civil servants are drafting all the replies stating we know nothing about any of it."

Jim shook his head. "I can't see that working with the Spanish, sir. They're not stupid."

"No, they're not, but things like this die down after a while if we string them out for long enough. So now, what do I do with you? David Orwell, my predecessor, has briefed me on some of the amazing tasks you undertook for him. We have agreed that you each deserve a medal and, if you agree, I will have my people process that for you all."

Jim leaned forward again. "Thank you for that, but if I may speak frankly, I have no interest in medals. All I want is to be let out of the army again to resume my life in Canada. What I would like from you is a firm promise I will never be called back again."

Ivan nodded beside Jim. "That goes for me, too. I just want to go back to Wiltshire to finish repairing my church roof and I don't want to have any more of these adventures either."

The PM looked a little startled. "I thought soldiers liked medals? My mistake, apparently. What about you, Staff Sergeant? What reward would you like for all your efforts?"

Geordie grinned. "A nice shiny medal would be very nice, but how the hell could I explain why I got it? And the question would come up every time anyone saw my dress uniform. So like the others, no thanks."

"Well I'm damned." The PM sat back in his chair and looked at each of them in turn. "All right then, for you two I promise I will never call on you again and if my successor needs a team, I will forget all about you. How's that?"

Jim looked at Ivan, who nodded. "That's just fine with us, sir. Thank you."

"Good, two down and one to go. Geordie, isn't it? Right then, Geordie, no medal for you, but your name will be on the list at the next promotion board. Since you are still in the army, I may call on you again."

The PM stood and walked around the table. "Thank you for all you have done." He paused. "And if you ever need anything from this office I think we still owe you any support we can give." As he shook their hands he said, "There will be someone outside to see you out."

They left the Cabinet Room and were taken back out the way they had come in. As they reached King Charles Street on the far side of the Foreign Office Jim paused and looked at his two friends.

"Gents, it's been a privilege as always, but right now we need to drop out of sight and stay that way. This contract could be a real problem, but I suggest we split up and all deal with our own part of it. Geordie, I'm sorry your actions have caused this, but I'm not sorry you shot that bastard. Carmen deserved that much."

They shook hands one last time and then went their separate ways.

One More Time – Author's Notes

One of the reviewers of my first book commented on the anomaly of using US spellings and terminology in a book with British heroes. My previous publishers and I debated this point and we decided that we would use US standards. I hope my readers who are more used to the Queen's English will forgive me and I hope it did not affect your enjoyment.

As with all my books, I try to be as factual as possible and this one is no exception. This chapter will give you the facts I have used when constructing this adventure, so that you can make a judgement about whether my story is credible.

Chequers, in Buckinghamshire, is the official country residence of the British Prime Minister. It has been the private retreat of the Prime Minister since 1921.

The Treaty of Tlateloico does exist and the UK is a signatory to it. During the Falklands War in 1982 a number of Royal Navy ships were deployed so rapidly that they were unable to offload the nuclear weapons they carried. The UK was able to justify this, to some extent, because Argentina had not ratified the treaty and did not do so until 1994. As far as I am aware the WE177 free fall nuclear weapons that were carried by Tornado aircraft have never been deployed to RAF Mount Pleasant in the Falkland Islands. These weapons were taken out of service by 1998.

RAF Mount Pleasant does exist and was built in the Falkland Islands to guard against further threats from Argentina after the 1982 war. Argentinians to this day believe that the islands they call Las Malvinas rightly belong to them. The islanders disagree.

It is true that in the year 1216, while crossing the Wash, a major tidal inlet in East Anglia, King John lost the wagon that was carrying his treasure, which may also have included the Crown Jewels. It strayed from the track and sank in quicksand. He died very shortly after this. The shape of the Wash has changed considerably over the 800 years since then and the area where the treasure was lost is now believed to be dry land. Treasure hunters have been looking for this hoard ever since. There are indications that it was found quite some time ago when certain families became very rich, very quickly, for no apparent reason. However, the search goes on just the same.

The Atomic Weapons Establishment (AWE) is located in Aldermaston in Berkshire. Its responsibilities today are fourfold. To maintain the warheads for the Trident nuclear deterrent safely and reliably in service. To maintain a capability to design a new weapon, should it ever be required. To complete the dismantling and disposal of redundant warheads replaced by Trident. To develop the skills, technologies and techniques that could underpin future arms limitation treaties.

The Forth Bridge, sometimes wrongly called the Forth Railway Bridge, is a stunning example of Victorian engineering at its best. It runs between

North and South Queensferry across the Firth of Forth near Edinburgh. Opened in March 1890, it is estimated to have at least another 100 years of life left at the time of writing. 190 to 200 trains a day use the bridge. It has been designated a UNESCO World Heritage Site.

The Atomic bomb dropped on Hiroshima in 1945 had an explosive yield of somewhere between 12 and 15 kilotons. The more modern WE177B free fall nuclear weapon had a yield of 400 kilotons.

KweKwe is a mining town in the Midlands area of Zimbabwe. Originally called Que Que, the name was altered in the aftermath of independence. It has a small airfield and good road and rail links. The Golden Mile Hotel and Conference Centre is just south of the town.

The war crime of shooting down the civilian Flight RH825 and then slaughtering the survivors is sadly true. The events unfolded much as I have described them in this book, though I have added my fictional observer of the massacre and put words into a survivor's mouth to tell the story. My source for the first hand account is *The Deafening Silence* by Hans Iver Mathinsen Hansen, who was actually on board the doomed aircraft. His book concerns much more than just this atrocity, but it is worth looking on Amazon to find it for more detail. There is also a more controversial book called *Viscount Down* by Keith Nell that tells the story from another viewpoint. It should also be noted that there are Internet articles that have sensationalised this awful event with claims of rape which appear to have been false. To their shame, western governments were silent about this atrocity and never condemned it.

Would a Police Inspector in Zimbabwe really try to drive someone off his land so he could steal his house? Sadly, yes. A great many farmers have been driven off successful farms to have them taken over by people who have no idea how to run them. In no small part this has contributed to Zimbabwe going from being the bread basket of Africa to a nation on the brink of famine. A very sad fate for a people who deserve far better from their government.

The Zimbabwean Air Force (ZAF) is small, but has proven to be effective in combat. As with many African nations, they have trouble keeping all their aircraft serviceable due to a lack of spare parts caused by funding issues and trade embargoes. The small fleet of BAe Hawks the ZAF has is grounded because they are unable to get spares from the UK for political reasons. They inherited aircraft from the Rhodesian Air Force at independence, but many of these are now quite old and difficult to maintain. The Alouette III helicopter is still in service and was used very effectively as a ground troop support aircraft by the Rhodesians during their long bush war.

The MI26 helicopter was a Russian design. Used mainly by military customers, there are at least two civilian companies using them for heavy and long distance work. One of these companies has a subsidiary in South Africa, a country with a good supply of experienced ex-military pilots. The aircraft has a range of some 1920 kilometers with a cruising speed of 255 kilometers per hour. It normally has a crew of five and is capable of carrying 90 troops, so the load and range needed for this mission are well within its capabilities.

The Air Force of Mozambique (*Forca Aérea de Moçambique*) is affected severely by serviceability problems for their small fleet of aircraft, so they would have had difficulty responding in the short time available to them in my story. Although their fleet of eight MIG21 fighters has recently been overhauled by Romania, it will take their pilots time to return to full operational capability having been grounded for so long.

The Cessna 172 is arguably the most successful aircraft of its type of all time. More of this type have been built than any other civilian aircraft. Primarily intended for flight training and private use, it has been designed to be reliable and relatively easy to maintain. Although later variants are more sophisticated, it remains a fairly simple and robust aircraft with a good safety record.

The British Army does have an Army Air Corps and, at the time of writing, they do their flying training at Middle Wallop in Hampshire. Potential pilots can join the AAC directly from civilian life, or serving officers and soldiers from other Corps and Regiments can volunteer to undertake a flying tour with them. The Corps operates mostly helicopters, but does have a small number of fixed wing aircraft for specialist tasks.

The red and white ships of the Hurtigruten Line do run along the rugged coast of northern Norway keeping the scattered communities linked to the rest of the country. The ships are comfortable and also take tourists from overseas who wish to see the remarkable beauty of the fjords and to try and catch a glimpse of the spectacular Aurora Borealis or Northern Lights. The food on board is good, but the bar prices are challenging.

The Nuclear Backpack Bomb, or more correctly the Special Atomic Demolition Munition, does exist. They were developed by both the USA and Russia during the cold war and they were intended to be infiltrated into enemy territory by Special Forces troops to attack key targets. For the US version, the bare warhead package was an 11 inch by 16 inch (28 cm by 41 cm) cylinder that weighed 51 lbs. (23 kg). The explosive yield of such a device would usually be in the region of Six Kilotons. There are presently strong concerns that the Russian devices are not under close enough control and even that a few may have been "lost". Strategic nuclear weapons are under control by heads of state, but by their nature small devices that can be carried by one man can also be detonated by that one man.

The Sami people do live in northern Scandinavia, roaming through the top of Norway, Finland and Sweden and even into Russia. They seem to divide into two main groups for their living; many fish, but a reasonable number do herd the reindeer. In the past they have not been treated well by the various governments, but things are now improving for them.

The 66mm anti-tank rocket is a lightweight weapon that is carried in a disposable metal tube that extends before firing. It is light enough to be carried by an infantryman in addition to all the other equipment he has to carry. It is simple to use and has the operating instructions printed along the top. It has been in service with US and allied forces since 1963 and remains in service at the time of writing. It is claimed that the HEAT warhead can penetrate up to eight inches of steel, making it remarkably effective for such a simple weapon.

The PIAT or Projector Infantry Anti-Tank was developed and brought into use by the British Army in 1942. Although it had a number of drawbacks, it was far more effective than Jim gives it credit for in the story. After the Second

World War it was found that approximately 7% of German armour put out of action had been hit by PIATs as opposed to only 6% by aircraft launched rockets. With a normal use range of around 140 meters, the infantryman had to get a lot closer than anti-tank troops do today. With a shaped charge warhead and the courage of the soldier, it proved to be effective and was used by a number of armies up until the 1950s.

The Bren Gun was a lightweight, magazine fed machine gun used by British and many other forces from 1938 until around 2006. It was certainly used in combat during the 1982 conflict in the Falkland Islands by both sides. Originally it used the .303 round, but was later modified to use the NATO 7.62mm round. Highly accurate and highly reliable, it was a very easy weapon to fire. A version of it is still being manufactured in India. My father claimed that his infantry section in the Grenadier Guards shot down a Stuka dive bomber in 1940 using Bren Guns and it was used in the anti-aircraft role as well as being vehicle mounted.

Denia is a town on the coast of the Costa Blanca in Spain. It is less tourist orientated than the town of Javea, which is on the other side of the Montgo mountain that sits between them. The area known as Les Rotes is situated on the south of the town and consists mainly of pleasant villas that are between the lower slope of the mountain and the sea. Slightly further along the coast there are some high sea cliffs. In these sea cliffs there are a number of caves, as there are throughout this area of tall rocky outcrops. Probably the best of the caves, and certainly the most accessible in the area, is just outside the village of Benidoleig and is known as *Cuevas de las Calaveras* or the Cave of the Skulls, due to the human skulls that were discovered in a side cave during an exploration. These caves have been used by humans since prehistoric times.

On top of the hills overlooking the sea cliffs of Les Rotes there is a ruined Mirador tower called *Torre del Gerro* or sometimes *Torre de l'Aiguadolc* that dates from the 16th century when pirates were a real menace along this coast.

The construction company known as ROC exists and at the time of writing is run, rather well, by Craig Downs. It operates up and down the northern Costa Blanca in Spain.

The restaurant called Mena does exist and sits right on the cliff edge in Les Rotes, providing some excellent views while you enjoy the very nice food. The viewpoint is there and does have a board detailing the wildlife in the area. It is true that four types of whales can be seen there.

The JU-87 Stuka dive bomber and the Heinkel He111 medium bomber were both used during the Spanish Civil War. Initially they were operated by "volunteers" from the German Luftwaffe, known as the Condor Legion. The Germans used this war to practice and hone the tactics they would use later during the Second World War. The aircraft continued in Spanish service after the Civil War and the Heinkel was built in Spain under license as the CASA 2.111.

The Heinkel was known familiarly as "Pedro" in Spain. German designed aircraft built under licence were equipped with Rolls Royce Merlin engines after World War Two, as the original engines were no longer available. The Stuka and the Heinkel were the bomber types used in the infamous bombing raid on the Basque town of Guernica that inspired the famous painting by Picasso.

The MG15 machine gun was fitted to both the JU-87 Stuka and the Heinkel He111 for self-defense. It was fitted with a double drum magazine for easy and rapid reloading that held 75 7.92mm rounds. It was relatively lightweight and later in the Second World War variants were used in the infantry role.

I mention in the story that aircraft engines of this time had hand cranks as back-up starters. I can vouch for this, having started a Pratt and Whitney nine cylinder radial engine fitted to a De Havilland Beaver aircraft with a hand crank when I served in Canada. It was scary with the propeller spinning so close and it was hard work, but it started the engine. The Daimler Benz **DB** 600Aa engine fitted to a Heinkel of this era has a hand starter at the rear of the engine that is accessed by removing the electric starter motor.

There were manual bomb winches mounted inside the bomb bay of some marks of Heinkel He111, to allow the bombs to be lifted into place from the trolleys they are moved on. This aircraft was also able to carry torpedoes so the bay would be large enough to accommodate sea mines, although the mountings would not fit without modification. The aircraft was also capable of carrying the V1 Flying Bomb and launching it from the air so the aircraft had the power to lift four heavy mines, but probably not easily.

During the Cold War at least one test was apparently conducted with a naval mine fitted with tactical nuclear warheads by the US Navy. The weapon was experimental and reportedly never went into production. Although, given the US expertise in keeping their black programs secret, that might not be true. In any event, the technology exists to make these devices a real possibility. There have been some reports that North Korea may be developing a nuclear mine.

The Spanish Air Force is equipped with a range of modern aircraft, including the American F-18 and the Eurofighter Typhoon. The nearest air base to Jim's escape route, though, is at Murcia–San Javier Airport from where they operate the CASA C-101 Aviojet. Although a trainer and display aircraft, this can be equipped with weapons. The military air base dates back to at least the early 1930s and is located at the northern end of the airport. It is used chiefly by Air Force piston and jet-engined training aircraft, including a well-known formation aerobatic display team which can often be seen practicing over the nearby Mar Menor.

The idea of concealing an aircraft hangar inside a mountain and having a road on the outside to act as the runway may seem fanciful, but it really isn't. The Swiss Air Force have aircraft concealed inside the Alps and they actually do use roads as runways. On a less grand scale, the Royal Air Force carried out exercises in Germany where aircraft were concealed in barns and forests and then wheeled out to use the Autobahns or major roads for runways. The Germans were aware of this as a concealment method in the 1940s and similarly hid their Me262 aircraft away from the massive allied bombing attacks.

There is an airfield in Gibraltar and it does have a Royal Air Force presence. The Spanish believe that Gibraltar should belong to them, but the British maintain it is theirs because of a long standing treaty. There are occasional incursions into the waters of Gibraltar by Spanish boats, but armed aircraft of the Spanish Air Force would almost certainly not fly into the disputed airspace without very senior direction.

The Dhekelia referred to in the story is one of the Sovereign Base Areas the British Military maintain on the island of Cyprus. The other one is at Akrotiri. There is a good rifle range at Dhekelia with a tall cliff behind the targets, making it one of the safest I know.

Could an aircraft of this age be made to fly? Possibly. Aircraft of the time were much simpler than modern warplanes with far less to go wrong. The lack of sophistication would work in favour of my story.

Might the British Government of the 1980s have decided to hide nuclear weapons in this way? Again, possibly. Throughout my military service there was a strong belief that the Soviet Union had every intention of attacking the western alliance. At the end of the Falklands War there was a militaristic feeling in the UK that might have encouraged such adventurism.

This book is the fourth in a series so Jim, Ivan and Geordie will put their lives on the line again.

I hope you have enjoyed this book and if so an honest review on Amazon, or wherever you bought the book, would be very much appreciated.

For more information about my books please visit my website.
http://www.nigelseedauthor.com/

Photograph "Courtesy of Grupo Bernabé" of Pontevedra.

Nigel Seed

Born in Morecambe, England, into a military family, Nigel Seed grew up hearing his father's tales of adventure during the Second World War which kindled his interest in military history and storytelling. He received a patchy education, as he and his family followed service postings from one base to another. Perhaps this and the need to constantly change schools contributed to his odd ability to link unconnected facts and events to weave his stories.

Nigel later joined the Army, serving with the Royal Electrical and Mechanical Engineers in many parts of the world. Upon leaving he joined the Ministry of Defence during which time he formed strong links with overseas armed forces, including the USAF, and cooperated with them, particularly in support of the AWACS aircraft.

He is married and lives in Spain; half way up a mountain with views across orange groves to the Mediterranean. The warmer weather helps him to cope with frostbite injuries he sustained in Canada, when taking part in the rescue effort for a downed helicopter on a frozen lake.

His books are inspired by places he has been to and true events he has either experienced or heard about on his travels. He makes a point of including family jokes and stories in his books to raise a secret smile or two. Family dogs make appearances in his other stories.

Nigel's hobbies include sailing and when sailing in Baltic he first heard the legend of the hidden U-Boat base that formed the basis of his first book some thirty eight years later.

The Other Books by this author

Drummer's Call

Revenge of a Lone Wolf

Simon Drummer is on loan to a bio-warfare protection unit in the USA when the terror they fear becomes real. A brilliant Arabic bio-chemist is driven to bring an end to the suffering of his countrymen. He believes that the regime that oppresses them could not exist without the support of the US government and the weapons they furnish. He needs to bring the truth to the American people in a way that will grab their attention. So begins his journey to bring brutal death and understanding to the USA. And now Simon must help to find him and stop him.

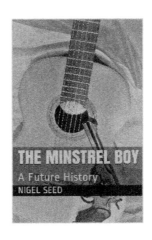

The Minstrel Boy

A Future History

Billy Murphy minds his own business and sings his songs in the pubs around Belfast. Then the IRA decides that he can be useful to them in preparing to restart the armed struggle for Irish unity. He finds himself caught up in their plots and learns the truth about the Troubles that he had never been told. But there are others who watch and take revenge for past atrocities. Billy must be careful not to come under suspicion and find his own life at risk from the terrorist killers he is working for.

The Jim Wilson Series

V4 – Vengeance

Hitler's Last Vengeance Weapons Are Going To War

Major Jim Wilson, late of the Royal Engineers, has been obliged to leave the rapidly shrinking British Army. He needs a job but they are thin on the ground even for a highly capable Army Officer. Then he is offered the chance to go to Northern Germany to search for the last great secret of World War 2, a hidden U Boat base. Once he unravels the mystery he is asked to help to spirit two submarines away from under the noses of the German government, to be the central exhibits in a Russian museum. But then the betrayal begins and a seventy year old horror unfolds.

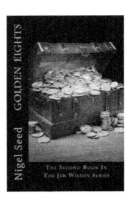

Golden Eights

The Search For Churchill's Lost Gold Begins Again

In 1940, with the British army in disarray after the evacuation from Dunkirk, invasion seemed a very real possibility. As a precaution, the Government decided to protect the national gold reserves by sending most of the bullion to Canada on fast ships that ran the gauntlet of the U boat fleets. But a lot of gold bars and other treasures were hidden in England. In the fog of war, this treasure was lost. Now, finally, a clue has emerged that might lead to the hiding place. The Government needs the gold back if the country is not to plunge into a huge financial crisis. Major Jim Wilson has been tasked to find it. He and his small team start the search, unaware that there is a traitor watching their every move and intent on acquiring the gold, at any cost.

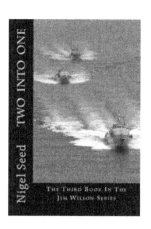

Two Into One

A Prime Minister Acting Strangely and World Peace in the Balance

Following his return from Washington the Prime Minister's behaviour has changed. Based on his previous relationship with the PM, Major Jim Wilson is called in to investigate. What he finds is shocking and threatens the peace of the world. But now he must find a way to put things right and there is very little time to do it. His small team sets out on a dangerous quest that takes them from the hills of Cumbria to the Cayman Islands and Dubai, but others are watching and playing for high stakes.

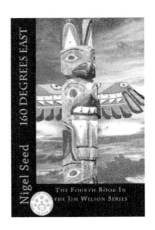

160 Degrees East

A fight for survival and the need to right a terrible wrong.

Major Jim Wilson and his two men are summoned at short notice to Downing Street. The US Government has a problem and they have asked for help from Wilson and his small team. Reluctantly Jim agrees, but he is unaware of the deceit and betrayal awaiting him from people he thought of as friends. From the wild hills of Wales to the frozen shores of Russia and on to the mountains of British Columbia Jim and his men have to fight to survive, to complete their mission and to right a terrible wrong.

One More Time

A Nuclear Disaster Threatened By Criminals Must Be Prevented At All Costs

Jim and Ivan have retired from the Army and are making their way in civilian life when they are summoned back to the military by the new Prime Minister. Control of two hidden nuclear weapons has failed and they have been lost. Jim must find them before havoc is wreaked upon the world by whoever now controls them. It is soon apparent the problem is far bigger than originally envisaged, and there is a race against time to stop further weapons falling into the hands of an unscrupulous arms dealer and his beautiful daughter. The search moves from Zimbabwe to Belize and on to Norway and Spain, becoming ever more urgent and dangerous as the trail is followed.

Twelve Lives

A Threat to Millions But This Time It's Personal

During a highly classified mission for the British Government, Jim Wilson and his two companions make a dangerous enemy. A contract has been put on their lives and on those of their families. Jim moves the intended victims to safety and sets about trying to have the contract cancelled. However, his efforts to save his family uncover a horrendous plot to mount a nuclear terror attack on the United States and the race is on to save millions of lives.

North of Fifty Four

A Crime Must Be Committed To Prevent A War

Jim Wilson is forced to work for a Chinese criminal gang or his wife and child will be murdered. While he is away in the north of Canada, his wife manages to contact Ivan and Geordie for help. The two friends set out to save all three of them, but then the threat to many more people emerges and things become important enough to involve governments in committing a serious crime to prevent a new war in the Middle East.

Short Stories

Backpack 19

A Lost Backpack and a World of Possibilities.

An anonymous backpack lying by the side of the road. Who picks it up and what do they find inside? There are many possibilities and lives may be changed for the better or worse. Here are just nineteen of those stories.

The Michael McGuire Trilogy

No Road to Khartoum

From the filthy back streets of Dublin to the deserts of the Sudan to fight and die for the British Empire.

Found guilty of stealing bread to feed his starving family, Michael McGuire is offered the "Queen's Hard Bargain", go to prison or join the Army. He chooses the Army and, after training in Dublin Castle, his life is changed forever as he is selected to join the 'Gordon Relief Expedition' that is being sent south of Egypt to Khartoum, in the Sudan.

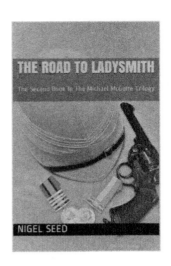

The Road to Ladysmith

Only just recovered from his wounds Captain McGuire must now sail south to the confusion and error of the Boer War.

After his return from the war in the Sudan, McGuire had expected to spend time recovering with his family. It was not to be, and his regiment is called urgently to South Africa to counter the threat from the Boers. Disparaged as mere farmers the Boers were to administer a savage lesson to the British Army.

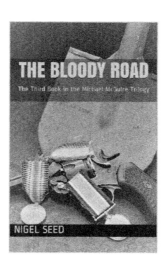

The Bloody Road

Michael McGuire has left the army, but as the First World War breaks out his country calls him again.

At the start of the war the British expand their army rapidly, but there is a shortage of experienced officers and McGuire is needed. He is sent to Gallipoli in command of an Australian battalion that suffers badly in that debacle. He stays with them when their bloody road takes them to the mud and carnage of the western front.

If you have enjoyed this book a review on Amazon.com would be very welcome.

Please visit my website at www.nigelseedauthor.com for information about upcoming books.

Printed in Great Britain
by Amazon